ROGUES
OF THE
EAST

Reading Ikenna Okeh's writing is like being held under the spell of a lucid dream; his descriptive powers in Rogues of the East sweep you across a raw tide of violence, dirty intrigues, and nerve-wracking suspense as he plows through the sacred and the sensitive with hard-hitting intensity. In this book, he has created a mix of the sweet, sour and surprising and characters that will leave you conflicted, enraged, amused and still living in your head long after you have closed the last page.

— David Hymar,

author of *I For Don Blow But I Too Dey Press Phone.*

This is something new and fresh on the African literary scene, … a most enjoyable read."

— Jindu Enugbe,

author of *Street O.T.*

Nothing interests like a story whose protagonist is a writer.

— Peter Hesen,

Ubuntu FM Africa.

'Rogues of the East' is keen with wild and intriguing brilliance.

— Kelvin Kellman,

The Stockholm Review of Literature.

Stunning … Nothing prepares you for the suspense and intrigue

— **Ever Obi**,

author of *Some Angels Don't See God.*

The best crime novel I have read in a long time

— **Dr. Onyeka Nwelue**,

author of *The Strangers of Braamfontein*

"A pleasurable read … a proof that literature in Africa has attained to a new stage of maturity"

— **Oche Akor,** author of *Apocalyptic Acapella.*

ROGUES OF THE EAST

A CRIME NOVEL

IKENNA OKEH

Abibiman
Publishing

New York & London

First published in the United Kingdom in 2023
by Abibiman Publishing.
www.abibimanpublishing.com

Copyright © 2023 Ikenna Okeh

Abibiman Publishing is registered under
Hudics LLC in the United States and in the United Kingdom.

ISBN: 978-1-7396934-9-7

This is a work of fiction. Names, characters, places, and incidents
either are the product of the author's imagination or are used
fictitiously. Any resemblance to actual persons, living or dead,
events, or locales is entirely coincidental.

Cover design by Stephen Embleton

Printed in the United Kingdom by Clays Ltd.

DEDICATION

To James Currey, for a life dedicated to bringing African literature to global attention; to Chinua Achebe, Christopher Okigbo and every other who took up the literary front-lines; and to Dr Onyeka Nwelue, for taking up the baton.

PROLOGUE

LATE AUGUST, 2012: SOMEWHERE NEAR OWERRI

A young man with large ears, pitch-black hair and a face tensed and roughened with worries and obvious lack of sleep sat, alone, like a speck, in the second pew on the centre column of the high-ceilinged church building. The stained-glass windows on either side cast a hallowed presence about the place. It was quiet everywhere except for a gust of cool evening wind intermittently rustling the fruit trees that dotted the uneven grassy landscape of the churchyard. Whenever the wind stilled, the silence weighed heavily on the young man's eardrums so much that he felt like screaming at the top of his voice just to break the quietness that threatened his sanity.

He wasn't a religious fellow; he had gone to church with his mother as a little boy, but those had been occasions to celebrate a wedding or a child's dedication, with coolers of steaming jollof rice and soft drinks to look forward to.

A glance at his wristwatch deepened the worry lines on his forehead. He never felt comfortable with shady meetings, and were it not a matter of life-and-death he wouldn't have considered coming in the first place to meet an unknown informant. He was already five minutes behind schedule; he hoped the fellow would not fail to show up as he had twice done; there was so much of the mess that had become of his life to clear up, and much more to lay to rest.

The dull echo of hurrying footsteps approached from behind, interrupting the young man's thoughts. He turned tentatively and, from his peripheral vision, glimpsed a middle-aged man hurrying in his direction. The newcomer's white clerical collar stood distinct against the blue of his loose-fitting short-sleeved shirt that flailed like a ship's sail with every advancing step.

With brisk steps the Reverend strode into the church, stretching his short legs to their limits as he hurried along. He was already running late for a meeting with the archdeacon; a man he inwardly loathed with as much bile as a priest could possibly allow in his heart. He hated that the archdeacon derived pleasure in making a scapegoat of him and running him hard like an arse; he believed it to be some sort of calculated attempt at continually asserting his authority about the place. Very much unnecessary trouble. Everyone knew already and no one contested the fact that the bald power-drunk fellow sat comfortably at the high echelons of the food chain; he was lord and king over the likes of the lesser clergymen. Even the bishop knew better not to cross swords with the man because of his wide connections within and outside the diocese. Any dumb priest or diocesan insider knew better than to be in the man's bad books. But would he let it rest there? The petty bastard. Who didn't know that the man was a weakling when it came to his own wife? It wasn't news any longer. Such juicy information had ways of seeping through unseen crevices in the walls of the most secluded parsonages. Everybody knew it, and they would exchange knowing glances whilst the 'venerable couple' kept up their public appearances with the assurance that their secrets were safe behind the closed doors of their bedroom.

He wished the archdeacon didn't preside over his fate, especially now when news making the rounds was of some diocesan appointments coming up real soon. The thought made him chew at the insides of his mouth - a habit he had for when worries claimed his peace. He was in desperate need for one of such appointments; at least as a chaplain in some important organization or a principal in any one of the diocesan seminaries or convents. It wouldn't feel right to sit by and watch his colleagues from the theological college surpass him that much. Only if he had a godfather higher up the clerical ladder to see to his interest.

A form seated in one of the pews caught his attention. Even though the church was always left open, he hadn't expected to see anybody in there. A parishioner meditating all alone was never a common sight. In fact, in all his three years serving in the parish he had never met one. The villagers contributed towards the church building. They still did. They gave their tithes and offerings and goaded their children living abroad into making generous donations. But that was as much religious as they were. They weren't given to prayers or meditations in the church building on any days or nights.

Strange things do happen, he reasoned as he approached, not slowing his pace, until he recognized the face. It was the same fellow from the day before, and still seated at the same spot! The face was that of a stranger, he could tell, because he had never seen it on any Sunday services. He appeared a troubled young man, a city dweller, perhaps, just returned to spend time with his parents in the village. But then, why did he have to sit all by himself? Were it not for the meeting with the archdeacon, he would have stopped by to have a word with the strange fellow. Who knows how much good could be gained in winning over this one soul. But he had only come to get some copies of the monthly financial report he was supposed to present to the archdeacon. He resolved to say a 'hello' as he walked by the young man.

On drawing closer, he noticed the youth had his eyes shut. The blackened thin lips moved silently too; he was murmuring a prayer. The Reverend thought better of interrupting him. Instead, he hastened on towards the altar brilliantly lit by the sunset seeping in through the huge, stained altar windows. He parted a portion of the heavy purple curtains by the altar and disappeared through a small door.

The young man had recognized the clergyman from the previous day; he still wore the same short-sleeved shirt, with the white clerical collar, tucked into black trousers meticulously ironed that they stood stiff with a razor-sharp line running vertically in front. He had feigned deep meditation on noticing the man approach in a bid to discourage any sort of discussions. He opened his eyes in time to see the priest hurry in through a small door by the magnificent altar, and then he dropped his guard, but only momentarily.

Again he glanced at his watch. Another twenty minutes had gone already. He sucked air into his lungs and exhaled noisily, resolving to wait another ten minutes and no more. After then, he decided, he would have to leave and forget everything about this shadowy informant.

Two men strolled in through the eastern arched doorway, and he turned in the direction of their footfalls. They looked a most unlikely pair, these two men, and he was riveted by this striking dissimilarity: where one was short and stout, with bow legs that made him appear to waddle like a duck, his partner was skinny and tall with sunken eyes that made him look like a man from a prize-winning photograph of drought-stricken Somalia. If there was anything the newcomers shared in common, it was their dark complexion, the kind that was untended and told of an acquaintance with adversities. In their composure, they both seemed to contest for attention; the short one's pair of white trainers appeared too large for his size: they accentuated the oddity of his bow legs and his duck-like waddle. The tall one walked with a slight waver that made it seem inadvisable to allow him to venture outside on a windy day. They were both engaged in some heated argument, with the short one appearing to be gaining the upper hand. Their argument had softened to a low whisper as they strolled in, but then the whispers were still magnified by the emptiness of the church. They moved across the building, in the direction of the western arched doorway like two travelers using the church as a shortcut. When they came abreast the altar, they fell quiet, faced it and then genuflected before continuing on their way. Their heated argument picked up the moment they walked out of the church.

Twenty minutes had passed again and the informant had not yet arrived. The young man's patience wore thin. The fellow must know better not to be tardy in matters as this. It made one paranoid.

He got off his seat and made for the southern doorway. He favoured that exit because the short stairs offered a lesser view of the church building to an observer down the hill, unlike the other more conspicuous entrances.

On the third rung of the wide steps, a sharp sting bit into his stomach. He doubled over instinctively, clutching his stomach in both hands. It was seconds later before the shot rang out loud and clear against the evening wind.

He had been shot!

You never get to hear the bullet that killed you, a friend's habitual saying went, and so he thanked God he was still alive. An angry bee wheezed past his temple at that instant, only grazing the tip of his right ear. The accompanying shot rang out seconds later.

Another shot!

He made to hurry into the church, but it was too late. Another bullet tore into his right shoulder just as he had straightened up a fraction. He fell, facedown upon the steps. The pains came surging through his body at that instant. It felt as though someone had poked a red-hot branding iron into his stomach and shoulder. He crawled up the steps on his belly, determined to get into the sanctuary of the church before the unseen shooter finished him off. With every determined effort to get away, the pain seared through his body, clouding his vision. He fought to climb into the church just as he fought to stay awake, but as much as he tried, the darkness, like a blanket, descended on him. Everything stood still and peaceful in a strange way different from the quietness inside the church.

Two men hurried towards the body sprawled facedown on the church steps. The short, bow-legged one nudged the limp body with the sole of his big white trainers. His locally-made pistol, still smoking from its wide rusty muzzle, hung down his arm. He dared not tuck it into his belt just yet lest the hot metal scald his skin. But for the layers of rags tied around its butt, he couldn't have been able to hold onto it after firing off the first shot.

"Is he dead?"

He tilted his head to throw a sidelong look at his slim companion standing next to him. It was the kind of look a man would give his son for asking a stupid question.

"Before *nko?* Don't you have eyes? Or do you think he is Rambo?"

"Let me shoot him another bullet again, just to be sure."

The short one stopped him before he could take aim. "What is wrong with you, *sef*? Don't you know that bullets are bought with money, or do you think they *shit* them? You just wasted some bullets and you are still not satisfied."

"Who told you I wasted bullets?"

"Do I need to be told? Don't I have eyes?"

"Was I not the one who shot the bullet that finished him off?"

"Which one?"

"The headshot."

"You dey craze, abi? Look at his head. Can you see any wound?"

The tall one examined the victim's head. "Only a small wound."

"When did *ear* and *head* become one? Maybe on your way growing towards the skies, you forgot your brains at your knees."

"Hey! Hold it there! Don't try to insult me again even in your next life."

"Why then should you act like someone who never went to school?"

The tall one hissed in resignation. "So you win, *abi*?"

"Yes *na*. You will be the one to give me three bottles of beer."

The short one was still brimming with triumph as he signaled for them to leave. Their pistols had cooled down considerably. Each man tucked his piece into the waist of his trousers as they began the calm descent downhill like two common villagers. They had begun their argument anew, the evening wind wafted bits of their sentences over the distance. Nobody was to know that they were assassins, light-hearted in the knowledge of a job well done and the promise of payday.

The Reverend hurried out of the small office. The last-minute decision to put some careful touches to the financial report had robbed him of some valuable time. He had felt the cost incurred in hosting the visiting foreign missionaries for one week might alarm the archdeacon. It would be unwise to give the petty fellow something to hold onto, and not especially now when the man would be looking for some excuse to deny him a place in the new diocesan placements.

The distant gunshots had come to him while he was absorbed in doctoring the figures, but he had dismissed them to be one of those crazy university cult boys at their thing again. He had only sacrificed a few seconds to ponder why people placed little value on their lives only to cling onto it in desperation in those few minutes when they were about to lose it. And then he had returned his full attention to the figures again.

At the steps of the southern doorway, had the Reverend not halted just in time, he would have tripped over the body lying still in the hallowed premises of the church. He recognized the lifeless body. The sight was too strong for his senses to withstand. It had to be a miracle he missed suffering a heart attack at that instant.

The young man he had seen praying only a few moments ago now lifeless and bleeding on the steps!

Looking about, he struggled to gain control of his quivering limbs and his frayed heart that threatened to leap from his mouth. Thank goodness there was no one in sight. He stepped over the lifeless body, careful that his shoes did not so much as brush against it, and then he flew down the hill, a slim file containing the printed financial reports clutched under his arm. God forbid he would be the one to bear the news of a murder in the church. Someone else would have to bear that cross.

ONE

JULY, 2012. PORT-HARCOURT

Luciano knocked on the towering black gate; three rasps in slow succession. It was the second time in that week that he had stood before the now familiar gates. He nervously patted the edges of his small oiled afro, dabbed his forehead with the back of his hand, and tugged at the tweed jacket he was wearing in spite of the promise of a warm morning. His nervousness unsettled him; he didn't like the feeling. It had a way of sneaking up on him moments before any meeting with a prospective sponsor for his book project, especially one as important as Chief Ofodile.

The clang of a bolt being slid back startled him. Impulsively, he took a quick step backwards. The gate opened a fraction and a small head of a man poked out. It reminded Luciano of a tortoise. A dismissive frown was plastered over the leathery face marred by the indents of a woven pattern, obviously from sleeping on a mat. Luciano recognized Ali the security man. His eyes had that wildness that came from being roused from slumber. Luciano braced himself for the hostility that would surely follow.

Ali sized Luciano up, and then snapped: "*Ehe? Menene? Wetin be that?*"

"Errm. I'm here to see Chief Ofodile."

"*Him don commot.*"

"What?"

"*You no hear wetin I talk?*"

"But I was supposed to meet with him," Luciano pressed, the panic seizing him. "We have an appointment for this morning."

"*Bana jin turanci. I no hear all that plenty oyinbo you dey talk.*"

"Oh, sorry," Luciano said, and flashed an imploring smile. "*I suppose see Chief Ofodile today. Na him say make I come.*"

Ali appraised him again as though gauging the truthfulness of his claim. "*Toh. Wait here. I dey come.*" He retracted his head, clanged the gate shut and rammed the bolt in.

Luciano dug into the pockets of his trousers, more to hide his quivering hands than to strike an impressive pose. He hoped Chief Ofodile wasn't trying to avoid him. All these important people and their methods of saying 'no' to a proposal. Or could it be that the gatekeeper was only acting silly in a bid to throw his weight around? It was nearly impossible to comprehend why important people made themselves unapproachable by keeping idiotic hounds around them. He had had such experiences while searching for jobs; the illiterate morons at the gates would act so tough and assertive that if you eventually met the person who called the shots, their simplicity would break your soul. He only hoped Ali wasn't out to spoil his morning. Getting to meet with Chief Ofodile had been tougher than he had anticipated, with the arrogant Ali telling him on every one of those visits that Chief wasn't around. His desperation had led to his stalking Chief Ofodile until four days ago when his efforts had paid off.

Chief Ofodile had listened with uninterrupted interest to his proposal and then had scheduled an appointment for this morning. He fought off the mounting possibility that the man was now attempting to put him off. And if it came to that, he resolved, he would simply give up the idea of ever becoming a published writer. He would go look for something else to do with his youth, even though he had no clue as to what that might be.

The bolt slid back again. Ali stood aside, holding the gate open for him. "*Shiga mana!*"

He didn't understand a word of Hausa, but he conjectured that Ali asked him to come in.

The compound was smaller than he had anticipated. He made towards a white-painted duplex with freshly watered potted flowers marking the way to the entrance, and knocked timidly on a heavy wooden door. It opened just at once as though someone had been stationed behind it, awaiting his arrival. And truly, it was Chief Ofodile himself. He held the door long enough to say a hasty welcome to Luciano, and then hurried back in, leaving the door wide open.

Luciano followed him into the house, past a small and cosy dimly-lit sitting room, onwards through a spacious irregular-shaped hallway with reflective floor tiles, and then into a kitchen designed after some exotic pattern, complete with hanging planters. The red digital readings on a large refrigerator caught his eye. A modest-looking dining table with three polished wooden chairs claimed the centre stage of the kitchen. Luciano took in the details of the kitchen, conscious that his lower jaw wasn't hanging down. Everything held his attention as though he was perusing the surreal photographs found on the glossy pages of a magazine.

Chief Ofodile unhooked a chequered apron from the kitchen door handle. Luciano watched him drape it over his head, securing the strings behind his back as he made towards a gas cooker. Luciano came alive to his surroundings, and that was when he perceived the smell of frying eggs coming from a medium-sized wok on a gas cooker. On the marble tabletop, some half-cut lettuces lay on a wooden chopping board beside a little pile of diced onions. There was a gleaming knife amongst the lettuces. Luciano watched Chief Ofodile grab a stainless steel ladle and stir the contents of the wok in a frenzy, his back turned to him.

"Make yourself comfortable, gentleman," Chief Ofodile said without turning to face him.

Luciano settled into one of the dining chairs. The aroma of the eggs was a welcome sensation. It had been a while he perceived the aroma of fried eggs, but then Chief Ofodile's cooking stirred the emptiness in his stomach.

"You could help me with cutting some more lettuces for an extra mouth."

"No, thanks. I'm actually not hungry."

"Nonsense!" Chief Ofodile suspended his stirring long enough to stare at Luciano. "I'm about going into a partnership with you. It would be helpful we developed something personal between the both of us, or don't you agree?"

Luciano nodded and went to work.

Outside, in the streets, a vehicle, obviously a truck, chugged noisily along as Luciano washed his hands in the sink, pressed the ends of the green leaves onto the chopping board and then sliced through. The knife was heavier and sharper than he had thought. He made a mental note to keep his fingers as far away from the cutting edge as the task would allow.

Chief Ofodile came around, scooped up a handful of the diced onions and dumped them into the wok from which the smell of burning eggs emanated. He stirred again, with some aggression this time, scraping the wok as he did. Then he returned to the remainder of the diced onions, scooped them all up, dumped them into the wok, and clapped over the hissing wok to shake off every bit of onions clinging onto his palms. He wiped his hands on his apron, and then attacked the wok once again.

Luciano, with some effort, restrained himself from pointing out that the onions seemed too much for the amount of eggs.

Soon enough, a strong smell of cooking onions mixed with the smell of burning eggs filled the kitchen with such pungency that assaulted the palate.

"You have to be fast with the lettuce. The eggs are almost done."

"I'm done, sir."

"Good."

Chief Ofodile scooped up the sliced lettuce, tossing everything into the wok. It would appear that he was a wizard adding a very active ingredient to his potion. He repeated the exercise twice and all of the sliced lettuces were gone from the table, and then he continued the stirring with renewed zest. "Being alone could really be messy sometimes," he said.

The sudden statement startled Luciano. He didn't know what to say in reply. He shifted his weight uncomfortably onto his other foot and then leaned against the table. The knife hung loose in his hand. "Anyway, you wouldn't know. It's not like I expect you to. We're just two different people in two separate worlds. We might not be able to understand what inward battle each one of us has to contend with in our individual worlds and with every passing day."

Chief Ofodile turned off the gas cooker, hefted the wok from the cooker, and dropped it rather roughly onto the dining table. The ladle still stuck out from the mass of the wok's contents. He walked to the refrigerator and returned to the dining table with a loaf of bread secured under his arm, and tins of milk, one in each hand. One of the tins was obviously half-full, the holes on opposite sides of the lid were sealed with bits of moistened paper torn off the tin's label. He let down the provisions on the dining table and then went off to one of the closets high up on the wall. Rummaging through tins and bottles, he found what he was looking for: a tin of *Horlicks*. "But either way, life is never a bed of roses, not for you and definitely not for me," he lectured on as he returned to the dining table and settled into one of the chairs. "Take a seat, and please pass me the knife. I will need it for the bread."

"Oh, sorry." Luciano reached across the table to hand him the knife, with the handle first.

"Thanks."

Chief Ofodile swiped the flat sides of the blade twice on the apron, across his small pot-belly. "But then, like I was saying, it is a hard life either way. For me, and as much as I can guess, for you too. You see, as for me, even though I wish for more money, I don't wish for more of the many inconveniences it appears to … oh *shit*! I forgot the mugs." He slapped his forehead in mock frustration. "Please, my dear, they are in the closet there." He pointed with the tip of the knife to the closet on the wall behind Luciano.

Luciano went about the task of fetching them.

"And some spoons too," he called out.

"Sure, sir."

Luciano found the mugs and the spoons as Chief Ofodile had directed. He got two saucers too, but they were all covered in a film of dust and thin threads of cobwebs. He washed them in the sink and settled down at the dining table opposite his host and prospective patron. To escape the uneasiness which his host's strange demeanour was causing him, he busied himself with spooning some *Horlicks* into his mug. With the tip of the knife, Chief Ofodile bored two holes on opposite ends of the full milk tin and slid the milk over to Luciano. The jug on the table was empty, and so Luciano had to go to the sink to refill it with hot water whilst his host made a crude sandwich from two slices of bread and a generous amount of the wok's content.

Luciano returned to the table unsure of how his tastebud would react to the first bite of one of Chief Ofodile's *sandwiches*. He thought he could feel the man's watchful eyes as he went about making his own sandwich, and as he took a bite.

"You aren't used to the cooking of a lonely ageing man?"

Luciano chewed animatedly, mindful not to offend his host. "Not that bad." Even to him, the compliment did not sound convincing enough.

"Come on, you don't have to hide it."

Chief Ofodile chuckled before biting into his *sandwich* with relish. Luciano chased down every bite with generous sips from his steaming mug of sweetened tea.

"You will be wondering why a man with plenty of money lives by himself in a big house and doesn't hire a cook. I can only imagine what sort of a miser you must be thinking me to be."

Luciano thought it over before replying: "It is probable that you like the exercise of making your own meals."

Chief Ofodile laughed and bit into his sandwich again. From the corner of his eye, Luciano observed the man gulp down mouthfuls of his culinary disaster with such gusto that made him put up a considerable bit of effort to restrain himself from shuddering, especially when the man smacked his lips and licked his fingers.

"For the record," Chief Ofodile said after a considerable while, "I don't like cooking for myself, and it is no exercise." He wiped the corner of his mouth with the knuckle of a forefinger. "Let me let you in on a little secret. Out there, many people wish to be me, but they wouldn't wish for the torturous and insipid life I lead. That is if they knew."

Luciano listened like an attentive student, biting into his sandwich. But his mind wasn't entirely with the man's lecture; it was beginning to dawn on him that he might have stumbled onto a man with some serious issues. Unfortunately, he would have to sit through it all, and if this was the cross he was to bear for tapping into the man's deep pockets, then it was a small price to pay. Many successful people are known to have borne much heavier crosses along slippery slopes.

"You see, all my life," Chief Ofodile went on, "I have always been the envy of many. I got a scholarship to study Economics in the United States when many of my friends were still hoping to be accepted into the universities in Ibadan, Lagos, and Nsukka. I got married to a Canadian, my girlfriend from my university days. Her name is Ella. A very beautiful lady. You could see yourself clearly in her eyes, and she had such legs that carried her gracefully as though she was an angel walking on clouds.

"Anyway, we had children who looked like they stood astride two different worlds. Then, I was a celebrity amongst my friends back home. Every single one of them adored me. I could see how they would nearly prostrate on the earth I trod on. It was like I had many badges of honour bestowed upon me by virtue of my having sojourned abroad, studied there, married a woman who isn't African and had interracial kids. I must confess to you, it felt princely those days. But to be honest, I wasn't seeing what they saw. Deep down, I had real issues to contend with. I returned to the country for good, and three months later, I took up a job with the Nigerian Customs Service. I made good money, enough to convince Ella and the kids to join me here and to a comfortable life insulated from the troubles of a country that was progressively lumbering and tethering towards systemic failure."

Chief Ofodile bit into his sandwich and chewed, and then he washed it down with a gulp of tea.

Luciano waited patiently for him to continue, never so much as taking another bite from the *sandwich* hanging limp in his hand.

"I acquired properties in nearly all major Nigerian cities," Chief Ofodile said, "and that was because I wanted an inheritance for my children. Yes. I was a good father. I brought them close to their roots, gave them privileges which most other Nigerians abroad can't even afford their children. Well, so I thought, but then this life could be tricky most times." He sipped from his mug; it was the last drop.

"I had the kids study in Nigerian boarding schools, but they went on to Europe and Canada for university studies, and that was it. Kelly got married to some Colombian boy whom she met in school, and the last time I heard, they were living in Zurich. Suzanne, my favourite, got married to one guitar-playing, carefree Briton. I guess they live in some obscure rat-hole in rundown Budapest. You know, hers breaks my heart the most. I have always had a partiality for her right from the night when we were stuck in traffic on the way to the hospital and Ella had given birth to her in the car, with only me doubling as the panicky driver and care-giver." Chief Ofodile let out a quiet laugh as though the memory amused him. "Information getting to me says that the vagabond Briton, her husband, plays his guitar in parks while she holds out his upturned withered hat to passersby to throw in their worthless pennies, and shriveled notes and what have you. That is how they get money for cheap transport to tour all the rat-holes in Europe so he could sing out his *bloody* heart in smoky bars, underground train stations and in all the rotten parts of the Western world which we don't get to see on television. What a way of life for a daughter with a secure future in Nigeria, her own fatherland?" He wiped his brow. In spite of the last bit of sandwich in his mouth, he sighed before continuing: "Of course, it isn't just the two of them I have. There is Melinda. She is a lesbian. She plays basketball in the United States and absolutely cares for nothing else."

He sighed and went about cutting out another two slices from the loaf, in the hope of making another sandwich. Luciano watched on.

"I thought you have a son?"

"Yea, regrettably," he said. "That one lives with his mother in Quebec. He hates Nigeria so much. The hatred he has for his own country is so glaring that a bat would see its clear outlines in broad daylight. Ella tells me that he is a *photographer*. He cares for no other thing, just like his siblings, except travelling the world and taking shots of anything that catches his fancy. The last time I heard he was in Paris, taking pictures of naked women who are willing to pose for him for a few Euros. All these for a senseless project. I hear some women even offer to pose for free. Imagine! The little rascal gives Africa a wide berth and refers to it in such derogatory terms like *the heart of darkness, the land where the sky isn't blue* and all such phrases which leave me wondering as to where he picked them from. At times I wonder what wrong a man could have done to deserve such punishment as this in his old age. I still ask, for whom have I laboured all these years? Surely not for myself for I wouldn't have laboured that much nor would I have taken certain risks in the past."

Luciano knew of nothing to say.

"Well, the world is a crazy place," Chief Ofodile continued. "Only a thin piece of glass separates reality from illusion; it all depends on what side of the glass you are standing. We will have more to talk on a subject indirectly related to it, but I will have to finish my breakfast first." With that, Chief Ofodile continued from where he had left off with his breakfast. He ate greedily in silence, as though the spilling-out of his emotions had both dampened his spirit and whetted his appetite.

Breakfast done, they retired to the sitting room. Luciano hadn't offered to do the dishes and his host hadn't seemed to be in the mood for them; he had instead dumped them in the sink and saddled with the weight of a full stomach, ushered Luciano to the sitting room. They were seated in deep sofas opposite each other.

Chief Ofodile cleared his throat. "You know, I like enterprising, brave young men who decide to take charge of their own destinies instead of lying in wait for handouts. You are one hell of a tough young fellow. I admire that, and honestly, I must confess to you that it pains me to see that those qualities aren't always rewarded as they should be."

Luciano sat tense in his seat. He could only attempt wild speculations as to what Chief Ofodile was driving at. Probably the man was only politely turning him down, and if that should be the case, Chief Ofodile would still be a good man after all, better than the others whom he had earlier approached for funding; it was only he who had shown such hospitality in inviting him to partake of a culinary mishap and then taken the time to soothe his mood with some encouragement before dropping a polite 'no'.

"But seriously, you got me thinking after our first meeting."

Luciano's heart did a quick flip-flop, but he braced himself for that moment when the man would eventually come around to saying that he wasn't interested in investing his money in some youth's wild fantasies. "I have a principle of not lending money to people, especially for wild shots as this one you propose. But then, we could work out something of immense benefit to the both of us. It's a proposal that will leave none of us feeling indebted to the other."

What is he really trying to say? Luciano's mental antennae went up, searching, feeling, and probing the air for the slightest hint of the obscene. "You could see it as a job and one which comes with a handsome reward."

Hope the man isn't suggesting something out of the ordinary?

"Come with me, Luciano. Let's take a walk outside. This is my house, but I have never trusted walls all my life; they seem to hear too many secrets that they get tempted to tell."

And so, Chief Ofodile led the way out of the house. At the gate, Ali blinked with surprise at the prospect of Chief Ofodile not leaving the premises in any one of the four SUVs parked about the compound.

"Don't lock the gate, Ali. I'm in the vicinity."

"*Tòh, Oga. Allah ya sa kaje lafiya ranka shi dede*; may you go well." He was bent over with reverence as he held the gate open.

Surprisingly, the weather looked gloomy in spite of the earlier promise of a break from the intermittent rains. Only a few people could be seen about the neighbourhood, skipping along, over the many little puddles of murky floodwater and soft muddy spots dotting the narrow street. They kept to the side of the narrow road where the earth seemed firm.

Chief Ofodile exchanged no words with Luciano along the way until they arrived at a sandy football pitch. A team of young men was engrossed in some football training. Some joggled footballs, some did sit-ups and some kicked their legs in the air, all under the watchful eyes of a thin coach standing akimbo with a whistle between his lips. There weren't any spectators about except for three children hawkers on the side of the sandy pitch, their trays of groundnuts balanced upon rolled cloth-pads atop their heads as they pointed and gesticulated at the training footballers.

Chief Ofodile and Luciano stood across from the hawkers. To a cursory observer, they were a young man and an older man, probably his uncle, whiling away a Wednesday morning.

It was Chief Ofodile, with hands stuck deep into his trouser pockets, who spoke first: "I have a proposition for you." Luciano remained still, looking straight ahead. "By the way, how much is it you said you wanted?"

"Five hundred thousand naira."

"That is plenty of money we are talking about here, but I could live with parting with the sum." He paused. "If only you consider my proposition."

Excitement shot through Luciano's nerves. It was with some effort that he kept from punching his fists into the air.

"Yes, I will."

"I am glad you will. I was counting so much on getting this response from you."

"Anything," he managed to say, as a wide smile broke upon his face.

"Anything … I will do it."

"That is good. This is my proposition: I have a son. Not the one in the Canada, but another one here in

Nigeria." He heaved a sigh and looked straight ahead. Luciano could tell from the man's countenance that he wasn't seeing the footballers, even though he was looking in their direction. "He should be a little younger than you are now. I think, twenty-five. You see, we were having a difficult time in our marriage, Ella and I. The children were in school and Ella had taken the opportunity to vacation in Turkey. She said she needed the time away to figure her stand on the direction our marriage was headed. I was broken inside and out. I feared that our marriage of a decade was as good as ended. Well, on that day she left for Turkey, I began to expect a divorce suit. In the midst of my troubles, I fell into a romantic situation with a cook I had hired. Uduak. That was her name. I guess it still is. Oh! Such a young woman with so much fire bottled up inside of her. She did so many things to my body and mind, the kind of things Ella knows absolutely nothing about. Anyway, the good news as at then was that she got pregnant. We lived together in the house and I had never been any happier; not when I got my degree, and even though I am a bit ashamed to say it, definitely not when my favourite child was born. Sorry for digressing." He let out a light cough. "Just when I was settling down with Uduak, I got a call from Ella; she sounded very much different from what I had earlier envisioned. Her emotions sounded mashed up and remorseful when she told me over the phone of her resolve to come back home. She told me that she had befriended a psychologist in Antalya, a city in Turkey, and that their acquaintance had advised her new resolve. You can imagine my dilemma; I could have told her then about Uduak, but I had children whom I loved. It was these children who influenced my decision, and funnily enough, they have turned out to be the rot in my ageing bones."

He breathed deeply, scratched his left ear and joined his hands behind his back. "Well, it happened that Uduak had to go. You might judge me in your heart all you want, but since it won't change a thing I don't see how it should mean anything to me." He shifted his weight to one foot. "She sent word across when the baby came. It was a boy, and I kept my promise of setting her up comfortably and giving her a generous monthly allowance on the condition that she kept the existence of the baby and our past affair secret. Well, to cut the long story short, things had been the way I had hoped for until some months back when she told me that the lad, our son, was having some revolutionary tendencies. I didn't lose any sleep over the matter. After all, he was my bastard, dispensable and of little significance. That had been the situation until Ella left me to join that wanton son of ours in Quebec. I contacted Uduak, for I wanted to make amends for my past mistakes. But the stupid woman told me that my boy had disappeared. You could imagine the way she was casual about telling me that she knew nothing of his whereabouts and couldn't contact him in any way. Before now, I hadn't retained any contacts with Uduak other than the bank account with which I religiously transferred money for her upkeep and my son's. There was the occasional phone call every now and then, though. I haven't even set eyes on the boy ever since he was born." He flashed Luciano a defiant look. "Save your judgments; they will amount to nothing. I want my son. I will want to approach my grave with the knowledge that an army of strangers will not invade the fruits of my lifelong toils." He sighed, drawing plenty of the cool morning air into his lungs. Again, he looked at Luciano standing still, in rapt attention, next to him. The look of excitement was gone. In its place was an expression that hinted at an ongoing battle in his mind. "Will you look for my son for me?"

If Luciano had brought himself to look into Chief Ofodile's eyes, he would have seen the plea in them, but he was too taken over with deep contemplation. He opened his mouth, but he hadn't decided on what words to speak and so he shut it. His eyes darted sideways to the other side, away from Chief Ofodile. The confusion was mounting, but he tried not to appear as evidently stupid as his speechlessness was already making him feel.

"I know it is too much of a task," Chief Ofodile said, "and that is why I am willing to pay handsomely for it."

"You could go to the police. They will help you with it."

"And make a media scandal of the whole thing? Do you know who I am? Every journalist will want to reap off such a piece of news as this?"

"But why me? I don't even know how to go about searching for a lost stranger."

"I believe you can. I went through the copy of the manuscript you left with me and I saw a person who could look at the ordinary and see beyond what every other person sees. You have a nose. You can poke into places where a dog wouldn't."

"I am only a writer."

"You're more than that."

"Where is this son of yours?"

"That is why I am hiring you. If I knew the answer to this your question, we wouldn't have been talking in the first place."

Luciano shook his head in dejection. *The solitude must have gotten into this man's head to think he could send me on a quixotic search across uncharted territories.*

"Okay, I understand your reluctance, but here is the deal. I will make sure you don't run out on operational expenses. As a reward for carrying out this assignment successfully, I will furnish you with all the money you need for your book. You just have to find my son and convince him to come to his father. If you decide to take on the assignment, I will equip you with the information you need to go on."

"I don't see any …"

"Just go home. Think it over. I will be waiting for your reply. Take your time. I am a patient man."

Luciano nodded, and when he stepped out, he was grateful to have left the presence of Chief Ofodile. Already, he was beginning to feel sore thinking about how privileged folks were in the habit of riding a desperate fellow really hard.

"Just think about what you stand to gain," Chief Ofodile called after him.

He heard the parting words as he walked across the sandy pitch over to the other side, but he never made any sign of acknowledgement.

The footballers were seated in the sands, exhausted. They passed on bottles of water amongst themselves. The children hawkers were beginning to stroll away from the edge of the pitch, towards another day of traversing the lanes and streets of Port-Harcourt, hopeful that the day would provide customers for their salted groundnuts.

TWO

Dear Luciano,

Thank you for your email, and for giving me a look at your manuscript. I appreciate your patience as I have taken the time to consider your material.

Unfortunately, I'm afraid I must pass. Though you have a strong premise, the opening pages didn't quite pull me in.

Thank you again for thinking of me, and please accept my best wishes for your project's success.

Sincerely,
Mercy Willow T.
Wonderbridge Literary Agency
Sydney, Australia.

Luciano stared long at the words on the computer screen. They appeared to dangle and swim before his eyes when he wasn't focusing. He wanted to fold himself away from all eyes, to cry out his frustration, and to bottle up the disappointment that tore at his heart. He had come to know the feeling that came with the same responses from literary agents and publishers whom he approached for his novel manuscript. For a fleeting moment, he considered venting his emotions on the stained walls of his rented room but thought it sensible to pardon the thin suffering walls. And he didn't cry because he couldn't; his tear glands had run dry a very long time ago.

There was hardly any foreign literary agency or publisher he had spared a meticulously tailored query, and then he had helplessly watched on as his query letters began to take on the tone of abject desperation. But none of the agencies or publishers considered the story, *Igwemma,* for even the most ridiculous offers in the publishing industry.

The local publishers had been worse off in their response; they had simply ignored him even when he sent multiple queries that relayed his mounting desperation. He didn't blame them; at least he tried not to. They were as frustrated as the stranded prospective local authors clueless as to what to do with something they believed to be nature's rare gift of storytelling bestowed upon them. He had read somewhere that the local literary publishers kept day jobs too, and publishing, to them, was likened to a woman frying fish heads in a pan of hot oil; they kept a safe distance because they knew it was a risky venture. If there was any real publishing to be done, it had to be either the more guaranteed academic texts for school curricula, 'bankable' Nigerian writers successfully published abroad, or nothing. Dipping into their pockets or taking loans and risking debt to fulfil some writer's lofty dream was utter madness, considering the costs to keep up with; there were office spaces to pay for, telephone and courier services, distribution and warehousing, employee salaries and the constant supply of diesel needed to run imported power generators on. And so, they had all given up in despair like most of the sensible local writers, to concentrate on the business of 'getting by'. At least that is the story with nearly every one of them. And this lot would rather that the writer showed enough confidence in his project to bear the financial burden of making his dreams come true. They floated imprints for these. Vanity presses, they called them.

There wasn't anyone to blame for this situation and nobody would want to shoulder any blames. The local paper mills weren't any longer functional. Everything needed for printing had to be imported, and they came in through the wharves under the sponsorship of the importer spoiling for huge profits. Should a publisher be crazy enough to publish some writer's novel up to international standards, no ordinary Nigerian would desire to commit three thousand naira for a book when that same amount could insure a thrifty fellow against hunger for a little over two weeks. Getting published overseas still meant that the books wouldn't be available for the average local reader when the high cost of clearing printed materials through customs was considered.

If only he could get published abroad. If only he could be like the privileged few who caught the eyes of foreign audience and got invited over to an American university to lecture on African Studies or African Literature or anything of the sort. It didn't matter if no Nigerian audience read his books. It would never matter for as long as he found himself far away from the frustration that threatened to squeeze the essence out of his sanity.

He had awoken late that morning, as usual, and was seated at the plastic desk set against the wall farthest from the bed, which was actually a mattress laid on the carpeted floor of his room. He was prepped up to do some new round of editing on *Igwemma* but had decided to check his emails; perchance there was something new waiting for him. The rejection letter stood out amongst two other unread messages, and by the time he was through with digesting the sugar-laced rejection, his zeal for *Igwemma* momentarily faded into the air. Getting off the plastic stool, he made towards the clothes' hanger, rummaged through the pockets of an old coat he no longer wore and whose pockets now held what bits and ends he could easily stash into them but was met with disappointment at the empty cigarette pack. Now, not to his surprise, he usually found succour in cigarettes whenever the frustration became unbearable.

With his hands akimbo, he contemplated on dipping into the two thousand naira in a pocket of the coat. It was the money Oge, his girlfriend, had left on the table before leaving for her place; that was her way of giving him money without bruising his ego. Torn between the fear of starvation and the hankering desire for the taste of nicotine, he stood and bit his lower lip in contemplation.

Maami's shouting interrupted his thoughts. Of all the neighbours in the yard, she was the loudest. Her voice filtered in through the thin wall that demarcated his room from the one she shared with her six little children. No doubt, she was in a sour mood this time, but she could be a jolly good nosy fellow when all was right with her.

"Girlie, you are a wicked girl!" she screamed.

He knew that she was at it again with her first child and only daughter, Girlie. He could tell from experience that soon enough, the teenage Girlie's shrill voice would rise in calm defence, but it could be lost to him if he didn't strain his ears well enough.

"When I was your age, I cared for my mother but I don't know where you picked this wickedness from!"

"Maami, I have told you, I don't have any money."

"Why don't you have any money? All those men who come to pick you, don't they give you money? Or do you give it to them for free? What do you use the money for? Where do you keep them? It is not like you feed your baby. I do that for you. I feed her ... I pay the electricity bills ... rent ... everything that is to be done in this house with the money I get from my man friends. Don't tell me you don't have any money!"

Luciano willed his ears to go deaf to Maami's shameless ranting. He just couldn't understand Maami's household; he didn't know much about the middle-aged woman with the bleached skin, but he knew she didn't have any husband. It was rumoured that not any two of her six children shared the same father. Girlie, just fourteen, supple and beautiful, with a close-cropped hairdo, breastfed an eight-month-old infant already. None of the children went to school. One could tell that a man was with their mother whenever one saw all of the children outside, playing or idling away, never entering their one-room apartment until the strange man was done with whatever business he conducted with their mother behind closed doors. On some nights, Luciano's mind would be disturbed with wild, pleasurable screams seeping through the walls into his room. He could tell Girlie's softer moans and suppressed whimpers from Maami's vulgar pleadings for whoever wielded the pestle to grind harder and deeper.

He reached for the money, took a five-hundred naira note and left the room. He desired the open air outside, to sit by the Fulani mallam's shop, puffing at a stick of cigarette, dreaming of being rich and famous and escaping every element of the present world around him.

In all of his thoughts, he never considered Chief Ofodile's proposal. The visit and the man's absurd proposition were relegated to that part of his mind where irrelevant memories were discarded, never to be revisited. The memory of that visit, to him, was likened to the first day he had barged into the communal toilet without knocking and had stumbled on Maami defecating into a bucket that once held custard.

THREE

"Baby."

The word came to his sleepy head like an echo from an abyss. "Baby."

"Huh."

He rolled away from Oge seated on the edge of the mattress. She had passed the night at his place.

"Baby." She nudged him a bit roughly on the shoulder.

"What?"

"Wake up. It's morning already."

An eyelid popped open. The dreamy eye regarded her momentarily as his sleep-addled mind took in the fact that she was dressed for work already, and then the eyelid slapped shut as abruptly as it had opened.

"Wake up na. Don't you know it is daybreak already?"

"I know."

He rolled over, burying his face in the pillows. They reeked of his stale sweat.

"Then wake up!"

"And do what?" The pillow muffled his voice so that he sounded like an antagonist in a zombie movie.

"Get up first."

"But I have been up all night, working."

"Baby, I want to talk to you *now*."

He knew better not to try waving her off when she sounded vexed. It just wasn't possible. Turning over on his side, he propped his head against his arm and faced her. He noticed her white miniskirt and the black coat over a white blouse that held out her full bosom suggestively. He gulped at the sight.

"What is it?"

"It is about you."

"Me?"

"Yes, you." There was an edge of finality in her voice. "You will have to do a rethink on the choices you are making with your life. You have to go out there and take a job, a proper one like everybody else is doing."

The sleepiness vanished completely from his eyes. "Baby, but we have had this discussion a long time before now."

"It isn't working, Luciano. You just don't have to stubbornly cling onto one particular plan all your life, even when it isn't working. You don't have all the time in the world. And it is not like you will live on forever so you can correct your mistakes when you are forty.

No, it is not so. You have to face reality. If one path isn't working out, you try another. Be flexible. They all lead to one destination after all."

He sat up abruptly and wheeled on his buttocks until he was seated next to her. Then he spoke in a pacifying voice: "Baby, we just have to exercise some little patience. We are this close to a breakthrough." He formed a pincer in the air with his thumb and fore-finger. "There's this publisher in Ibadan. I hear he will be interested in taking a look at my kind of writing."

"There you go again. This is exactly what you said the last time. The only difference was that the publisher was based in South Africa. From all I can see, we haven't progressed any farther than that."

"Baby, don't speak that way. Let us just be patient a little more. We will only have to exercise some little faith. It is surprising that you don't see the things I see. I see the light at the end of the tunnel. I see you standing next to me as I walk up the podium to take up awards, with the spotlight focused on the both of us, *me and you,* baby. Me and you. Doesn't this sound good? I see us on a book tour, walking the streets of Paris, London, New York, Sydney and all those wonderful places we to see on TV. It is beautiful life, Baby. A peaceful one. I will just write and we will have a wonderful life from the proceeds of my writing. You would never have to hastily dress up every morning to go pine away at some lousy job, enduring sexual harassment and derogatory treatment befitting only a stray dog, and all just for a begrudging salary. I will write from home and keep you and our children company. What other definition can we ascribe to the word *bliss*?"

"That is exactly what I am saying. You just have to wake up from that fantasy and take up a job, at least for me. Every other person is doing it and at least they are responsible enough. They can feed themselves and pay their own bills. See, I am not getting any younger either."

"Oh, is that what this is all about? *Marriage*?"

She frowned and turned her face away. "I just want to know where I stand with you. Period! "

"I have told you that I don't see a future without you." His tone dropped. "We could just get married in a marriage registry any time. You don't have to be in doubt that I love you with every string of my being."

"I cannot be married off just like that! In some marriage registry! Listen to yourself, Luciano! We are Nigerians, and not Europeans. We have to do things the normal way. We have a culture, for Christ's sake! I don't care about the ideas that spring in your head … I don't care what you choose to believe in as a writer, but I am not getting married off in some registry. God forbid. Not me, Ogemdi. "

"See, you are putting me in a tight corner the same way every one of your modern kind puts every other young man. The culture of getting married with hilarious amounts of money isn't favourable to this generation. We just have to revolt, albeit peacefully, by our actions, by being blatant in our opposition of all our cultural shackles and all those steep demands which we impose on ourselves and which mocks our attempts to escape the clutches of poverty into which we are born."

"If you were born into poverty, Luciano, I was not. I am not poor. Please! I don't share in your negativity. And I can't confess to being poor."

"That is it, the attempt to shy away from the reality staring you in the face. This new evangelical mindset possessing everybody isn't amounting to any good. "

"Baby, please stop that. I hate it when you begin to sound like you are set to change the world. It only makes you appear like a failure hiding under the ambition of a social crusader. It makes you sound like there is no hope with you, honestly."

Luciano looked pained, but he tried not to show the impact of her words. "But I am still young. I haven't reached my journey's end, and as such you can't say if I have failed or succeeded."

"I know. I believe in you and that is why I am asking for you to make some more effort in the direction of success. I wouldn't want to get pregnant by you outside of wedlock. I am tired of all these constant precautions."

"Baby, let us look at it this way; I need just a little over three hundred thousand naira to print a thousand copies of *Igwemma* with one of those vanity presses, but the requirement for the marriage rites is just so astonishing to the point of sounding like an outright joke."

"What are you driving at?"

"Didn't we both go through the items on the list? One hundred and twenty tubers of yam, forty whole stockfish, eight bags of rice, yards of wrappa, more than twenty-five crates of beer … trinkets, umbrellas, goats, chickens and just so much that I really can't remember without having to consult the list again. I think there was a motorcycle included on the list too. Did we not calculate three hundred thousand naira halfway through the list? Not including the stipulated cash payment of fifty-three thousand naira for what I can't still remember? If I had such money, wouldn't I have self-published my manuscript and live this dream that makes a hell of my world? Honestly, at some point, I begin to reason if that list isn't a ploy by your people to discourage our marriage since I didn't show up in a car."

"It is just too early to get into a quarrel with you. As you can see, I am on my way to work. I don't want you to wish me bad luck today. I simply wanted to let you know how I feel about the life you are leading."

With that, Oge got to her feet and strode out of the room, never uttering another word.

He heard her shove her feet into her high-heeled

shoes and then slammed the door with the mosquito netting shut. Luciano knew that the prospect of sleeping an extra hour before sitting down to do some editing on *Igwemma* wasn't going to be achievable. The morning had been soiled already.

FOUR

Three days had passed, but Luciano had not heard from Oge. He sent her a laconic text -- *call me back* -- but she never did. When he called at her apartment, nobody answered the door even when he could swear that she was in. He was becoming frustrated with her determination to avoid him. He needed her desperately. If for anything, he was starving.

He held nothing against her; not for her recent behaviour or for the confrontation on that morning three days back. Most times he questioned the sanity of his choice in being a writer wholly dependent on his writing for survival. There were moments when his mind was assailed with doubts; he feared his dreams were simply not dreams in the right sense of the word, but dreams to be lived only in his sleep. But then, the real fear had come when it began to dawn on him that Oge was intentionally avoiding him. She had been his only support for a long time, longer than he could recall. The fact that she had lost faith in him, and at this moment, was a mutiny, a betrayal too diabolic to consider.

The night before had been passed in deep contemplation. Luciano had strongly considered dusting off his certificates and heading to Trans-Amadi Industrial Estate to knock on the gates of factories in search of a job. The prospect had gotten him perturbed. It unearthed memories of past experiences at some job. Eventually, morning had come and the night's resolve dissipated with the break of dawn.

Luciano had worked in a biscuit factory owned by a Nigerian but run by a team of expatriate Lebanese. That had been months ago. It had been one moment of his life when he had been confronted with such realities that made him question everything about getting by in a civilized society. The factory workers were ridden hard like dispensable bits of machinery and for wages just sufficient to keep them alive and available until the next payday. He was astonished that the workers were grateful to be working on a job, glorying in the pride of not being 'jobless' like the 'less-privileged' others. Overwhelmed with the world about him, he learned to let out his spirit wander onto territories that existed only in his head while he worked mechanically at the packaging unit of the factory. At night, he would force his exhausted body and mind to plough through the pages of American novels by candlelight in his rented room; only when Maami and her family weren't in their foul element. He feared that his soul pined away as the days dragged by. During work hours, he would catch himself lost in space, conjuring up flawed characters. There came with it the nagging feeling to put those flawed characters and their imperfect worlds into writing, but it seemed there was no time or energy enough after long hours at the factory. Alone in his room every night, he would only write for a few minutes before he caught himself dozing off. Time dragged by and he grew more discontent. Those imaginative spells at work became more frequent until he began to get in trouble with the young Lebanese supervisor. They had quarreled one morning. That was when the supervisor threatened to whip him for being lazy and Luciano punched the over-bearing man in the face and fled the premises before the security guards at the gate got any wiser. That had been his last day at work.

Jobless, he had had all the time to indulge the fantasies of his imaginations so that he had completed the first draft of *Igwemma* in twelve weeks. Many people thought him crazy because he abandoned a job when there was an army of capable, young boys out there willing to give anything for a chance to earn an honest living. He thought himself crazy at times too. He knew he wasn't normal, and that he wasn't like every other person. To his understanding, the others never saw the big picture; they were too busy, with their snouts in the dirt, poking and foraging for a stray morsel to nibble at while life went by. He knew he had raised his head from the dirt, seen the horizon, and was crazy enough to have embarked on a journey to meet it. He never believed himself to be cut out for crumbs; he thought of himself as a human being, cut out to live. But it was only when doubts stood like a faint mist in the far distance that he felt pessimism gnaw at his heart.

The morning had begun with another round of fine-tuning of *Igwemma*. Two long hours had been spent poring over some sentence constructions and punctuation, deleting whole paragraphs to make the plot sound more close-knitted and logical. He worked until he found himself unable to articulate properly. He stretched and yawned, and his back ached from sitting for long on the plastic stool. Hunger gnawed at his stomach. All night, he had eaten nothing; he was doing his best to stretch the remaining five hundred naira in his pocket for as long as possible pending when he resolved the issue with Oge. Taking a walk sounded more like what he needed to ease his strained body and mind. He wriggled into a pair of grey combat shorts and a shirt that smelled slightly of stale sweat. He had just secured the padlock on his door when he noticed Papa CY, the landlord, waddling into the yard through the dimly lit narrow passage. If only he had noticed the loud-spoken, pot-bellied man on time, he would have ducked back into his room. But the man had already spotted him.

"Haa, neighbour! I don find you tire."

"I've been around."

Luciano was never at ease with the man; he never stopped by to chat with Luciano except when there was some new levy to be imposed on the tenants.

"I been knock for your door two times, but you no open. I come feel say you dey with that your fine nwa baby. Na so I just comot, make e no be like say I dey pour sand-sand for your garri."

Luciano managed a weak smile. Papa CY reciprocated with a conspiratorial smile that revealed a large pair of yellowed incisors forked sideways. "You know say everybody dey contribute money for the new transformer? Na him make I dey find you." He scratched his pot-belly peeking through a couple of undone buttons of an oversized long-sleeved shirt. "Your own share na three thousand, two hundred naira."

"Three thousand wetin?! Haba, Oga Landlord!"

"Na so we share am. Point by point."

"How many points do I have?"

"I no know, but I know say you get fan, pressing iron, computer, bulb."

"But my fan isn't working."

"Na wetin I see wey I count."

Luciano held down the irritation. He hadn't remembered welcoming the man or any one of the man's sons into his room. How come they had an inventory of his material goods? Nosy, jobless people!

"Where is the bill for the yard? I would like to see it."

Papa CY scratched his belly again. His forehead wrinkled with the strained effort of wracking his memory. "I no know where CY keep am."

Luciano saw his window of momentary escape. "Okay, I'm on my way out now. I will come to take a look at the bill when I return late in the evening."

"No wahala. But you go come back, abi?"

"Yes na."

"Na work you dey go?"

Luciano pretended not to hear Papa CY's last question. He hurried on towards the dimly-lit passage, eager to put as much distance between himself and the landlord. *The meddlesome bastard! Always poking his nose into other people's affairs.*

He was still seething with resentment as he fought to adjust his sight to the long, near-dark passage with rooms on either side rented out to tenants. The passage looked like a tunnel even in the brightest of afternoons, and then it was always stuffy with the aroma of food cooking on the many kerosene stoves set up beside each tenant's door. On Sundays, the aromas were mostly of curry stews, but on other days it often was the aroma of some pale soup being warmed over stove fires so that an experienced nose could tell that the weary soup had been stretched for far too long so as to sustain a household of little means and many mouths to feed.

As he picked his way along, he cursed the electricity company for wanting to install the new transformer. All the months there hadn't been any electricity, no one had died, and instead, life had continued without the extra burden of electricity bills. Besides, he didn't have three thousand naira to spend on electricity, which was guaranteed to be in unsteady supply.

FIVE

Luciano laid siege by the rusty brown gates of Oge's compound all afternoon of the next day, even though he was sure she would still be at work. He was intent on reconciling with her. His whole worldly goods amounted to a hundred naira and the remainder of a small loaf; leftovers of a sparse breakfast. Starvation was closing fast on him; it left him with no choice other than a reconciliation with Oge.

He saw Oge alight from a tricycle taxi, pay the driver, and would have breezed past him in feigned oversight had he not stepped on her path.

"Oge, why have you been avoiding me?"

"Please get out of my way!"

"This isn't you, Oge. What has suddenly come over you?"

"Luciano or whatever you may decide to call yourself, I don't know about you, but I take my own life seriously …"

"Oge, this isn't the way to go about things. We can sort out our misunderstanding together and amicably. This is no issue, and you are overplaying it already. Let us sit and sort it out as we always do."

"No. I have sat down and I have taken enough time to sort mine. I have been trying to sort out yours for you, but you fail to see it. Maybe you take me for a fool because I brought myself cheaply to you. Maybe it is because I don't make any demands on you. That's no problem. I have learnt my lessons. It is now up to you to sort out your life on your own this time." With her hands akimbo, she turned her face away. Luciano noticed that she was blinking in suppressed agitation.

"Okay, tomorrow, I will go looking for a new job, I promise. Would that be okay?"

She snickered. "Too late, dreamer. You woke up just when the party is over. And come to think of it, how is it supposed to be my business anymore what you choose to do with yourself?"

"Come on, Oge. Why are you talking strangely?"

"Luciano, I am getting married to someone else."

It seemed like that split second after a hard-used pillow had been slammed into your face; Luciano stood rooted as the numbness swept over him. He blinked repeatedly as though to revive his stunned senses.

"Oge!"

"And I must warn you to keep away from me. Should

I find you stalking me ever again, I will make sure you don't live to repeat it."

"Oge, please …"

She would have run him over had he not stepped aside just in time for her to brush past. He stood by, watching her stomp away, rounding the block of flats to the servants' quarters where her one-room apartment was.

FIVE

The next morning saw Luciano headed to Chief Ofodile's house. He met the gate open as a black Nissan Armada eased out of the compound in reverse gear. Chief Ofodile was at the wheels. His eyes lit up in recognition when he saw Luciano.

"You are coming to see me," he said after he had rolled down the window on his side. It was more of a statement of fact than an enquiry. The devil-may-care smile underscored the point. Luciano nodded in the affirmative. "I am on my way out, but that business can wait. Let us meet inside."

He changed gears and drove back into the compound. Ali shut the gates while Chief Ofodile ushered Luciano into the mansion. As they walked, Luciano noticed Chief Ofodile looked older than the last time he saw him, even though it was only days ago. His well-tended greying hair stood out, and he hobbled slightly to the left. He noticed also that Chief Ofodile never locked the front door of the house when he went out.

"Hope it isn't too early for a drink?"

He was making straight for the small bar at one corner of the small sitting room, close to a shelf stacked full with gleaming leather-bound volumes.

"Malt will do, sir."

Chief Ofodile had been reaching for a glass on a lower shelf when he suddenly stopped. With an astonished look on his face, he turned around to his guest. "You don't take alcohol?"

"Yes, sir, I drink alcohol. I am just not up for it at the moment," Luciano said, lowering himself into one of the deep leather sofas, grateful to rest his wearied feet after walking the entire distance from his place.

"That's better. I never would trust a man who doesn't drink."

Chief Ofodile poured himself a generous measure of scotch, and bearing it in one hand and a can of *Maltina* in the other, he strode to a sofa opposite Luciano. He slid the cold can of *Maltina* across the low table to his guest just as he eased himself into the sofa, suppressing a wince from a pain in his knee. He sipped his drink.

"You have considered my proposal?"

"Yes, sir. I have."

"Good."

Luciano pulled the ring on the can, slurped the

foam that erupted and proceeded to drink greedily. In an instant the can's content had gone down his gullet and sated his stomach, which was raw with hunger; his last meal had been a little piece of bread on the night of the previous day. He suppressed a belch.

Chief Ofodile, pretending not to notice his visitor's voraciousness, had his gaze fixed on the scotch glass in his grip.

"I'm just curious," he said. "What exactly advised your decision to accept my proposal?" Luciano absentmindedly circled a finger around the rim of the empty can, but said nothing. "Is it because of money?"

Luciano offered no reply still. He was beginning to feel uneasy at the thought of Chief Ofodile circling him like a hound teasing a cornered prey. "I thought as much. It has to be money." Chief Ofodile paused, and shrugged. "Alright, we will get down to business if only you excuse me for a second." He eased himself from the sofa, hobbled out of the sitting room and disappeared through an arched doorway.

Luciano's gaze rested on the man's drink abandoned on the glass centre table. *Is this old man simply careless or does he think himself invincible?* As for him, Luciano, he wouldn't make such a mistake. An uncle was said to have done the same and had come back home vomiting, only to die on that same night shortly before a swift messenger had arrived dragging a herbalist along.

Luciano saw Chief Ofodile re-appearing, a brown envelope dangling in his loose grip and he returned to his seat. His wincing wasn't as pronounced as the first time. He noticed Luciano's attention focused on a goatskin hand fan on the wall. A bold inscription was stitched around its circumference: *Onwa n'etiri ora 1 of Aniasa.*

"My ceremonial hand fan," he said with pride. "Reminds me of glorious days long gone, those days when they used to call me *Onwa*. Some people still call me that title, though, but that isn't the issue for today."

He upturned the envelope and its sole content spilled onto the centre table. It was a small-sized photograph of a boy posing on a photographer's stool. Tossing the envelope aside, Chief Ofodile picked up the photograph with reserved care, and gazed at it for a considerable while before passing it to Luciano.

"There he is. His name is Aniete. Aniete Ubong. His mother named him after her own people. He is studying at Imo State University. If my calculations are anything to go by, this should be his second year studying Food Science."

Luciano studied the glossy picture. In it, the boy seemed to be somewhere in his mid-twenties. The face was fair, beardless and slightly oval, and the well-oiled bare scalp glistened in the daylight. His eyes looked mischievously carefree like he had some secret to hide but enjoyed the thrill of keeping it concealed.

"Is this picture recent?"

"Yes. I asked his mother for it a few weeks ago."

"When was the last time you heard from him or saw him?"

"Like I told you, I have never heard from him nor seen him … except in this photo."

"What if this isn't your son?" Luciano asked. "What if this your mistress is onto some scheme to fleece you of money?" He started regretting this spontaneous speech even before its completion. As crazy as this whole quest sounded, he had decided to embark on it as a desperate measure to escape dying of hunger. This quest promised money, security, and much more money if it was successful; money he was in desperate need for; and discouraging Chief Ofodile wasn't in any way making his life any better.

"It is not possible … This is my son." Chief Ofodile's voice was laced with sentiment, and he jabbed a finger into the air to emphasize every syllable. "By the way, what does she stand to gain in making me go on a search for the missing boy? It isn't like she is asking for funds to organize a search party."

"Of course, I was just testing the logic of the whole thing. He has your eyes, I mean the boy."

Chief Ofodile heaved, perhaps in relief, and then settled back into his seat. "You see why I have faith in you? You have a nose and eyes that seek things out of the ordinary."

Luciano remained indifferent to the flattery. "So, what's the deal?"

Chief Ofodile clasped his hands together and leaned forward. "Here it is. Every week, I will make a deposit of thirty thousand naira into an account of your designation. The money is for operational expenses. Here is my business card." He leaned to his side to get out a lean brown wallet from his hip pocket. Out of the wallet, he fished out a business card and tossed it to Luciano. "You will call me every two days to fill me in on your progress. I will warn you, young man, if you dare play me in any way, you will force me into going back on some past I would rather not."

Luciano pretended not to have been affected by the threat. "And if I complete the assignment?"

"Yes, if you do complete the assignment, and I'm optimistic that you will, you will have six hundred thousand naira to yourself. I have decided to throw in the additional money for motivation."

Luciano focused hard on the photograph in his hand. It was an attempt to hide his eyes from Chief Ofodile; he didn't want the man to notice the excitement in them. It was a difficult task, but he congratulated himself on doing just fine. In holding down his simmering emotion.

"So when do you start off?"

"Immediately … I am commencing immediately, sir."

"Good," Chief Ofodile said, and nodded in undisguised contentment. "Good." He dipped into his pocket again and fished out a wad of naira notes. "This is to set you on the road." He handed Luciano the money. "Take it as a token of goodwill, not part of your allowances or payment."

Luciano nodded his gratitude and tucked the money into the recesses of his trouser pocket. He couldn't tell exactly how much it was. But from the bulge, he could guess it was about fifteen thousand naira. However much it amounted to, it was good money; it had been a long time he had that amount of money to himself. The gnawing hunger in his stomach faded into nothing at the thought of the reassuring bulge. Didn't they say that a hungry man who had hope of eating never dies of hunger?

"I hope our deal is fair?" Chief Ofodile asked.

"Yes … Yes, sir. It is fair."

"Just bring my son to me."

"I will do my very best."

"Call me to give me the account number for depositing your allowances. And remember, I want you to be the one calling every two days to give me situation reports."

"Sure, sir. I will be doing just that."

"Thank you."

Luciano knew that the meeting was over, and so he

stood to leave. The man returned his attention to his drink on the centre table just as Luciano made for the front door.

Out in the streets, Luciano had just one destination in mind: a restaurant to treat himself to a sumptuous meal such as he had never had in a long while. After some refreshment, he would immerse himself into this quest. As crazy as it sounded, he had no more reservations against it. After all, it was an all-expense paid expedition with some good reward in view at the end of it all.

THE SEARCH

SIX

OKIGWE ROAD, OWERRI.

The taxi dropped Luciano off at IMSU junction. He dipped his hand into his pocket and handed his fare to the driver.

"I don't have change," the taxi driver said, his face contorting in irritation at the two hundred naira note Luciano held out. If he noticed the impatient honking of the other cars behind his, he never showed it. Even the obscenities hauled at him for taking up the small parking space for too long did not cause him to be civil. Or perhaps he was, implausibly oblivious to these savage noises. It was Luciano who felt embarrassed for attracting attention.

"Never mind, keep the change," Luciano said to the driver.

The taxi driver, grateful for the rare generosity of his passenger, steered his smoking car onto the road amidst nerve-shattering honking. An irate taxi driver leaned hard against his car door and screamed into his face, "*I wu onye apali!* You are a fool!"

"Your mother's genitals!" he bawled in Igbo before speeding away into the afternoon.

Luciano leapt over a wide-open drainage gutter and began to make his way uphill towards the university gate, joining a throng of gaily-dressed students walking to and fro. Now and then, he found himself turning backwards and sideways at the many beautiful young women who were about the place. It felt like he was a child in a candy shop, staring at all manner of appealing things on display.

It was his first time seeing Owerri. He had heard a lot about the beautiful girls of the university in the city centre, and now he had begun to attest to the truthfulness of those stories. The city itself pulsed with noticeable exuberance; you could sense it the very moment you arrived. Life in Owerri was unhurried yet vibrant; the kind he had never seen in any other Nigerian cities.

At the Main Gate, he breezed past the armed uniformed guards more concerned with ensuring that none of the motorists evaded the toll fee. From the gate, he heard loud music punctuated by the distant roar of a thrilled crowd. The road ahead forked into a T with a black signpost at the head of the junction written in bold letters: INDECENT DRESSING IS NOT ALLOWED ON CAMPUS. He turned to his left and then right. Assured that there wasn't any risk of being run over by the many luxury cars he had seen driving past, he crossed to the other side of the road. He didn't know where exactly he was headed to, but he followed a throng of students walking on the paved sidewalks and onto one of the red-brick walkways crisscrossing a park dotted with life-size sculptures, shade trees and concrete benches, towards where he could guess the music was coming from.

Four loudspeakers stood amongst the statues, directed towards the four cardinal points of the park. A disc jockey scratched away at his equipment, entertaining a crowd of jolly youngsters standing in a thick human ring as they cheered and jeered at some activity going on at the centre of the ring.

Luciano couldn't see through the dense crowd of spectators and so he climbed onto one of the concrete benches. Five youths, obviously students, were dancing, in fierce competition, to the Dancehall music blaring from the loudspeakers. They were three girls and two boys. The dancer who seemed to attract the most attention was a dark, fat boy. Such a good dancer he proved to be, swinging his hips and belly to the rhythm of the music with such fluid and effortless grace that was capable of putting a belly-dancer to shame.

"Kingston! Kingston!" rent the air as he danced on, thrilling the crowd even more.

An emcee called off the music and the crowd unanimously voted for Kingston as the overall winner. He was awarded a free pass for the Ladies Free Night at some night club in town. Luciano hadn't gotten the name of the club when the emcee called it, but he thought it sounded *Nollywood,* or was it *Hollywood Nite Club?*

As the emcee began announcing another round of competitions, a drinking contest this time, Luciano walked away from the merry crowd and decided to savour the life of the campus. Through the park, he strolled, keeping to the leafy shades until he came to a line of fruit trees bordering the edge of the park. A yellow building stood across on a patch of eroded land. A rusty sign high up the roof read *Faculty of Humanities* in faded blue letters. He made for the building with the intent of looking around, and that was when he heard the familiar chorus of voices and drumbeats. It was the same drumming and hearty singing that had stolen his young, teenage heart a long time ago.

He was fifteen and in secondary school when he first heard the Kegite Club of Nigeria play. The occasion had been at Grandma's burial and the Kegite Club of Nigeria had attended because Ukachukwu, his big cousin, was a member at *Ilya Du Elephant,* as the Abia State Polytechnic branch was referred to. They had come with their drums, their blue-and-white ill-tailored regalia, sonorous voices and merry hearts. They had beaten their drums and danced in circles after Mother had presented them with a generous mound of *fufu*, a small cooler of bitter-leaf soup with bits of beef and a fifty-litre can of fresh palm wine as Ukachukwu had advised.

The villagers, even old men and the other music troupes in that had come for the burial ceremony had abandoned every care and worry as they danced in circles and sang along with the Kegite Club members. In the spirit of merriment, more cans of palm wine and beer had found their way onto the arena, disappearing almost immediately in gentle sips down jolly throats. Middle-aged men and young people left their homes that evening; and so, tipsy and merry, everybody had danced and sung heartily far into the wee hours of the next morning. There and then, Luciano had fallen in love with the Kegite Club. He had nursed it in his heart to get initiated the very day he got admitted into the university. But then he got admitted, and for the four years of his undergraduate studies he was never initiated; he had observed that the many fraternity boys on campus were members of the Kegite Club, and so his dread for them had kept him away from satisfying that teenage desire.

"Don't you know that the Kegite Club is a house of assembly where the Buccaneers, Black Axe, Vikings, Ku Klux Klan, and even the stinking *joo* gather?" Luciano's roommate, Nwobo, had said this to him when the issue had come up on one of their many heated arguments.

His non-membership, however, didn't stop Luciano from watching the club members sing and dance in circles whenever he had the opportunity.

Luciano followed in the direction of the song. Around the yellow faculty block, he went past the obsolete-looking Law Faculty blocks with the flower trees hugging the dusty asphalt on either side to form a light overhead canopy. He turned to the left, continuing uphill until he came to the green signpost that read ILYA DU LAKE. This meant he had arrived at the Kegite shrine. He crossed over to the opposite side of the road and stood under a line of pine trees marking off a dilapidated-looking basketball pitch dotted with make-shift photo stands where sugar-tongued photographers hustled everybody within sight.

With his hands stuck deep into his trouser pockets, he watched from his vantage point. The Kegite culture hadn't changed one bit. The members drank from palm wine gourds and danced in circles around four frenzied drummers. Some of the members, all young men and women, blew cigarette smoke into the air as they danced along with glee, lost in the fellowship of merry-making.

A pair of girls walked up some metres close to Luciano. They settled against a pine tree to observe the Kegite members too. Luciano edged closer to them.

"Hello, I am Luciano."

The girls exchanged looks even as Luciano's outstretched hand lingered in the air. The one closest to him took it gingerly after a moment's hesitation.

"Hi." Her smile seemed to be forced. She slipped her hand off his light grip almost the same instant they made contact.

"Hi," the other fair-skinned one said, and took his hand. "I am Miranda."

"Nice name."

She smiled. "Thank you."

"You ladies study here?"

"Yea. I am in up school."

"Sorry?" he asked, confused.

"Oh." She let out a small laugh, doing nothing to hide her embarrassment at his ignorance. "Industrial Microbiology."

"And your friend?"

"*Down school* … Education Biology."

"Why did you say *down school?*"

She pointed at the buildings downhill. "Down there, we call them *down school*. They are the Arts, Social Sciences and Humanities faculties. Up here is *up school* and it houses the faculties of Sciences and Medicine."

"Oh."

"Yea. That is what we call them here."

"Nice. The campus is really in a jolly mood today,"

he observed, tugging involuntarily on the strap of his leather satchel.

"You really don't school here. Do you?"

Luciano snickered. "No. I'm a first time visitor."

"Oh. That is how it is here every Wednesday. Lectures end at noon and social events take over for the rest of the day."

"Hmm. Interesting. This is more like where I should have schooled."

"Where did you school?"

"Nsukka."

"Oh."

He saw the awe in her eyes. "Very boring place. Stale and lifeless. Please don't envy me. You have a better life here."

"Really? But they have much better academic standards than we have here."

"I will not be too hasty to agree. An insider knows that the university is thriving on past glory. In fact, the only thing to find in Nsukka today is rot. Everything there is rotting."

Miranda paused, as though contemplating his words. "Are you here for postgraduate studies?"

"Me?" Luciano scoffed. "I wish I were. Actually, I am looking for my nephew."

The girl's eyes narrowed as though she had been given an unexpectedly dull answer. He guessed she was trying to be civil in not wanting to sound interrogative, but then for the purpose of stoking what seemed to be a lively relationship, he offered to explain more: "He schools here. We haven't heard from him for some time now and his father, my brother, is worried. I am here to search for him. It's funny coming here in search of a grownup, right?"

"Yea, it is funny, but something must have made him unreachable. What is his name? He might be popular enough for me to know."

"Aniete Ubong," Luciano said.

Miranda rolled her eyes as she ran the name through the database in her head.

"Do you know him?"

"I think I have heard the name somewhere," Miranda said.

"Where?"

"It could be anywhere, but the name stands out amongst the many Igbo and English names on campus," she said.

Luciano sighed. He thought he had gotten a juicy lead, but it was clear his hopes had risen for nothing after all.

"He might have been robbed of his phone or lost it outrightly."

"Pardon?" Luciano snapped out of his disappointment. He hadn't got the girl's drift.

"He may have either lost his phone or he might have been robbed. Hence, he can't get across to home. You know, it happens all the time around campus and in town. People get robbed every time."

"But then he would have called with some other's phone or come back home when he runs out of money, or do they hand out money to students on Wednesday afternoons too?"

The girl let out a boisterous laugh. And he laughed too, not that he saw anything funny, but the girl's unrestrained laughter seemed very contagious. Her companion was engrossed in the Kegites members' dancing. Luciano didn't bother about her. He had earlier ruled her out as being totally unsociable; it was either that or she was just some girl with strong issues against male strangers who didn't match her tastes.

"No. They don't give us any money. I suggest you check him out at his department. I hope you know his department?"

"Yes. Food Science and Technology."

"FST. It is down there, at the Faculty of Agriculture." She pointed in the left direction, *down school*. All he could see in the blurry distance were buildings. "You will hardly find anyone there at this time, but I can show you there in case you might have to check back tomorrow."

"I will be grateful."

He flashed her a smile and tipped his head slightly

in a mock bow. She returned the smile, nudged closer to her friend and whispered something to her. Luciano noticed the reluctance which the nameless, priggish snob wasn't trying to hide, but then she consented grudgingly. She tagged along as Luciano and Miranda chatted on, walking effortlessly downhill in the direction from which he had come.

The Faculty of Agriculture stood on a small expanse of land that appeared to be an appendage of the university campus. The surroundings bespoke near-total neglect; the elephant grass grew tall and uninterrupted around buildings that looked like makeshift structures hastily knocked together in expectation of some important government official's visit. The weakened fragment of a broken fence stood like a lone, naked, war-torn soldier after the rest of his comrades had fallen with the enemy in a bloody battle. Even though the roads in the university were paved, the asphalt didn't get to that part of the campus so that red dust readily settled onto one's shoes. True to Miranda's suggestion, there wasn't a soul to be seen about the deserted-looking faculty premises.

"You will have to check back tomorrow morning. His coursemates could give you some useful information."

They stood side-by-side close to the fragment of a fence, observing the dismal surroundings.

"Thank you very much. I am grateful for your kindness."

"Never mind."

"Do you mind if I show my gratitude by buying you a drink?"

"I would have…" she began, but the noise of an approaching vehicle interrupted her. It was a silver-coloured Nissan Altima, and they watched as it screeched to a halt in front of them, raising a cloud of dust.

"Hey, baby, hop in!" a dimpled lad called out from behind the wheels of the car. He had rolled down the window to peer at Miranda from above the rims of his designer sunshades.

Luciano could see that the fellow was handsome. He noticed the biceps taut against the sleeves of the white T-shirt embroidered in gold.

Miranda waved him goodbye as she skipped around to the passenger's side of the car and hopped in beside the driver. Her nameless friend had already taken the backseat and was tapping with intense concentration at her Blackberry. The driver rolled up the window and screeched away; all the while he hadn't paid Luciano any acknowledgement.

There was nothing left for Luciano to do with the rest of the day. The watch on his wrist read 3:23 p.m; he would have to look for somewhere to pass the night. He began making his way towards the main gate, for he had achieved the much he could for the day. Tomorrow looked like it held some promise. In his heart, he knew this whole business of looking for Chief Ofodile's son would be over in no time; he would just get to the lost boy tomorrow and then convince him to come to his rich daddy who was suddenly missing him. He would tell the boy of all the unimaginable riches the privilege of birth had bestowed upon him, and only God would have to tell what kind of a retard the boy would be to refuse hopping on the next bus bound for Port-Harcourt.

SEVEN

IMO STATE UNIVERSITY, OWERRI.

Luciano was back again at the Faculty building next morning. His head ached from lack of sleep; he had spent a fitful night in a cheap hotel room somewhere on Douglas Road. The lone window of the hotel room overlooked a lively open-air bar where a highlife band, complete with trumpeters and drummers, had played until the wee hours of the morning. He had tried to endure the smelly sheets that pricked his skin so much that he had hoped desperately for the approach of daylight. The groaning overhead fan had done very little to dispel the heat in the room. And sleepless, he had tried to do some work on *Igwemma* but endless minutes went by with him doing nothing but stare blankly at his laptop screen and wishing that the highlife musicians drop down at once. It had worsened when the hotel power generator went off. Immediately, the mosquitoes swarmed around the room like some battle-crazed infantry surging through a breach in the enemy's defenses. They seemed to be giving vent to their pent-up frustration for the revolving ceiling fan which had forced them into hiding all the while. The heat and the whirring mosquitoes forced him into giving up the work on *Igwemma* and seeking refuge under the prickly and smelly sheets instead. Almost immediately, he felt hot and suffocated under the sheets pulled over his head, but he couldn't bring himself to confront the vindictive mosquitoes spoiling for his blood. And when the sun rose with the cockrows the next morning, he bathed, standing on the tiled bathroom floor because the bathwater of the previous night hadn't yet drained from the bath. The toilet wasn't flushed properly either and he had to leave the hotel room with the image of floating bits of faeces in the water closet.

With his leather satchel slung across his shoulder, Luciano strode down the faculty premises. Three small groups of students squeezed into benches in the shade of a mango tree gripped his attention with their boisterous conversations and hearty laughter. Some others milled around in smaller groups, joking and laughing. It was a pair of boys engaged in some low-toned, seemingly-confidential discussion that Luciano approached.

"I go try sort that course," Luciano overheard one of the boys say to his companion. The speaker had a long finely cut face marred only by a receding hairline, too early for his young age. His muscular frame contributed in lending him a hardy disposition. His companion was a little shorter than he, and was dressed in a Caribbean shirt.

"Good morning," Luciano said as he drew closer, and suspended their discussion. The hardy one and his companion regarded the stranger with guarded suspicion. They acknowledged his greeting with a mutter and a nod. "Please, are you two students of Food Science?"

"Yes," Hardy replied before his friend could bring himself around to answer.

"I am looking for Aniete. Aniete Ubong."

"Aniete," Hardy's friend repeated the name like a wine taster would, and then gave his verdict on the quality of some wine sample.

"He's in his second year," Luciano added.

"We are final-year students. The second-year students are having classes right now."

"Where?" Luciano enquired.

"There." Hardy pointed straight ahead to a small lecture hall that had a couple of large windows without shutters.

"Thank you very much."

Luciano strode in expectation towards the lecture hall. The walls were without plaster and the rough outline of exposed cement blocks bore witness to poor workmanship. As Luciano drew close, he could see the roof had no ceiling. A short bespectacled man sporting an unkempt greying goatee stood before a class jammed to capacity with students seated on the kind of desks found in under-funded secondary schools in some rural area. He was apparently the lecturer and commanded some air of authority as though he wielded the power over the destinies of all the students seated and who were listening to him in absolute reverence. Luciano imagined how the students coped in the hall when the tropical sunlight warmed the aluminium roofing above.

Luciano stood by the windows, away from the line of view of the lecturer who had turned to illustrate some complex diagram on the whiteboard stuck to the wall in front of the class. And as time passes, discomfort began to set in; all morning he had stayed on his feet. Now he wished for someplace quiet so as to do some work on *Igwemma,* but there appeared not to be any such places within sight. He remained standing, deciding instead to occupy his mind with the lecturer's lesson. But he couldn't because his thoughts drifted away too frequently.

Concern for the students assailed his mind. They were such a gullible lot, he reasoned, eager to follow through the carved-out education system so as to graduate with the best grades their aptitude for assimilation and regurgitation could guarantee. He imagined their hopes for a bright future at the end of their academic struggles, and then he thought of his own disappointment, of the persistent feeling of being conned by the system that promised much for the youth with a good university degree. Who would tell these ones the truth? And would they listen? Or should they be left like the ones before them? To realize these things at a much later age when they were either too broken in spirit by the harsh reality or too distraught to learn another new set of survival skills? He didn't blame the system, he blamed everyone. He blamed the government, the people, and every bit of a society that was many poles away from reality and its loud gospel of unworthy relevance. So much importance had been placed on acquiring an endorsement printed on a piece of embossed paper showing the degree of one's inability to sift through the grains of *wisdom* cycled and recycled by a guarded fraternity of academics. It was such *wisdom* that robbed the young of common sense, intuition, and basic survival instinct in a society of men, which to all appearances is a jungle except for a web of laws woven to set boundaries against the species existing on the lower rungs of the food chain. Getting just any graduate degree were perceived as a one-way ticket into a life of bliss, a sure opportunity to live happily ever after. So sold-out on this notion was the myriads of Nigerians that people paid heavily in scarce monetary bribes to secure places into universities. The tuition fees got hiked at will, and after the initial murmur of protests, everyone settled in to the new development like dust particles after some disturbance. Lecturers took advantage of the desperation of the students to blackmail them into parting with money and pride in exchange for good grades. The students, on their parts, ignored their talents and innate gifts as they dedicated their intellect to getting pass marks. Only years after graduation did the armour of deception wear out and then they felt as duped as they actually were, just as he had felt.

The students milled out of the lecture hall as soon as the lecturer breezed out of the class. He still didn't notice Luciano standing by the window. A group of girls followed the lecturer in mock pursuit. Perhaps they were in need of some favours, which if not granted, threatened or ruined their chances of good grades in the goateed man's course.

One of the students, a young man, strolling out of the lecture hall caught Luciano's attention. He had his eyes glued to the screen of his smartphone without losing his sense of direction. Tall and muscular, with biceps straining the short sleeves of his black shirt tucked into close-fitted faded jeans; he stood out easily amongst the throng of his fellow students. His bare scalp glistened in the brightness of the day, in sharp contrast to his pencil-cut beard the colour of the leather-bound diary in the crook of his free arm. Luciano approached him and said, "Excuse me, please."

The youth lifted his gaze from his phone, stopped and turned to face Luciano. He stood head above Luciano who then noticed that the boy looked younger than his physique suggested. Luciano thought that perhaps the lad was a little below his own age bracket. This presumption emboldened him to fight off the intimidation of that imposing height and physique before him.

"Please I'm looking for Aniete Ubong. They say he is your coursemate."

"Yes." The youth appraised him with a hint of suspicion.

Luciano noticed the blackened lips and the husky voice; tell-tale signs of habitual marijuana smoking.

"Do you know where I can find him?"

"I don't know. I haven't seen him this morning."

"You mind if we take a walk?" Luciano asked. Alertness flashed through the youth's eyes. "It's nothing. I just want to ask you some questions … I want us to go somewhere cool and quiet so that we can talk … a canteen … a bar. I just need to sit down. I've been standing here for the past one hour."

The boy appraised Luciano less suspiciously this time. He appeared a little convinced of the absence of any threats, but the tension in his pose didn't diminish.

"Okay. Let us go to the Coca-Cola Spot."

"I don't know the place, my brother. I am a stranger here."

"Don't worry. I will show you."

EIGHT

The Coca-Cola Spot stood on an elevated bit of land, with a large veranda overlooking the traffic coming from the St. Joseph's Catholic Chapel downhill, all the way to the Vice Chancellor's office. It was one of the few places on campus where the sale of beer was permitted. They sat at one of the branded tables on the veranda already bustling with students drinking beer and Smirnoff Ice so early in the day. They chatted noisily about campus activities and other things which might be of concern only to students. Luciano could overhear one group's discussion about an ongoing Student Union campaign, and another, something about a course rep intentionally raising the price of their textbooks, for his personal gain.

"What do I get you?" a female attendant asked. She had walked up to them the very moment they settled into seats.

"You get Harp? Luciano's companion enquired with a hint of flirtation.

"Yes."

"Give me one."

"Coke," Luciano said when the girl looked at him in silent enquiry. She disappeared inside the bar.

"I am Luciano." He offered his hand across the table.

"They call me Stone"

Their hands clasped in a warm but formal handshake. Stone seemed more receptive in the hospitable environment of a bar.

Their drinks arrived and with them, a glass for each man, but the attendant would not leave their table.

"Your money is three twenty, sir," she addressed none of them in particular. Luciano gave her a five hundred naira note and she disappeared inside, to get his change.

"So, Stone, as I was telling you earlier, I am looking for Aniete." He paused long enough to fill his glass. "Actually, I am his cousin. We all live together, with his parents, in Port-Harcourt, but for some months now we haven't heard from him. His parents are getting worried and so I am here to see Aniete, to be sure that he is alright."

Stone nodded his understanding as he let down a half-empty glass. With the back of his palm, he wiped off a thin line of foam from his upper lip and then went about refilling the glass with remarkable dexterity that the glass, when full, was topped with no more than a thin head of foam.

"I'm surprised that Aniete wasn't in the lecture hall this morning," Luciano continued. "Tell me the truth, what kind of life does he lead on campus? Does he attend classes?"

"Yes. He attends classes, at least most times."

He lifted the glass to his lips again.

"Sir, no change o." The attendant was at their table again; Luciano hadn't noticed her approach from behind him.

"How much is my change?" Luciano asked.

"One eighty."

Luciano foraged in his satchel; he believed the taxi driver had given him some loose change that morning. He found them.

"Bring another bottle of Harp for my friend." He handed her a fifty naira note and a twenty. She disappeared into the bar again. In a moment, a defrosting bottle of beer stood next to another almost-empty one before Stone. "I will need you to help me find him so that I can go back to my business in Port-Harcourt."

"I don't know how I can be of help to you," Stone said, "but I will tell you all I know. I hope it will be of relevance to you." And then with eyes darting sideways, he leaned forward and dropped his voice to a whisper: "Aniete hasn't been coming for lectures for a very long time now. There are lots of others like him on campus, so it is no big deal, and nobody really cares. Have you checked in his hostel?"

"I didn't see any hostels when I came in."

"Are you new to this place?"

"I only came here for the first time yesterday. I told you I'm a stranger here."

"Alright. The university provides no living accommodation for students. We rent accommodations outside the campus. Aniete stays around Bishop's Court, in a building called Pentagon Lodge."

"Where is Bishop's Court?"

"I will point the place out to you, but I won't go with you into that part of town."

Luciano resisted the urge to ask why, but he had the good sense to restrain his curiosity and not push his luck too far. Maybe Stone was a member of a school fraternity and was reluctant to step into a rival's territory. In his student days he had watched these guys from a distance and heard a lot of stories about them to have an idea of as to how they operated.

When their bottles were drained, Luciano and Stone made their way in the direction of the Main Gate. Luciano noticed the unmasked excitement in Stone's voice as they chatted and walked; the beer had loosened up his tongue somewhat. He strode like he had lost that conscious carriage with which he had borne his toned frame earlier.

Outside the university gate, the road sloped steeply. Luciano and Stone took the uphill direction, walking slowly as their thighs and calf muscles strained with the effort, and when they came to a crossroad, Stone halted.

"Follow this way," Stone said, pointing to his left. "Pentagon Lodge should be the fourth building on your left, with a blue roof. I can't go any farther than this. I have a lecture to attend in ten minute's time."

Luciano could swear that Stone was lying, but he was grateful nevertheless. "Okay, thank you. I'm grateful for your assistance."

"No problems, bro."

They shook hands and snapped fingers.

"I owe you another drink."

"I will always welcome it."

They both laughed. And Stone turned around, heading back the way they had come. Luciano continued in the direction he had been pointed to.

Pentagon Hostel wasn't difficult to locate. It stood at the very spot where Stone had said it would; it was also the only building with a blue roof in sight. But Stone did wrong in never mentioning that Pentagon Hostel did not look like the American defence headquarters it conjured to the imagination. It was a two-storey building abandoned midway to completion. There were two flats on each floor with block-and-mortar hedges for balcony railings. The second floor made one speculate that a moron posing as an architect had taken over the plan from where a more articulate one had left off. Crude scaffolds of decaying bamboo sticks stuck out of the building, forming a framework around it that made one think of a radical experiment on acupuncture. There were other buildings within sight, but Pentagon Hostel caught the eye as easily as a ragged old woman in a colourful ceremony would. One would have thought nobody lived in such a place, but the balconies bore evidence of active habitation; clothes hung out to dry on the balcony hedges and on the scaffolding lent a form of mundane but colourful, festive air to the melancholia of the building. A young fellow, naked from the waist up, sat on the balcony of the first floor, his legs dangling dangerously over the world below. From his precarious perch, he seemed to be engrossed in the view of slow-moving cars plying the bumpy, gully-ridden street.

Luciano made his way into the compound through the space where a gate was supposed to have been in the weather-battered fence. In the compound, a young woman stooped over pots and pans, her back to the yard, and she scrubbed to the rhythm of the hearty song she was humming. Her skimpy shorts and sleeveless vest exposed her fair skin that seemed to hold the daylight.

"Good morning, sister," Luciano said.

She turned to look at him. His sudden presence must have startled her. She straightened up, impulsively tugging at her vest so as to conceal her exposed stomach. Her face was as fair as the skin on her body. It was such fair complexion enhanced by a calculated application of cosmetic treatment. He caught himself staring. She wasn't beautiful. It wasn't her face that caught and held his attention but the outline of her firm and full breasts against the light fabrics of her cotton vest. The nipples stuck out visibly. He felt a lump rise in his throat and a stir in his groin.

"Are you looking for somebody?"

"Yes … Aniete. I am looking for Aniete, please."

"Climb upstairs. His room is in this flat." She pointed to the flat right above her. He fought a losing battle against the desire to steal a look at her bosom as she raised her hand.

"Tha ... thank you."

"The staircase is there, to your left."

He followed her direction to a bare staircase. The faint smell of marijuana hit his nose almost immediately. Taking the stairs two at a time, he came to the first landing and then to the balcony. The half-naked fellow was still seated on the hedge, kicking his feet in the air. Luciano noticed the crucifixes and daggers tattooed on the young man's taut muscular torso. Even though he did not see all of his face, he placed the lad somewhere in mid-twenties.

"Good morning, brother."

The young man turned, facing him, and that was when Luciano saw the big joint of marijuana between his fingers. He wondered why the fellow would be playing truancy, smoking marijuana so early in the day, whilst others were on campus attending lectures.

"Good afternoon, bros." His voice had that characteristic hollowness of habitual marijuana smokers.

"I'm looking for Aniete, please."

Truant took a drag on his joint, regarding Luciano through eyes dimmed against the wafting grey smoke. "Who you be?" The smoke came out in short bursts through his mouth and nostrils as he spoke.

"I'm his cousin."

"Is he expecting you?" he asked, switching over to English.

"No. I have a message from home."

"Okay. Let me show you his room."

He swung off his precarious perch and led Luciano through a doorway into the open flat. The space that was supposed to be the parlour was bare, dusty and uninhabited, but it was the three bedrooms and the kitchen that had been fitted and rented out to students in need of cheap accommodations. A toilet and bathroom filled the flat with an objectionable stench. Luciano held the saliva in his mouth as Truant led him to the door of one of the rented-out bedrooms. It had a big padlock fastened to the lock. "He is not around," Truant said.

"Do you know where he has gone to?"

"Lectures."

"But I'm from his department and they haven't seen him for days now."

"He's been around." Truant blew at the end of the joint; it had almost died out from momentary neglect. "Who do you say you are to him again?"

"I am his cousin."

"Okay. If you check back in the evening, I'm sure he will be back by then."

"That will be fine. I will check back. Thank you very much."

"No problem." Truant dragged on his joint. At the balcony, he resumed his perch as Luciano continued down the staircase and into the compound. The young woman whom he had seen upon arriving was nowhere to be seen in the compound.

NINE

At four later that evening, Luciano repeated his visit to Pentagon Lodge.

The building looked very much alive than when he had visited earlier in the morning. He was conscious of the curious stares he received as he walked into the compound. He considered them to be the look of appraisal one would give a stranger; humans are after all as territorial as lizards, if not a little more. Quite naturally, he continued walking towards the stairwell. There wasn't only Truant on the balcony this time; three other boys were crowded about on stools. They lounged leisurely, passing around a marijuana joint. His heart jumped when he saw the marijuana-smoking gang, but then he recalled that marijuana smokers were not violent. If anything, the marijuana sedated them.

Truant's face lit up with recognition on seeing Luciano. The others regarded him with obvious disinterest.

"Is he around?" Luciano asked. He was grateful that his voice didn't quiver.

"Yes."

"Thank you very much."

Luciano waved a greeting at the three others on the balcony, and they grunted their reply, making room for him to edge his way through.

Aniete's door stood wide open but for a pale blue curtain flailing in the light breeze apparently coming from the open window on the opposite side of the room. Luciano parted the curtain a fraction, enough to permit his hand to knock on the coarse wooden door.

"Come in," a voice called, a bit too eagerly, from inside the room. The owner sounded like he had been expecting the knock. Luciano parted the curtain and entered.

The room was brightly-lit by the evening light coming in through a lone window with the glass slid open. A dark-complexioned young fellow was seated on a mattress on one corner of the carpeted floor. Something didn't feel right to Luciano. He suspected that it had something to do with the sole occupant of the room. Maybe it was the way he sat alert and fully dressed in a pair of blue jeans and expensive-looking long-sleeved shirts complete with a pair of leather boots. He looked the dandy student, the kind Luciano had earlier noticed walking with exaggerated swagger round the campus.

More shocking was the fact that he didn't look anything like the face in the photograph safely stashed in the small compartment of Luciano's satchel. The room didn't look lived-in either; the air hung heavy with dust as though it hadn't had any occupants for many months.

The curtain behind him parted and Luciano watched with horror as all the boys he had seen smoking on the balcony trooped in menacingly, with Truant among them. It was Truant who secured the lock on the door when they had all filed in and it was at that moment when the door swung closed that Luciano saw the lock dangle from a single nail; it had been burgled.

"Sit down!" one of the boys ordered, gesturing towards the bed. He was slender, quite small, and with a face that made one think of a fuming bull. His voice had a steely arrogance to it, unbefitting of his stature. The others stood guard, never interfering. Truant had gone to stand by the window. He slid the glass shut and drew the curtain. The dandy one had slid over to one end of the bed and, like the others, kept silent guard.

Luciano made to protest but the small fellow reached under his shirt. A silver pistol gleamed in his hand when he brought it out.

"Are you sitting down or not?"

Meekly, Luciano lowered himself down on the mattress. Sweat broke out on his forehead and he made no attempt to hide the quiver in his limbs.

"Your bag!" Silverpistol commanded, his forefinger on the trigger of his pistol aimed at Luciano's chest. Luciano obeyed, unslinging the satchel and holding it out to Silverpistol. It was Dandy who snatched the satchel, unzipped it and upturned it on the floor. The laptop tumbled out with a thud, causing Luciano to jerk impulsively as he made to reach for it. But Silverpistol jabbed the muzzle of the pistol into his chest causing him to settle back on the bed, thankful that Silverpistol had not been itchy in the forefinger.

A thorough search of the bag revealed a shirt, a pair of undershorts, a toothbrush, a roll of loose change, a mobile phone and the photograph of Aniete. It was the photograph and the phone that caught the attention of Luciano's captors. Dandy handed the photograph and the phone to Silverpistol who only threw a cursory glance at the photograph and then tossed it onto Luciano's lap. The phone, he pocketed.

"Who are you?" Silverpistol asked Luciano.

Luciano opened his mouth to answer, but it seemed his mind had given up on him. Everything was happening too fast for him to keep pace with. "*Who send you?!*"

Luciano still couldn't bring himself to answer.

Silverpistol dug into his trouser pocket with his free hand and then tossed some seedy things onto Luciano's lap. Luciano recognized them to be bullets. He got the message loud and clear; Silverpistol was trying to warn him, to tell him that the gun was loaded. "Speak now or I blow you."

"My name is … Luciano…"

"Why are you looking for Sly?"

"Who?"

"Sly." He gestured with a flicker of the pistol to the picture now lying on Luciano's lap.

"His father sent me… "

"I am warning you, you better tell the truth."

"I swear to God, his father has a message …"

Silverpistol looked at one of the boys standing aloof with his back to the closed door. "Make we move am."

The boy nodded, opened the door and stepped outside. Dandy took the boy's position behind the door. "Now listen. We are moving out," Silverpistol said. "There is a car waiting outside. We will all walk out of here and get into that car like normal people. If you try anything funny, I will have to shoot you in the back of the head. Do you understand?"

Luciano nodded his acknowledgement. The sweat was running down in streams down his face and neck. He doubted if his quivering legs would carry him even if he ever attempted to flee. A car honked, just one short blast. Truant stooped on the floor, returning the laptop and every other bit into the satchel, slung it across his shoulder, and strode over to the built-in wardrobe with curtains for doors. He parted the curtains and chose a shirt from a sparse collection of clothes hanging from plastic clothes hangers on an iron rail that ran horizontally overhead across the length of the wardrobe.

"Let us row," Silverpistol said. He stuck his pistol into his belt and tugged Luciano by the arm. Luciano could feel the strength in the small fellow's grip. Dandy held the door open as everyone filed out of the room.

Out in the compound, the other hostel occupants paid no more than a cursory glance at the small procession. A girl was hanging some underwear on a clothesline. Truant halted his progress long enough to pinch her round bottom clad in a pair of yellow shorts that revealed her nakedness underneath. She screamed playfully and made to slap his hand, but he stepped aside and out of her reach just in time.

"Spoilt boy! *Ashawo!*" the girl said.

Laughing contentedly and paying no more attention to her, he ran to meet up with the procession that had gone on without him. A red Toyota Camry idled outside the compound. They let Luciano in, and Silverpistol and Truant sat on either side of him. Dandy came hastening to the car. He took the front passenger seat. A few paces away, on the large bit of loose earth beside the gully-eaten road, some boys played football without boots. For goalposts, they had two cement blocks set apart. Not one of them paid the slightest interest to the red Toyota Camry pulling away to join the slow-moving traffic along the bumpy road. It dawned on Luciano that he was being kidnapped right under public view. He could still be led to a slaughterhouse and nobody would be wiser, and he, like a lamb, had not even uttered a word of protest.

He feared that he wasn't going to be making that call to Chief Ofodile. He feared if he ever would.

They drove through the town, keeping to quiet streets and lanes until they came to a wide dirt road. The driver pulled over to the side, and as though it was a signal of sorts, Truant put a hood over Luciano's head, and then gave the go-ahead for the driver to proceed.

Luciano remained alert. He made a mental map of their route, taking note that the car made a U-turn after driving for a few seconds, continued on a straight course for a little less than half a kilometre and then made a series of turns to the left, some more to the right and then to the left until he lost count and gave up on the idea of keeping track. He believed they were intentionally driving in a labyrinth to put off any of his attempts at trying to commit their route to memory.

The car slowed and braked. Firm hands helped him out of the car and guided him along. The ground felt uneven, rising and falling here and there so much that he feared he would sprain his ankle at every step. A tuft of something brushed against his trousers. *Grass*. One of his guides stepped onto something that gave a crunching sound. *A plastic bottle*. He bumped his toes against something hard. *A stone, perhaps*. At all of the times, the firm hands of his guides held him steady from stumbling onto the uneven ground or fussing over his bruised toes. He counted forty-seven short strides and then they began to ascend a stairway. Their footfalls echoed with every upward step. *A house not much inhabited*. Fifteen steps more and he perceived from the wide level space that they had ascended onto a landing. The hands led him on again. Sixteen more steps up an echoing stairway, they halted. One of his captors knocked at a door a few paces from his face; two sharp knocks immediately followed by a bang. Some sort of signal.

A bolt slid back loudly, followed by the creak of a door swinging open upon rusty hinges. His guides nudged him forward. He could tell it was some room he had been led into. It smelt heavily of an uneven blend of humanity and cement dust suspended in the damp air. A chair scraped against the bare floor and then he was helped into an armchair. He felt grateful to be seated and he leaned against the backrest. Surprisingly, much of the fear had left him; he was no longer as scared as he previously was. Fear was replaced with weariness and the resolution to stand up to the very worst that could possibly happen; it felt useless expecting help at this point when it was clear there wasn't any to be expected.

The hood was lifted off a bit too roughly. Luciano blinked as his sights adjusted to the near-darkness. Just as he had guessed, he was seated in the middle of a room with unplastered walls. The only pair of windows was crudely boarded up with sawn planks, and mosquito netting nailed over the planks to keep out night insects. The room was virtually empty except for a lean mattress on one end of the bare floor, a crude wooden table set against one of the windows, and the armchair in which he was seated. His captors stood round the room; Silverpistol stood next to the table, his whole weight leaned heavily on one foot as he tapped furiously at the keys of a Blackberry phone. There was a new face too; a tall girl seated on the mattress with her long legs folded yoga-style. She was probably the one who had let them in. Luciano noticed she made no attempt at concealing her interest in him; it was the kind of close examination which told of a determined effort to absorb every detail of him, to commit them to her photographic memory for a later time. He tried not to return her look. Silverpistol signaled for her and she came to him. They stepped aside to the window and discussed briefly in whispers, and then she left the room. Silverpistol walked slowly around, in deep contemplation. He leaned hard against the table again, fixing a hard stare at the ground at Luciano's feet. It was clear that he was pissed off with something the girl had told him. He looked up suddenly at Luciano.

"Now, you will give me answers to my every question." His voice was cold. "Why are you looking for Sly?"

Luciano knew he would have to tell Silverpistol all he needed to hear, and quickly.

"A man hired me to look for him," he blurted out. "He offered to pay me well if I can convince Aniete … sorry, Sly." The fear was beginning to rise anew. "He wants me to convince Sly to come to him. Please I don't want any part of it anymore. I am no longer interested in searching for Sly. Please let me go and, I swear, I will forget ever having met you people … I beg you."

"Where is he?"

"Who?"

"Where is Sly?"

"I … I don't know. I swear to God." He silently prayed that he sounded convincing enough.

"You lie."

His heart nearly failed. The perspiration trickled down his ribs beneath his shirt stuck to his skin like one who had been drenched in a drizzle. "If I knew where he is, I wouldn't be looking for him."

"Then what do you know of his whereabouts?"

"I don't know, I swear."

"Who are you?"

"I am … I am Luciano."

Silverpistol's menacingly wild gaze returned to him. "I am a nobody … a writer …"

"A journalist?"

"No … no … I swear I am not … I … I'm hoping to be a … writer … a novelist."

"I don't give a fuck. Where is the money?"

"What?! What money? I don't know what you are talking about."

"You think I am joking?" He pressed the muzzle of the pistol point-blank against Luciano's chest "You have to start talking before I count to four. One…"

"Please … I …"

"Two!"

"Chai! My God, is this the end of me?"

"… Three!"

"Please, my brother. You are a good man. Don't do this to me … I don't know about any money… I swear to God." The tears streamed down his cheeks as the image of himself lying stiff on the floor of some obscure criminal hideout flooded his mind.

"Four!"

Luciano pressed his eyelids shut.

Click!

The world stood still for an instant. He could still breathe. He was still alive! No bullets had come surging through the barrel of the pistol to tear into his body and take the life from him. A true miracle. He began to weep hysterically as relief, combined with the realization that he had been kicked around and kidnapped with an unloaded gun, washed over him.

"I believe you," Silverpistol said and then strode out of the room. The others who had been standing guard, silently observing the drama, followed after him. Luciano was left all to himself. He felt nothing anymore; not fear, not relief and certainly not hope. He no longer cared for what would come next; he had come very close to death. And now that he was back to life, the land of the living felt strange to him. The door creaked open again and his captors filed in, with Silverpistol taking the lead. He walked around to the table again, facing a jarred Luciano. The pistol wasn't anywhere within sight.

"We are looking for that bastard too. Do you have any information that might help us? We will appreciate if you share with us. "

"No. I don't. Honestly." His reply was calm and composed this time. Gone was the hysteria.

"The man who paid you to search for him, who is he?"

Luciano thought for a moment, his good sense was telling him to give them every piece of information about the crazy Chief Ofodile who had been so devious with his money as to send him on such a suicide mission. But he decided against it. "I don't know him. He just came up to me one day and asked for me to go in search of Sly."

"If you don't know him, how are you supposed to be relaying your feedback to him?"

"I don't know exactly. He just asked for me to drop a message with Sly if I get to meet him."

"And what is the message?"

In that split second, something came to his head. It was a codeword he had once come across in some espionage novel. "The fox is in the nest."

"The fox is in the nest?" Silverpistol looked to his colleagues as though he ached to ascertain whether they could decipher this unfamiliar codeword. They stared back at him, clueless. He returned his attention to Luciano. "And how do you intend to receive your money?"

"He said he will be doing the fund transfer directly into the account I gave him."

Silverpistol remained silent for a moment. "I will need your help."

"Me?"

"Yes. Sly is a wanted man. We had a deal with that bloody civilian, but he double-crossed us. He betrayed us and made away with all the money. Now we are broke. Our cover is blown, two of my men have been deleted and all the others are now in hiding. I need that bastard badly. He owes us more than he knows."

"Please I don't want any more of this. I'm not interested, I'm not continuing with looking for Sly. I thought it would be just as simple as the man had made it sound."

Silverpistol kept silent as though weighing some options in his mind. "Okay, we will let you go."

He looked at one of the boys standing behind Luciano. Without warning, the hood was suddenly put over his head again. He was helped to his feet and guided out of the room. They led him down the staircase and into a car; he guessed it was the same car they had brought him in. The car engine came alive and they began to drive slowly along a bumpy road. He guessed the road was different from the one they had taken on arrival. They came to a level road and the car gathered speed. They drove through labyrinth-like roads until the driver pulled over. The hood was lifted off him and he saw that they were parked to one side of a highway. Silverpistol turned in his seat beside the driver.

"This is Egbu Road. I hope you can find your way?"

He nodded in the affirmative. Yes, it was a lie, but it never mattered. Anywhere away from his captors was better than being here with them. Truant tossed the satchel onto Luciano's lap. The weight of his laptop was reassuring; that (and his life, of course) was all that mattered to him.

Dandy stepped out of the car to make way for Luciano. He crawled out hastily, and hardly had Dandy taken his seat in the car than it shot away, joining the fast-moving traffic into the gathering dusk.

Luciano rummaged in the satchel. Everything was intact, even the photograph. But it was the mobile phone he reached for. He dialed the familiar number. It answered just when he had thought it would go unanswered.

"Hello." The voice sounded drowsy.

The crazy bastard, to be taking a nap when I was close to taking a bullet to the chest.

"Hello?"

"Good evening."

"Yea, good evening. What progress have you made?"

"Enough."

"That's good. Fill me in on the details."

"I got kidnapped and had a close brush with death, all thanks to you."

There was silence on the other end. "The details of the events of this evening are convincing enough to make me tell you with confidence that my life is much more valuable than what is needed to sustain it."

"But then, consider …"

"To hell with you! To hell with you for thinking your money makes you lord over other people's lives. You can leave the comforts of your contained existence and come look for the results of your sexual frivolities yourself. Don't trust anybody -- least of all, me -- to wipe your own *shit*!"

He severed the connection and returned the phone into his satchel. He felt much lighter. Even the evening wind had a rhythm to it, which he had been oblivious to all the while. For once in his life, he had spoken his mind to someone important, and it had counted. It made him feel a sense of accomplishment. The man owed him for protecting his identity from the vindictive criminals. He couldn't tell why he had done it, but he congratulated himself for being such a good liar.

The street lights overhead suddenly came alive; rows of yellow dots shining against the cloudy evening sky. He would have to get going. Port-Harcourt was out of the question for the time being; not only because of the lateness of the hour, but the city seemed to have too many ghosts haunting his mind.

Orodo came to mind. It had been quite a while he visited Aunty Eliza and her husband in that rural part of Owerri. The last visit had been a couple of years back when Aunty Eliza and her husband returned finally from Kaduna. Visiting Aunty Eliza felt like the best thing to do. He would seize the opportunity to fathom what next to make out of his life that was getting more meaningless with each passing day.

Along the paved pedestrian walkway and under the yellow street lights he walked, on his way to the closest junction where he hoped to ask people for any bus headed to Orodo.

TEN

ORODO.

Luciano arrived at Orodo in a taxi. The traffic at Amakohia had lasted for hours;he arrived at Orodo at that time when shop owners were packing up for the night. He counted himself lucky to find a cyclist idling astride his bike. A lone *mallam* fanned the embers in his crude barbeque grill. He would occasionally dab the grilling slabs of meat with oil, causing a spell of fire to leap over the sizzling meat.

"*I na-aga*?" the cyclist asked in a hopeful tone. A baseball cap hid much of his face. One couldn't tell whether he was fat or thin from the layers of protective clothing that made him appear bulky.

"I'm going in the direction of the church."

"Whose compound exactly?" the man asked in Igbo, kicking his bike to life and revving the engine.

"Gorilla's house."

Everybody knew the one whom they called Gorilla. He was Aunty Eliza's husband. The mat of thick black hair covering every inch of his muscular body had earned him the nickname. Only a few people still remembered that his real name was Ejiogu.

"Okay. I know the place ... hundred naira."

"No problem," Luciano said, climbing behind the cyclist. He suspected that the man had hiked the fare because of the late hour, but it didn't matter.

They tore along the smooth, dark road bordered by what appeared in the dark to be abandoned farmlands on either side. The cyclist took the dangerous turns and bends like a maniac so that Luciano had to nudge him to slow down a bit; he feared the man might run into another reckless oncoming driver.

They turned onto a dirt road, and then onto a narrower one littered with leaves from the overhanging canopy of large pear trees hugging the path on either side. By the time the cyclist braked in front of Aunty Eliza's bungalow, Luciano's ears felt woozy from the chilly winds rushing past them all through the adventurous ride.

The entire neighbourhood was shrouded in darkness and stillness. Not even a light bulb broke the monotony of old bungalows spaced unevenly by fragments of cassava farms. The noise of the bike engine caused no doors to be thrown open to check on the new arrival.

And for a moment, Luciano feared Aunty Eliza no longer lived in the village with her husband. *If only he had called her before coming.* He had banked on the possibility that she would still be holding onto her love for rural life; her husband had been a worker for the textile mill in Kaduna, and when the factories shut down he returned with Aunty Eliza to the village where they completed a long-abandoned three-bedroom bungalow with the little pay-off money the labour union had succeeded in exacting from the begrudging government.

Luciano asked the cyclist to wait and then he ascended the wide front steps and knocked on the front door. Almost immediately, a male voice called out harshly: "*O bu onye?* Who is that?"

"It is me, Luciano."

"*Onye?!*"

"Chikadibia," he said, recalling that nearly none of his family members knew him by his Christian name.

"Is that Chika, *nna m?*" another voice enquired from inside the house. It sounded older, a little bit hoarse, but there was no mistaking the voice of Aunty Eliza, his mother's younger sister, who had babysat him and doted on him all through his childhood.

"It is me, Aunty." He felt elated to know that he hadn't arrived at a deserted house.

A bolt slid backwards, and then another. The front door swung open and Aunty Eliza came through with her arms spread wide open in a welcoming embrace. *Had she grown shorter or was he the one adding a few inches to his height?*

She enveloped him in a hug so tight he would have choked had she been a little stronger. Luciano wrapped his arms loosely around her, inhaling the faint odour of wood smoke.

"Why are you coming in at such an hour? Where are you coming from? How is …"

The cyclist honked impatiently. Luciano realized it was by the dimmed lights of the bike's headlamp that the family reunion had been going on. He descended the steps, rummaging a side pocket of his satchel. He fetched a handful of crumpled naira notes, sorting them out by the light of the bike's headlamp; he singled out a hundred naira note and handed it over. The cyclist confirmed the money by the headlamp. Satisfied, he deposited the money into an inner part of his jacket, did a wild U-turn and, throwing Luciano and Aunty Eliza a cursory *'ka chi fo'*, he zoomed away into the black night.

Luciano ascended the steps where Aunty Eliza stood waiting for him. The silhouette of her husband, Gorilla, stood in the doorway. In his grip was a double-barreled gun with the muzzle pointing to the ground.

"*Nnoo*," he greeted Luciano, and switching the gun to his left, he proffered his right hand for a handshake in the near-darkness broken only by the light of a big blue hurricane lantern that Luciano hadn't earlier noticed burning in the sitting room.

Luciano took the outstretched hairy hand in a warm handshake. Gorilla appeared pleased to see Luciano whose gaze lingered on the barrel of the gun, the sight of which had set his heartbeat on a race. "Nna, come inside," Gorilla said, gesturing and taking the lead.

Aunty Eliza led Luciano to the sitting room, her hand against the small of his back. "Where are you coming from at this hour?" she asked again.

"I was in Owerri for some business and so I decided to seize the moment to come see you."

That seemed to please her, for he noticed a broad smile spread across her face as she turned around to secure the lock on the front door.

"You have done well in coming to see me after this very long time."

"The way you say *very long time* makes it sound like it's been up to a decade when in actual sense it's only been something close to a year, that's if I'm not exaggerating."

"Is one year not a long time, this boy?"

He laughed and, with the front door secure, Aunty Eliza led the way through the sitting room and into a narrow hallway that opened onto a spacious backyard.

"How is work in Port-Harcourt?"

"It's not been easy, Aunty."

"I understand. Life in big cities has never been easy on a struggling fellow. I doubt it will ever be."

Everything appeared a little changed from the last time Luciano had visited. A log fire burned in a thatched shed erected at one side of the backyard close to a fence; it served as the kitchen. It was to this kitchen Aunty Eliza led Luciano. She offered him a stool and took another one close to a pot cooking over the log fire. The sweet smell of cooking stockfish assailed Luciano's nostrils, reminding him of how long he had gone without food all afternoon. In the light of the log fire, he could make out a wire-gauze basket hanging from the rafters over the cooking fire. Some corn in husks dangled from the rafters too. Balancing his satchel on his lap, Luciano settled as comfortably as he could on the lowest stool he had had to sit on in a very long while.

Aunty Eliza stoked the fire. "But you should try to visit more often."

"I know. I am always busy at work … it's not easy, Aunty."

"I understand, but you have a family here and we will always want you to be in touch. It doesn't matter that your parents are gone, you are not alone in this world. So, bear in mind always that there are people who are concerned about your welfare."

Luciano said nothing. He had come to feel nothing when references were made to his parents' early death. It had happened not too long ago when he was at university. Ezindu, his elder brother and only sibling, had been the apple of their parents' eyes. His tuition through medical school had cost the family a fortune and they were already deep in debt by the time he got to his final semester. Five months after graduation, Ezindu again made the family proud when his name was shortlisted for the compulsory National Youth Service Corps program. If only anyone had foreseen the pogrom that would happen in Kano a few months later. They said the northerners were not happy with the outcome of the Presidential elections and so they took out their grievances on the Youth Corps members, killing and bludgeoning to death every one of *the infidels' agents* as they could lay hold on. The shock had been just too much for the family. Father suffered a stroke. Much of the two million naira compensation money for Ezindu's murder from the government went to hospital bills and drugs. Six months afterwards, Father died. Mother began to sound and act detached from reality. She couldn't keep up a conversation without veering off to the abstract. She soon began to care less for her appearances, going for days on end without a shower and would be seen muttering to herself and laughing at nothing in particular. People began to say she had gone mad, that a screw had gone loose in her head. One morning, she didn't wake up with the household, and everyone secretly breathed a sigh of relief.

"So when will you be bringing a girl to show us?" Aunty Eliza's eyes lit up in mischievous expectation.

While awaiting Luciano's answer, she got off her seat and took the lid off the cooking pot. Using one of the flaming logs as a torch, she stirred the soup with a metal ladle, beat it against the edge of the pot and then, blowing the hollowed end of the ladle with her breath, ran her tongue along it. Evidently satisfied, she returned the dying log to the fire and stashed the ladle in the rafters above. She returned to her place on the seat. "I asked you a question."

The log fire wasn't bright enough to reveal Luciano's embarrassment. And for that, he felt grateful.

"There's nobody, Aunty." He focused on the earthen floor next to his feet so as to avoid her eyes. "There's no one for now."

"What is wrong with you boys of nowadays? You hang around with everything that has firm breasts, yet you sound like you walk around with your eyes shut."

Luciano let out a strained laugh. "When the time comes, Aunty."

"If you need somebody to tell you, it will have to be me. And I am telling you that the time is now. It has come, whether or not you realize it. You think your father was yet your age when he came to marry my sister?"

"Aunty, you know that I haven't made money yet."

"Nonsense. What have you been doing with the money you earn from your job?"

Luciano laughed heartily.

"I think I know your problems, Chika."

"Aunty, what are my problems?"

"All those *shakara* girls you township boys follow around like green flies, that is the problem. They confuse you. Never mind, there are many homely young girls in the village here. They are from respectable homes. I will make sure you have the best amongst them for a wife."

Luciano nearly toppled over with laughter. Gorilla stooped into the low-thatched kitchen. He didn't have his gun with him.

"*Nwanyi* a, why not take Chika into the house so that he can keep his bag? Is it proper to convert him into a woman?"

Aunty Eliza asked turned to Gorilla. "Is he complaining?"

Luciano intervened, flashing a reassuring smile. "Never mind, sir. I am okay." Gorilla regarded him in the light of the burning log fire.

"I am okay here," he reassured Gorilla.

"I will soon be done with the cooking and you can have him to yourself for all your manly talk," Aunty Eliza said.

Ignoring his wife, Gorilla turned to Luciano. "If you say you are okay here, I will let you be. Just be mindful that the smoke doesn't get into your eyes."

Aunty Eliza waited for her husband to leave the kitchen before continuing with their discussion: "Have you in any way come by Obichere?"

"No, Aunty."

"*Hmm*," she sighed, folding her arms across her breasts.

"He still hasn't come back yet?"

"My dear, we haven't set eyes on him. All other of his mates who traveled to Gabon, Cotonou and even Chad often come home at least once in two years. But not him."

"When did he leave?"

She rolled her eyes, and then looked thoughtful. "I can't remember, but you were only learning to walk about the house with unsteady steps then."

"That must have been a very long time ago."

"*Mtchw*," she hissed, sharply sucking air between closed teeth. "He would have chosen some other place than Panya to travel to. They say that any young man who finds himself there is as good as forgotten."

Luciano grinned. "Where is this Panya of a place?"

"I hear that it is in Equatorial Guinea. My dear, they say that life in that place is very sweet. Too much partying, cheap food and drinks, and easy life. I hear also that the women are very beautiful, with wide hips, loose morals and very much unlike our women. They will keep a man in the house, and feed and clothe him. That is the reason our men never get to think of home again the moment they get a taste of Panya."

Luciano's eyes widened with the revelation. He

secretly desired such a place where life was so easy, and free of the kind of worry that he had come to know. It would never matter if the world he left behind spent all eternity keeping count of the length of his absence. "I thought you must have seen him one way or another. That is why I asked."

"I would have walked by him if we met on a road. I don't even know what he looks like."

"But I thought there are such things you people of nowadays do with this new kind of computers you now hold like bibles in your hands." She made a small square in the air.

"Laptops," Luciano offered. He dug into his satchel for his laptop. "Something like this?"

"Yes. Exactly. Although, Ikodiya's son's own is a bit bigger than yours. He said that with it, he could connect with many people all over the world. He even showed us pictures of Ezeora, one of my in-laws living in Lagos, and I saw many others of our kinsmen living in Kaduna, and in London."

Luciano smiled, "I believe it is Facebook."

"He didn't mention the name, else I would have recalled."

Gorilla was back again. He held a wine keg by one of its curved arms and two drinking cups in his other hand. Aunty Eliza reverently passed her stool on to him and stood up in search of another for herself. She settled with an overturned small wooden mortar.

"My inlaw, I have brought palm wine for us here since you choose to keep your aunty company in the kitchen." He handed a cup over to Luciano and kept the other for himself. Luciano noticed Aunty Eliza hadn't been included to partake of the palm wine. She went about rummaging in a bamboo shelf high up against the kitchen wall. She uncovered some plates, emptied their contents into the boiling pot of soup and stirred with the ladle. Replacing the lid on the pot, she returned to her seat on the upturned mortar.

Gorilla placed the palm wine keg on a slab of wood used for chopping meat, removed the leafy stopper in the mouth of the keg and poured himself a liberal measure. He drained it at once and smacked his lips.

"Sebastian still remains the best in the business of tapping wine. Try it."

Luciano obliged. It was the second time he had tasted undiluted palm wine. The first had been in Enugu. He couldn't recall the occasion, but it had come with the delicious *abacha* prepared with tenderized stockfish and plenty of pepper. "I heard you discussing Obichere," Gorilla said, reviving the discussion that had died with his arrival. Luciano chose the moment to take a sip. Aunty Eliza made no comments.

Gorilla licked his lip. "Panya, as I have heard is not a place for young men. Obichere was a little younger than you when he left. He should have known where he came from. He is supposed to know that much is expected of him back home. If that place isn't favourable for him, he should just come back, or better still, relocate to Gabon where his mates are doing well." He paused to take a sip. "When we were much younger, three of my uncles traveled to Panya. They stayed there for a very long time that even when their mother died, there was just no way to relay the news to them. For a very long time they stayed away from home, so long that the little children they left behind had grown beards. Still they hadn't come back, even for once. Their only brother at home died one day, and since he had other brothers alive, his body was to be preserved until any male member of the family was present to bury him, and to preside over the responsibility of the family. A delegation of two men and Nwando, a young lad, was organized. Every villager was levied a tin of palm oil and the money realized from the sale was handed over to the delegation. Eze Iloabuchi, the king that time, and the oracle offered their blessings to the noble men who were to go on the mission to bring back our lost sons. And so, saddled with money and blessings, each of these men bid their families farewell. Three months passed, and at the beginning of the fourth month, our lost sons arrived. But little did we know that we had exchanged one problem for another; only one of the men from the delegation had returned with the robust-looking missing brothers. Panya took Nwando and the other man. They sent word with the returning party that they would be coming back to the village at some later time. You should know the other older man who stayed back with Nwando."

Clueless, Luciano stared at Gorilla's sitting form in the light of the log fire. "It was my late father," he said, with a hint of a smile. "He came back in his old age, when life's vigour had been sapped out of him. As for Nwando, his mother rained curses on her enemies up till the day she died. Nwando is yet to come back home till this moment. Who knows if he is still alive." He chuckled as he raised the cup to his lips. Luciano's mind was preoccupied with images of a paradise where one could escape from the travails of his world, and in that moment, he envied Nwando and Obichere.

With her bare hands, Aunty Eliza brought down the pot from the fire and then clapped them sharply together. Luciano looked on, aghast. There was no way he could attempt such a stunt without getting his palms charred and spilling the pot's contents.

"Chika, you are not drinking," Gorilla observed.

"It is quite strong," Luciano answered.

Gorilla laughed. "Very tricky drink, sweet yet very strong."

Aunty Eliza dished some soup into a black clay gourd and into two other soup bowls. Luciano noticed that she had dished the soup in three places. He had always known Aunty Eliza to eat from the same plate with her husband. Could there be an ongoing quarrel between them that he hadn't noticed? Was it the reason for her not partaking of the wine?

"Let's go and eat inside, or would you prefer here?" Aunty Eliza asked Luciano.

Why the deference to me? "Here is okay for me, Aunty."

"Me too," Gorilla said.

Aunty Eliza left the kitchen and returned shortly with two wooden stools. She placed one before her husband and the other before Luciano. From the bamboo shelf, she produced covered plates of *akpu* and placed each man's portion before him next to his plate of steaming soup. They washed their hands in a bowl of water.

"The food is for the both of us o. Don't finish it before I return," Aunty Eliza said to her husband as she made for the house, bearing a bowl of soup in one hand and a plate of *akpu* in the other.

"Aunty, where are you going to?" Luciano asked, puzzled.

Aunty Eliza stopped in her tracks, dumbfounded like one caught red-handed in the middle of some clandestine act. It was very obvious that she was failing in her attempt to cook up some defence. Gorilla cleared his throat, interrupting the tension.

"Nna m, this isn't something I would want you to

get involved with," Aunty Eliza said. She seemed to have found her voice, and he couldn't see the reason for the remorse in her voice. He looked to Gorilla. The hairy man was already studying his countenance. It dawned on him that he had stumbled onto some family secret which he wasn't supposed to dabble into.

"My in-law," Gorilla said at last. "I want you to come with me."

He led the way into the house with Aunty Eliza tagging along, the dishes borne in her hands like an offering to *Idemili*. Nobody gave any thoughts to their abandoned dinner.

ELEVEN

The room was fairly large but almost bare except for a small stool next to a wooden poster bed devoid of curtains on its railings. A small lantern glowed on the cemented floor. Its globe was clear of the slightest smudge such that the lantern seemed to give off more light than it was capable of. They hovered around the bed except for Aunty Eliza who sat on the edge of the bed, next to a manly form lying face up amongst the spotless white sheets. His stomach was swaddled in thick bandages. Another string of bandage went around his right shoulder, passing under his armpit. His right arm lay limp in a loose sling. But for the rhythmic rise and fall of his flat chest, the sleeper appeared as lifeless as a corpse. He was tall, Luciano noted, and his feet almost touched the end of the ancient-looking bed.

"I thought the sedative would have worn out by now," Aunty Eliza whispered to no one in particular.

"We chanced upon him in a more helpless state than this," Gorilla explained to Luciano.

"*Shh*, you will wake him up," Aunty Eliza cautioned. She looked like a mother hen fussing over her day-old chicks.

"Let us go back to our food," Gorilla suggested, tugging Luciano's arm. Luciano allowed himself to be led out of the room.

The fire in the kitchen had died down to a few live coal and a heap of hot ashes the moment they returned to the kitchen. Luciano settled down to his food as Gorilla fed two logs of wood and twigs into the dying fire, stoked it, and like magic, little flames materialized with the crackling of the twigs. The kitchen was lit and warm.

Gorilla washed his hands. "Your aunty found him last week. I think that should be six days ago."

Luciano foraged for a piece of fish in his bowl of soup. He had lost appetite. But showing it, he felt, would be a dishonourable thing to do.

"On her way back from selling fish in the market," Gorilla continued. "She stopped by the churchyard to pluck scent leaves. It was on the steps of the church that she saw him bleeding to death from bullet wounds."

Gorilla juggled between chewing, licking his fingers, swallowing and talking with such dexterity that neither his narration nor his food suffered unequal attention.

Aunty Eliza joined them; she dragged the upturned mortar closer to her husband and then settled down to eat.

"I will wait for the drug to wear off," she said before grabbing a handful off the mound of *akpu*. No one said anything in acknowledgement.

Gorilla continued where he had left off. "Your aunty did a most thoughtless thing, and that was to take the risk of bringing him to the house in her wheelbarrow. She wouldn't hear of my objection. You know how difficult she could be at times. We have had to be extra cautious since the day she brought the boy here. Since then, strange faces have appeared in the village making enquiries about a missing boy. At first, we thought it was the police, but we know all of the policemen at the police station and those faces do not belong with the police. Three people's homes have been broken into in the past five days. This is a rare thing to witness in this village, but the strange thing is that nothing was taken away in all of those break-ins." He licked his fingers. "I suspect that there are some dangerous people looking for someone, and that person is very much likely to be this boy we have under our roof."

Luciano rolled the morsel of *akpu* in his fingers absentmindedly. His stomach had tightened into a knot. The very thought of Aunty Eliza and her husband being in danger unsettled him.

"Yes, it was a thoughtless thing I did, but regrettably I would still have done the same thing were the occasion replayed," Aunty Eliza said. "It isn't my fault. Twenty-five years of being a surgical nurse makes you instinctively reach out to people when you see them in need of medical attention. If I hadn't brought him here, he sure would have bled to death out there and in the house of God. His wounds weren't as mortal as I had feared. He had been shot, but the round metal bullet had lodged itself close to his stomach without rupturing it. Thank God it wasn't a pointed bullet. It was a challenging task, but fortunately I extracted the bullet. Another bullet had torn through his shoulder and left off through the other side. It is just some tissue damage, but it missed his shoulder blade by only a fraction."

"When will he be fit to leave?" Luciano asked.

"His wounds are healing fine. In two days time, he should be able to leave. Though I suggest he rest for a long time, and avoid anything that will put any strain on his body."

"Aunty, but it was dangerous to have brought in a person suffering gunshot wounds under your roof. What if he is a wanted criminal?"

"What should I have done under the circumstance? There was no way I could have let him die there. I couldn't have lived with that on my conscience. And come to think of it, only a living person can be prosecuted for a crime."

"Have you reported this matter to the police?"

"Chikadibia, this patient needs intensive care. I can't leave him all to himself simply to go all that distance to the police station."

He knew Aunty Eliza was just being ridiculously protective; he doubted she'd ever take the matter to the police.

Someone sneezed inside the house, and like a herd of antelopes unsure of the direction of approaching danger, everyone pricked their ears as they listened and waited. Nobody dared to breathe. They exchanged questioning looks as though to ask, *Did it really come from the house*? Aunty Eliza was the first to reach for the bowl of water. She washed her hands hurriedly and made for the house. Luciano followed, with Gorilla almost breaking into a trot close behind.

In the room, they crowded around the bed. The form on the bed was awake. His eyes shone with surprising agility for an injured patient.

"How are you feeling?" Aunty asked.

"My head is woozy," he replied with an air of relaxed familiarity.

Luciano's ears picked out a trace of the Efik lilt. The patient's gaze met Luciano's and held. Aunty Eliza noticed it.

"This is my nephew, Chikadibia. He works in Port-Harcourt and he came to visit."

"Good evening, sir," he said.

"Good evening. How are you?" Luciano said. He hoped the apprehension didn't show in his voice.

"I feel pains."

Luciano flashed him a broad smile.

"You are doing great. Your wounds are healing fast," Aunty cut in. "I will have to change your bandages for the night. Chika, please help with the lantern. I need a clearer look."

Luciano held up the lantern as Aunty Eliza went about the task of tending to her patient's wounds. He stole the chance to study the patient by the lamplight. He was younger, twenty-two or twenty-three, and his face was strikingly familiar.

The face!

Luciano didn't have to wrack his memory for long; there was no mistaking it. It was the same face in the picture stashed away in his satchel.

TWELVE

Luciano hoped to do some work on *Igwemma,* but he dropped off to sleep. Perhaps he should blame the gentle breeze lifting the white curtain and cooling his head, or his characteristic indolence? Surprising lack of imagination? How long did he stare at his laptop screen without typing a word? Thirty minutes? One hour? He wouldn't know, but he remembered with a shudder that the sea of words displayed on the screen had appeared to be a jumbled mass of calligraphy to his unfocused vision. He had to shut down the laptop to conserve the batteries for some other time when his head would be neither foggy nor troubled.

Images of the patient's face haunted his head. It stole his sleep as he laid down on the mattress brought into the sitting room for him. He was sure it was Aniete on that bed. *The wanted Aniete under Aunty Eliza's roof!* Just when he thought he was done with trouble, it seemed to trail him wherever he went. He thought he had wiped his hands off Chief Ofodile and his *shit*, but this problem had proven to be stickier than camel's dung. He laid on his back, trying to make out the ceiling in the darkness as he thought of the potential danger his relatives were bringing upon themselves in harbouring Aniete. Do they actually know that their patient was trouble? Was it the reason for their paranoia, the double-barrelled gun and the hush-hush atmosphere about the house? Gorilla had said he suspected the staged robberies to actually be a desperate search for the boy. He had to be right. There was no better explanation for the robberies. But then, how did the boy, Aniete, get himself riddled with bullets? Who were those staging the robberies in the neighbourhood? They definitely weren't Silverpistol and his gang. There were lots of questions whose answers Luciano needed. But one thing was certain: Aniete must be of immense value to be wanted so desperately by some mean people, including his own father.

The sun had crept over the horizon when Luciano stirred awake. He stared at the ceiling as he collected his wits. Recalling the events of the previous night, he sprang out of bed and made for the bolted door.

The compound was obsessively swept and tranquil this morning. A bird chirped in a guava tree behind the house. Another bird, similar in tone, answered. A light breeze rustled the leaves of a mango tree, dislodging a yellowed leaf. It descended onto the patterned sand; those patterns created by sweeping palm fronds had always been one aspect of rural life that stole his heart.

He met Aunty Eliza seated in the shade of a young soursop tree, making brooms; she would expertly run a small sharp knife twice along the blade of a palm leaf and as though it were some magic trick, a fresh broomstick would be wavering in her hand. A pile of fresh green broomsticks lay on the ground to her left and a larger pile of palm leaves to her right.

"Aunty, good morning," he said as he approached.

"Nna m, good morning. Did you sleep well?"

"Yes." He squatted on the sand besides Aunty Eliza. He was not bothered about the ground soiling his boxer shorts.

"You should have gotten a stool."

"Don't worry. It is not every day I get to enjoy the freedom of unadulterated village life."

"I cooked yams for breakfast. Hope you like it. I made it with *ugba* and *utazi*."

"Hmm, I like it, but I haven't washed my mouth."

"You came with a toothbrush? Or would you like to use an *ugiri* branch?"

"I will use my toothbrush."

"Why not do that while I dish the food. There is

toothpaste by that window." She pointed a window facing the backyard. "I hope there's something in the tube."

"Okay. I will do that later. I am not hungry yet."

He yawned and made to scratch his crotch, but caught himself midway and sat out the impulse. There was no sign of Gorilla, and so he enquired from Aunty Eliza.

"He went out for a meeting early in the morning," she told him.

"And your patient? How is he?"

Aunty Eliza laughed, catching on the joke. "He will live."

Luciano kept mute. The front door banged open and Aunty Eliza snapped to alertness. It was Gorilla. He came through a second entrance that was a passageway into the backyard, a bundle of three freshly cut bamboo poles balanced across his broad hairy shoulder. A sharp machete dangled loosely in his left hand. He placed the poles against the wall close to the thatched kitchen, and picking out the bits of leaves clinging onto the hairs on his shoulder where the blue cotton singlet didn't cover, he stooped into the kitchen for a small stool.

"Good morning, sir," Luciano said as Gorilla approached the shade of the soursop tree with a low wooden stool.

"Good morning, my in-law. Hope you slept well."

"Yes."

He sat opposite his wife, peeled the singlet off his body and draped it across his thigh. He gathered some blades of palm leaves to his side and, with a pen-knife which he produced from the pockets of his combat shorts, he began the magical production of broomsticks with some show of dexterity than his wife could boast of. Luciano was seeing Gorilla closely in the light of day for the first time in a very long while. Apart from certain parts of the man's face, there was no other part of his body spared from the encroaching forest of black hair that made him appear pitch black from a distance.

"How was the meeting?" Aunty Eliza asked.

"Fine. We arrived at a consensus to take the matter to the police headquarters in Owerri. You know we haven't experienced this kind of house breaks before and people are becoming too recurrent for anyone's liking. You should have heard wild speculations being aired in the meeting. "

"Hmm," Aunty sighed. "It is becoming more dangerous for him."

"Why didn't you contact the police with information about Aunty Eliza's patient?" Luciano asked Gorilla.

"Your aunty thought against it, and then I thought against having to place us in a situation where we would be accused of harbouring a criminal."

"We don't know if he is a criminal. He is only a wounded boy. Just look at him. He isn't any older than Munachi. Imagine that it were Munachi, our own son. He could have been robbed and shot. Anybody could have been in such a helpless situation too," Aunty Eliza said.

"He is a wanted man," Luciano said.

"I can see that," Gorilla said. "He was shot and some people are breaking into houses in a bid to fish him out."

"I think there is more than just one party desperately seeking for him," Luciano pursued.

"Why do you think so?" Aunty Eliza asked, and studied Luciano's face with undisguised curiosity.

"Because I was looking for him too, at least until yesterday when I gave up hope of ever finding him."

Aunty Eliza and Gorilla had their full attention on him. "You place yourselves in the line of danger in keeping him with you."

"Chikadibia, you speak as though the wine your in-law gave you last night hasn't yet cleared from your head."

In any other circumstance, Luciano would have laughed, but he didn't. Instead he looked her in the eye. "That boy lying in the room has some kind of history which I am yet to know. Some rich man offered to pay me good money to search for his illegitimate son. I took on the job because I am starving, jobless and in desperate need for money. Only yesterday, I ran into another search party out for the same boy. They kidnapped me and interrogated me and when they found out I knew next to nothing about the boy, they let me go. They seem to be more desperately in search of him than his rich father. I called the boy's father and let him know I am no longer interested in the deal. That was why you saw me here late last night."

They were both silent when Luciano finished narrating his story. Not even a shadow of wind appeared to stir.

It was Gorilla who broke the silence: "So what do we do now? He isn't yet strong to leave. Is he?" He was looking at his wife in expectation.

"Just a few more days. For now, all he needs is rest."

Luciano fought down his irritation. Here was Aunty Eliza being stubborn in the face of trouble. She should have been concerned with removing the element of danger from her house instead of being heady. But he didn't say it. He did not even let his irritation show.

"We will have to keep our fingers crossed for the time being," Gorilla said.

Luciano considered asking his in-law to be more definitive of the word 'we'. If they weren't family, he would have taken his bag and walked away on them and from impending danger, but they were family and he would have to stick with them, even though it meant his not returning to Port-Harcourt on that day, as he had earlier planned.

He didn't leave the next day either; he spent the days that followed thinking on the next line of action and working on *Igwemma* whenever his mind was free of concerns.

THIRTEEN

Igwemma balances a clay pot on her head and walks to the river. Ezenwanyi, her mother, bought it only yesterday for her as a gift in remembrance of the morning of eighteen planting seasons when she was born. Igwemma sings to herself as she walks alone on the path. She swings her hips too, and the beads on her small waist rattle to the rhythm of her song. The footpath is narrow. There are cassava farms on either side. A gentle breeze makes their leaves wave in the noon sun.

The other girls don't like Igwemma. They say she is a proud girl. They also say she makes the young men pay them very little attention.

Igwemma gets to the Sister Rivers. Like always she stands on the little hill that looks like a small hunch on a giant's back and looks at the calm water stretching far into the distance. It appears as though the sky meets the water somewhere in the far distance.

She never stops to wonder at the strange, proud waters. She can see the thin ridge of dry land splitting the waters into *two lanes, with Ahama flowing on one lane and Ukpokiri on the other. The both waters never meet. If both waters are poured into a clay pot, it broke and the waters flowed into two distinct puddles, away from the other. If she came very early in the morning, she would stand on the hill long enough to listen to the flow of the waters. She likes the sound. It makes her think of two sisters quarreling. But it isn't quiet this afternoon.*

The girls washing at the banks of the Sister Rivers look away when Igwemma comes along. She gives them a wide berth. She lays her new pot very carefully on the sandy banks and then goes into the cool water to bathe her legs. She sings and swings her beaded waist and then she sees the woman's reflection in the water!

She is standing far down in the river where the water rises to her belly. Igwemma recognizes the woman. Her name is Myeine; she told her so in her dreams a long time ago. Myeine is always in Igwemma's dreams, she is beautiful. Her hair is very long, black and beautiful, like she applies some fine oil that makes it sparkle. It reaches down her back and into the waters of the river around her. She has very bright, small stones in her hair too. In her dream, Myeine always talked nice to her, and she would hold her hand as they walked along beautiful beaches with very white sand that shone brightly in the daylight. Igwemma looks up at the riverbank; the other girls are too busy, and they do not see Myeine. Maybe they cannot see Myeine.

"Igwemma," Myeine calls out to her. She is smiling like she does in those dreams.

"Myeine. You look beautiful. Can you make me as beautiful as you are?"

"I can never be more beautiful than you, my mistress. I am only your servant and guide."

"My guide?"

"Yes. I am sent to bring you to your household. Everyone is waiting."

"Who is waiting?"

"Your family."

"My family?"

"Yes, daughter of the household of the Sister Rivers. You have a mother and you have beautiful sisters too. They have patiently watched over you, especially Siniril, the eldest."

"But I have a mother and she loves me. She bought me a clay pot, a new one only yesterday. Can you see it over there?" She points to the clay pot resting in the sandy shore.

"Come with me and you will see the beautiful things that await you."

Myeine holds out her hand to Igwemma. Igwemma takes it. She steps forward into the water. It reaches up to her knees, her thighs, and waist and then... splash!

Screams of "Mammywater! Mammywater!" rent the air. All the girls scramble away from the riverbanks abandoning their clothes and clay pots in their flight. A few of the girls have seen the big tail fin of some strange fish break the surface of the water in a great splash. They had always heard from folk tales that mammywater lives in the Sister Rivers, but as they flee, they *know they have become living witnesses to the realities of such tales ...*

Luciano's back ached from sitting for too long. He shut down his laptop and, stretching and yawning, gravitated away from the fallen tree trunk, where he had been ensconced for a little more than an hour. His joints creaked from stiffness. The sun was overhead in the clear sky and he was already feeling the beginning of hunger pangs, even though it hadn't been up to four hours he devoured some ripe plantains. His mind went to the fruits in the basket Aunty Eliza had left for him before leaving to buy some drugs from the pharmacy across the main road.

It was the fifth day in Aunty Eliza's house and he had begun to enjoy the prolonged stay. Nothing out of the ordinary had occurred – at least not yet – and he was taken very good care of. Aunty Eliza fussed over him a lot and stuffed him with food. Gorilla told him many past stories over a keg of freshly tapped wine so he was tipsy for most of the time.

The patient was healing fast. Surprisingly, the boy's improving health was becoming an impending threat to the tranquility Luciano had been enjoying for the past days. It was becoming clear to him that the day was fast-approaching when he would have to confront the boy.

He had toyed with the idea of calling Chief Ofodile to make amends and restore the terms of their contract. He could be accused of being an opportunist, but he could still be excused for his intention to safely deposit the element of danger far away from his aunt and her good husband.

He made the call at sundown that day.

"Hello," Luciano said.

"Hello"

Silence.

"I am listening, Luciano."

"I have seen him."

"Who?"

"Aniete, your son."

"Great." There was a moment of silence. "Bring him."

"Do we still have an agreement?"

"Of course. For the fact you held up to your own end of the bargain, it means we still do. I can't claim to understand your recent outburst, but I think I can conveniently categorize it as an occupational hazard."

"But there is a problem."

"What is it?"

"Things are quite complicated here."

"Please do what you can. I am depositing all

accumulated allowances into the account first thing tomorrow."

"I will do my best."

"I am counting on you. Good luck."

The connection went dead.

FOURTEEN

It took a week and two days more before the patient could go about the house without bandages. A fresh stitch scar ran diagonally over the right side of his stomach. It looked like the imprint of a large centipede on his skin. A small scar spotted his right shoulder just under the shoulder blade, and at that same spot on his back, an ugly scar stood out where the bullet had torn away a chunk of tissue as it made its exit. The scar looked so fresh and moist that Aunty Eliza still covered it with some tape and cotton wool, but the boy looked fit. He no longer lay sedated on the bed but would go about the backyard and the rooms, although he kept away from the front yard and out of sight of the few visitors who called.

One wet evening, he sat with the other members of the household on low stools around the log fire in the kitchen, roasting and eating yellow corn on the cobs with pears being roasted in ash.

"You have not told us about your parents," Luciano dropped the subtle accusation without warning. He imagined the look of horror on Aunty Eliza's face, but he resisted the urge to look in her direction. As for Gorilla, he reasoned, he could hold up quite well.

The patient paused his munching long enough to offer his reply: "My father died two years ago. For now, it is just me and my mother. "

"Are you a student?"

"Yes."

"Which of the universities?"

"Nnamdi Azikiwe University."

"The one in Awka?"

"Yes."

Luciano eyed him. The patient gnawed innocently at his cob of corn as he floored the questions without the slightest hint of contemplation. *Maybe this boy isn't Aniete. Maybe I'm chasing after a shadow.* "You must be far away from school," he pursued half-heartedly.

"Yes." Aniete looked up from the stripped cob of corn in his hand and, on meeting Luciano's questioning gaze, he explained further: "I came with my study group on a field trip to test for soil samples in this area. The test was for a school project." He tossed the spent cob aside, pulled out a fresh one from the bed of live coals and whipped his hand repeatedly in the air to cool off his scorched fingers.

"Do you know who shot you?"

The patient hung his hand in mid-air long enough to flash Luciano a suspicious look. "No. I don't."

Luciano read the look and knew he might not be chasing after any shadows after all; he rose to the bait. "Did you see them?"

"No."

"What about your friends in your study group? Are they the ones searching for you?"

The patient's eyes came alive. "Is anybody looking for me?"

"Yes, and desperately so. Do you know them?"

"No." The streak of concern on his face revealed his anxiety.

"Are the people who're looking for you your friends in the study group?"

"I don't know."

"Did you know your father before he died?"

"Yes. He was a contractor with Nigerian Breweries."

Luciano nibbled at the cob in his hand. It tasted cold. *Is the boy genuinely naïve of the subject of his parentage or is he trying to mask it behind a shroud of deception like he is doing about his shooters and where he schooled?*

"I know your father."

The patient regarded him intently. The stunned expression on his face looked either genuine or ingeniously faked. He turned to Gorilla and Aunty Eliza for some explanation but their different degrees of helplessness stared back at him. "I mean the father you don't know," Luciano offered. "He knows you and wants to meet with you." The boy remained silent, but Luciano continued. "He knows I am with you even at this moment."

"I don't know what you are talking about. My father is dead," he replied in a careless tone.

"No. He is very much alive. He told me everything. It was he who told me that your name is Aniete. I have the photograph of you, which he gave me. It is in my bag. In fact, it is a long story, but I have been on the search for you for two days before I stumbled upon you just when I had given up."

Luciano could tell from the patient's silence that he was processing the information in his head. "He told me that your mother's name is Uduak."

He didn't miss the boy's blink of amazement. "Years back, your mother was his mistress, but he had to send her away…" Luciano paused in mid-sentence before continuing. "I think he will tell you the rest of the story when you get to meet him."

"You mean to tell me that I have a father and he is alive?"

"Yes, and he awaits your return."

"It is true that my name is Aniete. But I don't want to know how you came by that information. I don't care to know anything about the man you are talking about. I am not interested in meeting a father who never cared for my existence all this while!" All of his initial reservations evaporated in the heat of the rage that he gave vent to. "I have lived without him all these years. I have learnt to survive without him. He doesn't exist to me."

He rose from his seat and strode casually into the drizzling rain. He gave no thought to the cob in his hand as he headed for the room in the house where he had convalesced. He had naturally taken to the room. It had become his sanctuary over the period he had lived in it as a patient and a guest.

Luciano caught Aunty Eliza's accusing gaze. Gorilla was as passive as he could be, but he had the look of one who would rather not wish for any trouble playing out under his roof.

Luciano wasn't bothered about Aunty Eliza or Gorilla; at least not anymore. His concern was the fear of not completing the task for which he would earn some good money to guarantee a future for himself. "Come what may," he resolved, "there has to be a way of convincing the boy to come with me to Port-Harcourt."

That night, Luciano ate his dinner alone in the sitting room, with the yellow flame of the lantern for company. The rest of the family and Aniete, were having theirs on the veranda. Aniete had been avoiding him for the rest of the day and he didn't want to upset him anymore than he already had. The sound of approaching feet from behind caused Luciano to turn. It was Aunty Eliza. She settled beside him on the red cushioned settee.

"Hope you like the soup."

"Very much." He licked his fingers clean for emphasis before digging into the remaining small mound of *akpu*.

"But you are not eating the fish in the soup?" she observed, craning her neck to have a clearer look into the soup bowl.

"I am reserving it for when I am done with the *akpu*. You know, fish and meat are meant to seal a filled stomach. They will kill your appetite if you eat them while the main food isn't yet finished."

Aunty Eliza laughed. "You are still the same boy I used to know."

"But a bigger version, *abi*?"

"Yes."

The sound of a morsel of *akpu* on its way down his gullet resounded through the room.

"He said he would be leaving in the morning," Aunty Eliza said without prompting. Luciano returned a morsel of *fufu* back to the plate.

"Aniete? I mean, your patient? He is leaving tomorrow?"

"Yes. And he is no longer my patient. He is fully recovered now."

"Aunty, I want to ask a favour from you."

"And what would that be?"

"I want you to drug him by morning."

Aunty Eliza regarded him in utter disbelief. "*Bia, nwa a*, what has come over you? What have you grown to become?"

"I need to take him to Port-Harcourt with me, Aunty."

"Why not forget about this whole story of bringing home a lost son. You remember how close you told us you were to danger as a result of this whole business? Why not be grateful that you were spared instead of reaching out for more trouble?"

"Aunty, do you think I am making all these stories up?"

"No. I do not doubt you, Chika. I am only concerned for your safety. And it is looking to me like you are losing yourself over this whole business of bringing home a lost son. At some point, it is even sounding strange, like something that happens in the movies."

Luciano said nothing, but he continued with his food in silence, even though his mind was miles away from it. He would never forgive his failure in achieving his dreams if he came this near to actualizing them.

Later that night, while everyone slept, Luciano tiptoed to Aniete's door, tapped lightly and listened or any response.

Only the chirping of night insects reached his ears. He knocked again and then called out lightly, "Aniete".

He had come in the hope that Aniete would not be too petty as to keep malice with him. He knocked again, a little louder this time, just in case Aniete was deep in slumber. *Thank God Aniete's room is the one that opened onto the backyard, away from the one Aunty Eliza shared with her husband; they surely would have heard this very knock.* Thunder, like a giant's grumble, sounded in the blackened skies above. A gale of chilly wind swept through, the cold biting into his bones and causing him to shiver. He contemplated dashing back into the house for something to put on other than his boxer shorts.

He could swear he didn't hear the bolt slide back, but the door swung silently open. Aniete stood in the doorway and there was an interrogatory look in his eyes.

"Can I ..." Luciano was saying. But Aniete backed away into the room dimly lit by the same burning lantern with the wick turned low. Luciano hurried into the room, grateful for the warmth. He shut the door after him but didn't bother with securing the lock.

Aniete sat on the edge of the bed. He never offered Luciano a seat. Luciano read the air of contained hostility and settled for standing at the head of the bed instead. No one spoke for a while, causing the tension to build up so thick you felt you could cut into it with a knife.

"I am sorry to have upset you earlier," Luciano began. "I know how traumatizing it can be when you

165

suddenly come to realize you have been deceived into believing something different all your life." He could tell that despite his silence, Aniete was listening. "But then, my only offense is in being the bearer of the news, and for that I am truly sorry."

"My problem isn't with you," Aniete cut him short in a tone that was surprisingly low but devoid of warmth. His gaze was focused on the lantern on the floor. Luciano breathed a sigh of relief. He waited for Aniete to continue, but seconds passed and the young man wasn't showing any signs of saying any more than he already had.

"Your father wants you."

"Why now? What happened to all those years when I had to struggle on my own because I believed that I didn't have a father?"

"But I thought you had a father?"

"That was after he died."

"But you said he died only recently."

The boy kept silent. Luciano's brain was working overtime. Something wasn't adding up. He had earlier suspected that the boy was lying. But it was becoming clear he was such a pitiful liar.

"I lied." The confession was without remorse; the way an insolent, pampered, child caught red-handed by the housemaid would own up to actually dipping into his own mother's pot of stew.

"Tell me, what part of your story is true?"

"How is it your business?"

It pained Luciano to see Aniete act insolently. The boy was putting Aunty Eliza and her husband in the line of grave danger with his lies, and yet he was impenitent about it. His first impulse was to strike Aniete in the face, but then he thought better of it.

"I hear you are leaving in the morning."

"Yes."

"Where will you be going from here?"

"Back to school."

"Imo State University?"

Aniete shot him a quick glance and then looked away. The low light didn't offer Luciano the chance to read the look on Aniete's face. "That is another lie you said back there. Isn't it?"

"It isn't your business where I go from here."

"The people who shot you, do you know them?" Luciano asked, but Aniete didn't reply. "I know for a certainty that they aren't the only ones you should look out for." Even in the dim light, Luciano noticed the slight flinch. "There's another desperate group on campus. They are turning over every rock and looking into every crevice in search of you." He looked out for any reaction, but there was none. "Does a short, dark, mean devil wielding a silver pistol mean anything to you? I guess he is the don of some kind of *La Cosa Nostra* on campus."

Aniete remained mute and still. "What about a muscular, tattooed, marijuana-smoking, exuberant occupant of Pentagon Lodge?" Aniete shot him another glance, a longer one this time. "In case Aunty Eliza hasn't told you, there is another group, more daring than the others. They are even staging robberies in houses in the neighbourhood as they search for you. The last house they hit is the fourth one to the left of this house. My guess is that they know you are in hiding in this village. They must have some spies determined to smoke you out one way or another. You just might have a bullet tear through your skull before you venture half the distance to the motor park on your way to God-knows-where."

Luciano allowed his words to sink in. He could tell that he was doing fine, for Aniete sat still like a statue cut in stone. "You need help and I offer my help."

"It doesn't seem as though you are my friend. You have always thought me to be some criminal. I don't need your help."

"Don't be stupid. You know as much as I do that you are a marked man. You become a walking object for target practice the very moment you step out of here and into the open. You need help."

"Why do you want to help? What do you stand to gain? Why should I trust you?"

Luciano sighed inwardly. The boy was a clever one; he would give him that. "I have some money and a future to gain if you come with me to Port-Harcourt to meet with your father. But here's the deal. I will be your partner, I will watch your back for as long as it takes to deliver you to your father in Port-Harcourt."

"I am not interested in going to Port-Harcourt. I don't know the man you talk about."

"He is a lonely old man. His family has deserted him and defected abroad, to a better life."

"I am not going to babysit some old stranger who claims to be my father."

Luciano whispered his desperation: "For God's sake, he is a wealthy man more concerned with having an heir for his estates. My God! I wish he had claimed to be my father."

Aniete cracked his knuckles in turns. Luciano interpreted the gesture to be one of sparked interest. "You only have to present yourself to the man. Agree to be his son and he will open his treasury doors to you. You will live a life of no worries. Imagine the luxuries you will enjoy whilst awaiting the day he expires, which I am sure is not too far off. But if it takes too long in coming, you could just snuff the life out of him or something like that. Considering his age, it doesn't look like it is going to be a difficult job for you. Just look at what you stand to gain and you will see that coming with me to Port-Harcourt is the best decision you will make in your life."

Aniete remained still.

Luciano feared that he was going to give him the silent treatment, but he spoke eventually: "How am I to trust you?"

"Oh, come on, have I been doing a sloppy job in trying to win your trust all this while? You are worth nothing to me dead. I need you delivered to your father alive and in a good shape, so he pays me off. The rest will be up to you, afterwards to do as you please."

Aniete grinned.

"Do we have a deal?" Luciano asked expectantly, and Aniete nodded.

Luciano breathed a sigh of relief. He had never felt such satisfaction in a very long while.

That night, he dreamt he was in a hall, signing autographs for a long queue of enthusiastic fans. They each clutched a book in their hands. The book covers were glossy and beautiful. A fan in the queue looked like his mother. She stepped forward when it got to her turn, her face awash with awe. He smiled back at her and tipped his head in greeting. She laid her own copy on the table before him and that was when he saw the writing on the cover in beautiful and bold print:

Igwemma
A Novel
By Luciano D. Iloabuchi

She flipped over the book cover and he signed his autograph.

FIFTEEN

Morning came and Aniete was still in bed long after the rest of the household had risen.

Luciano met Aunty Eliza in the kitchen warming a pot of soup over the log fire. It was the remnants of last night's supper.

"Have you woken?" she asked.

"Yes."

"Will you have *akpu* or tea for breakfast? There's bread in the house."

"Tea."

"I think the boy will have *akpu* to sustain him on his trip," she said

"I guess so. I am leaving for Port-Harcourt this morning too."

If Aunty Eliza was surprised, she didn't show it. "Why the sudden decision? Does it have anything to do with the boy?"

"We are travelling together."

He stood to her full height, hands akimbo. "Chikadibia, I don't understand you anymore. You have become a changed person. What exactly has life done to you?"

"Aunty it is nothing. We both know that there are people out there looking for him. He is in grave danger. I don't know where he is going to, but I am just his partner to follow him with watchful eyes as far as Owerri, and then I will continue on to Port-Harcourt."

For a moment, she looked thoughtful, then sighed and said, "I hope you will be safe?"

Luciano smiled reassuringly. "I am a big boy now. I can take care of myself. Don't you know?"

"You will have to be very careful, please."

"I will. Where is my in-law?"

"Look at him there." She pointed at a tall palm tree in the distance. Luciano had not earlier paid notice to the *kpoi! kpoi! kpoi* echoing in the wind. He strained his sight to make out a figure leaning hard on his *ete* high up in the palm tree as he swung the blade of a machete at the base of palm fronds. "He is pruning off the leaves so the trees yield bigger bunches of fruits."

Luciano wondered how Aunty Eliza and her husband had come to adapt so well to village life. It was hard to believe that they were once government workers living in big cities sometime not too long ago. Luciano's phone beeped. He reached for it against the waistline of his boxer shorts. It was a bank transfer alert. Chief Ofodile had paid the money as he promised.

Aniete woke and went about preparations for his departure. There wasn't much of a preparation to make – since he had arrived without any baggage – except for a hurried bath. Aunty Eliza plied them with food and he obliged heartily. Gorilla had come down from his perch high up in the tree to learn of Luciano's hasty departure. He only apologized for not having any remaining palm wine in the house to toast to their departure. He offered them some money for transport fare but Luciano politely declined. Luciano noticed the struggle within Aniete to accept the money, and he was glad when the young man eventually declined too. Aunty Eliza took the better part of thirty minutes admonishing them to be careful and watchful on their journey.

At long last, they were on their way through a winding footpath to the market where they would get a bus to Owerri. Gorilla, menacing-looking and with a sharp machete, clutched in a vice-like grip, led the way. He was intent on escorting them as far as the point where the footpath opened onto the market square. They didn't meet anyone on the way as they trudged along in silence. The lonely path inspired Luciano to think of

Igwemma. Lately, the story had become too much of an over-demanding mistress, possessing his thoughts and begging for his every attention.

The girls run into the village screaming.

"Mammywater has carried Igwemma o!"

"Mammywater has carried Igwemma o!"

They scream to Ezenwanyi's house. They dash themselves to the earth in the compound and wail. Ezenwanyi, tall and beautiful hurries out of the hut, clutching her loose wrapper against her bosom.

"What is happening?" she demands in panic.

"Mammywater has carried Igwemma o," they chorus.

"When? Where?"

"At the Sister Rivers."

Ezenwanyi secures her wrapper firmly in a notch under her armpit. She runs downhill to the Sister Rivers, holding onto her breasts so they won't flap against her chest ...

The motor park was a small area at one corner of the market. It was a market day, and so the scene was packed full with a shuffling mass of humanity. Customers haggled, traders called out their wares, hawkers did the same, and to the corner that served as the motor park, conductors called out to passengers.

A conductor leaning against a dusty bus and holding his crotch in his hand, called out, "Aba! Aba! Aba!"

Luciano was elated; he hadn't expected getting a direct bus to Aba; the town closest to Port-Harcourt. But then, there were only two passengers on the bus. He sighed. He knew he would have to wait for God-knows-how-long it would take the bus to get filled up. There wasn't much he could do about it other than to take an alternative route through Owerri. But he couldn't tell how long he would have to wait for a bus to Port-Harcourt from Owerri to fill up. Better not to jump from the frying pan into the fire, he reasoned. He approached the conductor.

"How much?"

"Four hundred," the man replied with an air of indifference.

Luciano made to dig into his satchel.

"I'm not going," Aniete said from where he stood behind Luciano. Luciano turned around to face him, unsure of what he had heard. "I'm not going," Aniete reiterated.

Luciano signaled his apology to the bus conductor, and then guiding Aniete by the elbow, steered him out of earshot of the conductor. "What's the matter this time?" he hissed.

"I need to see somebody."

"Are you crazy? Can't you tell that you are exposing

yourself too much right now in standing in the open? Some fellow could have a gun aimed at your back even as we speak."

"I just need to see somebody."

Suppressed rage forced out some veins on Luciano's forehead. "Why? Who the *hell* is this person you want to meet at the risk of your own life?"

"My friend."

"Are you being serious right now? You think this is the best time for a courtesy call?"

"You won't understand."

"Okay, now make me understand while you are still alive before another shooter gets lucky this time."

"It is a long story."

"Of course, it always is."

"I have to go now."

He made to go, but Luciano grabbed him by the arm. "You think going out on your own like that is wise?"

"I need the money."

"Hold on." Luciano looked puzzled. "What money?"

"My own share. One million, three hundred thousand naira."

Luciano blinked in astonishment. "You didn't tell me anything about any money."

Aniete didn't reply. He made to go, but Luciano held him back. "But I still need you to come with me to Port-Harcourt." Aniete said nothing. He didn't force his arm away from Luciano's grip either. "Please."

"That will be after I get to collect my money from my friend."

"Promise?'

"Promise."

"Let me hear you say it."

"Say what exactly?"

"That you will come with me to Port-Harcourt the moment we are done with seeing your friend."

"I will follow you to Port-Harcourt the moment we are done with seeing my friend."

Luciano sighed and let go of Aniete's arm. "So, where are we meeting with this your friend?"

"Owerri."

"Jesus Christ! Owerri, you say?"

Aniete nodded. "What in bloody hell is the matter with you? Do you have a date with death?"

"Have you changed your mind?"

"No. It is just *fucking* risky. That place is a war zone. It's bloody *fucking* hostile territory!"

Aniete began to walk away and Luciano fell in step beside him. "I still want to know how you came by such money?"

"Not your business."

"How did you wind up in the village?"

Aniete didn't answer but kept on walking. Luciano fought to keep pace with Aniete's long strides. It was evident that Aniete never wanted to talk about the money or how he wound up in Orodo and so Luciano thought it best to lay his curiosity to rest for the moment. And truly, all of that wasn't meant to be his business. His business with Aniete only went as far as delivering him to Port-Harcourt, and he was going to remain objective in seeing to the task. In the meantime, he would have to keep his eyes open; there were just too many unanswered questions about Aniete. Inasmuch as they were partners for as far as the journey to Port-Harcourt went, he would never trust the sneaky bastard with his satchel - least of all his life.

They got a bus to Owerri, but it departed two hours later. Luciano looked out of the window for hours at the fleeting scenery until it was only fallow lands that met his gaze. The wind brushed past his ears as the bus sped along. He slid the glass shut. Aniete snoozed besides him. There was nothing else worthwhile to do, and so he took out his laptop.

SIXTEEN

Everything is bright and beautiful. In her whole life, Igwemma has never seen such beautiful things gathered together in one place. Everything in the palace is made of gold and many other things that sparkle in the bright lights. She is wearing a dress; long, flowing and studded with pieces of bright stones that catch the lights. It feels so light and soft against her skin like a spider's web. Her hair has suddenly grown long and black like those of the other girls and women about the palace and its magnificent courts. They have wound her hair into a bundle on her head. It doesn't look like the patterns she had always plaited from when she was yet a little girl. They have also stuck glittery carved pins to her hair. She looks into a big mirror. She likes what she sees. She touches the pins. They are smooth and they look like glass with water in them.

She has entered a large court filled with beautiful people. They turn to look at her in admiration. Most of them smile at her. She feels like she has known them somewhere. There is a beautiful woman sitting on a big chair that sparkles in the light. The crown on her head is the most beautiful thing in the whole court. The others bow before her in greeting.

Igwemma has not seen Myeine.

"Come to me, daughter. We are proud to have you visit," the woman with the beautiful crown beckons.

Igwemma obeys. She steps forward before the woman.

"You are welcome home, daughter. Your sisters and I are honoured to have you come to see your people. We have always watched over you. We have guided you and will always do so for as long as your sojourn in the land of mortals lasts. You are a princess of a great household that stretches over large territories, the envy of many. Your place is with us and not with the daughters of mortal men. I welcome you once again."

Every other person in the court listens to the woman with the crown. She waves her slim, beautiful hand and the court doors are thrown open. Women in colourful dresses file in. They are not wearing any gold or any of the shiny things the other women wear. They set long tables in the middle of the court and then they place glittery dishes on the tables. Igwemma recognizes Myeine amongst them. She smiles at Igwemma. Her teeth glitter; she has a gold ring in them. A banquet is set in a moment and everybody mills around the long tables. Twelve elegantly dressed women walk into the court. They walk as though they are floating in the air. The woman with the crown introduces them as the twelve daughters of the household and Igwemma's sisters. The girls are lovely. They talk sweetly to Igwemma. They give her a silver cup and then pour in some red wine; she likes the flowing sound of the wine in her cup. They have their own cups too: silver, gold, studded with sapphire, diamonds, rare-looking pearls and all the many glittery things that Igwemma hasn't seen before. They smell nice too, like strange flowers in a garden on a cool breezy evening.

Igwemma tastes the wine. It is red and sweet, very sweet and sweeter than the honey Ezenwanyi buys from the man who wanders into the bushes and comes out only to sell the rare things he finds before he disappears again for days. She loves the wine. They refill her cup and she drinks all of it again. They are delighted that she likes the drink. They like her and she likes them too. They sit around her and tell her tales of lands far away from the village where she was born, places she hasn't heard of. They tell her of other households, of other princesses less beautiful and of kingdoms less peaceful.

She is enjoying herself. Somebody is playing some music with some strange instrument. She loves the music, it's soft and slow. She hasn't heard anything of the kind, but it is pleasing to her ears. The music, the wine, the glittery court and elegantly dressed women, the princesses -- everything is so wonderful. They make Igwemma forget all about her mother, Ezenwanyi. This is where she loves. The woman with the crown claps her hand and the music comes to an abrupt end. Everybody turns to her. She stands to her feet. She is tall and very beautiful, and her smile would melt even a woman's heart. Her dress, blue as waters Igwemma has never seen, flows down to the ground about her feet.

"It is time to go back to the world of men, daughter," she announces, looking at Igwemma.

Igwemma wants to cry, she wants to say 'no', she wants to plead with the woman to let her stay forever.

"Hold your peace, daughter. Your earthly mother disturbs me with her wails. You have to go back. It isn't yet time for your return. Everything has an appointed time, and yours will come."

Igwemma cries.

Ezenwanyi is crying for her daughter. She runs up and down the riverbank, throwing her arms in the air. She has lost her scarf, but she doesn't care. Her hair is ruffled as she runs her hands through them in anguish. Her hair is like Ekpewerechi's, the mad woman's, but she doesn't care either. She cries for her daughter to be returned to her.

It was at that time of the evening when weary farmers returned home caked in soil and sweat. Igwemma walks home along the lonely footpath. Her body is wet, very wet and slippery. She didn't see her calabash. Maybe Mother has taken it, she thinks. Igwemma doesn't like the village, not anymore. It is not beautiful, it has no beautiful courts. The villagers are ugly, they wear their shorter hairs in patterns that are not as beautiful as she has seen, and they don't love her. They don't wear beautiful robes and rare jewels and they don't drink sweet red wine. They drink only palm wine and wear dull-looking calico and bland ivory for *jewelry. They don't have gold, silver, sapphire or all those glittery things that catch the eye.*

She meets people on the way. They look at her, and some of them run ahead to tell Ezenwanyi that Igwemma is back. Ezenwanyi shrieks for joy. She doesn't wait to think if they were saying the truth, but she runs down the path to meet her daughter.

"Did you see that girl, Igwemma, today?"

"Yes o, I saw her with my two naked eyes, my sister."

Two maidens gossip as they make the family's supper.

"Did you notice how beautiful she looks?"

"I swear, she looked like mammywater."

"Is she not one?"

"Hmm, Nkemdirim, say what you know o."

"Before nko? Who has heard of somebody disappearing for hours in a river only to return looking more beautiful than ever?"

The warning flashed on his computer screen, notifying him that his battery's charge remained only seven percent.

The bloody batteries!

He had earlier bought a brand new one only to discover that it was worse than the troublesome old one. He made a mental note to buy a Macbook when *Igwemma* became successful. He looked at Aniete snoozing next to him. His head was thrown back against the backrest and his mouth hung agape.

Luciano hibernated the laptop and stashed it away in his satchel. He willed himself to sleep through the journey, even though he knew that there was not going to be any sleeping for him. Ever since he began writing, the ability to sleep at ease had become somewhat alien. He settled down to look out the window at the trees, the grasses and fallow lands that hurried past. In them he saw a story of peace and harmony with the earth. They spoke of a world untainted by lofty ambitions, where every individual species is united in a single goal of survival.

A grunt escaped the sleeping Aniete's throat, causing Luciano to turn in his direction. In his sleep, Aniete chewed at some imaginary food and then fell back into peaceful slumber. Luciano held himself from staring too long at the sleeping fellow; he didn't want any other passenger to notice the stare. He had many questions for Aniete. The young man looked like one who had dabbled into messy things and his only motivation seemed to be money, and a promise of plenty of it. That part of Aniete's life was not his business to know, he cautioned. He only hoped they met with the friend he was so keen on seeing, so they could continue their journey to Port-Harcourt without further drama.

The bus arrived in Owerri shortly afterwards, but they were not to know of what surprises awaited them in that small city of many little pleasures.

SEVENTEEN

A STREET IN EGBU, OWERRI.

The dirt-road stretched quietly down a hill and up again like some contraption in an amusement park. Apparently, the construction of the road has been abandoned in its early stages just after the engineers had laid the bed of mud but hard use had made the road compact so that it was never dusty. High-fences hugged the road closely on either side, like the landlords of the towering duplexes were intent on never losing a meter of their land to the road. It was a suburb, the residential area for lecturers, senior civil servants and people who desired to live away from the contagious and subtle exuberance of the city.

Luciano and Aniete came to a twin two-storey building with a high fence topped with an unending coil of barbed wire. The big brown gate was cracked open a fraction. They let themselves into the compound, with Aniete leading the way. Aneiete strode with an air of confidence, towards a wide doorway that was the entrance to the building. They took a flight of stairs to a long, well-lit hallway on the first floor dotted by heavy mahogany doors on either side. It was a lodge meant for the rich ones amongst the university students who desired to live away from the vicinity of the campus. Instinctively, Luciano caught himself looking out for a boy with crude tattoos on his muscular torso; memories of the boy, Truant, were still fresh on his mind.

They came before a door that bore a titanium-coloured plaque engraved with the number 326 and Aniete knocked with his bare knuckles. He was about dealing out a second round of knocks when a key turned in the lock and the door swung open. A young woman with clean, ruffled hair held the door open. Recognition swept through her face on seeing Aniete, but that was all. She didn't smile.

"Where is Peter?" Aniete asked.

"Inside."

"Tell him I am here."

She grinned as though to say 'okay', and then closed the door. Luciano stood by, silently watching. He knew he had seen the girl somewhere. *Miranda?* Yes, it had to be her. She had seen him too, but she hadn't acted like they had met before. The pit of his stomach tightened into a knot. He sensed something out of the ordinary, but familiar nevertheless. *Was it danger? Or was he simply being paranoid?* He could see that Aniete appeared relaxed; it made him feel a flash of shame. He looked up and down the hallway. A boy in the company of two giggling girls staggered along, obviously tipsy. They came to a door; the boy yanked the handle and kicked it open. They all staggered into the room and the door was jammed shut. But that was all the activity about the place. Luciano began to relax.

It was taking longer than necessary, but the door to Room 326 eventually swung open again. A sturdily built young man in a punk-style haircut held the door open this time.

Luciano guessed that he was the one whom they called Peter. There was a hint of surprise in his eyes even as he ushered them in. Luciano didn't like the fellow. He couldn't bring himself to trust the face; it looked like that of a deceptive character, the kind he would create in a fictional story walking around with a loaf of bread tucked innocently under his arm but with a dagger concealed within its crust.

They entered an air-conditioned, spacious studio apartment. The blinds hung down. Four blue light bulbs high up on the walls gave the room a calm theatrical feel. A mute movie played on the LED TV screen on the wall. A soft male voice filtered in from the slender speakers of the home theatre set. John Legend, Luciano thought. The girl who had earlier answered the door laid propped up on her elbows on the twelve-inch mattress positioned against the farthest end of the room. Her beautiful face focused hard on the laptop before her was marred with a frown. Luciano craned his neck long enough to see a Facebook page on display on the screen.

"Where is the money?" Aniete asked immediately their host had shut the door.

Peter flashed a suspicious look in Luciano's direction. He seemed not to like that Luciano was busy mentally taking in every detail of his apartment.

"Don't worry about him, he is with me," Aniete explained.

Peter appeared to relax, leaving Luciano to continue with his scrutiny. A small kitchen was tucked away at a corner. Next to it Luciano could make out a shut door which he guessed to be a toilet-and-bathroom combination. To another end of the apartment was another shut door, adjacent to a built-in wardrobe. Judging from his observation of the building's architecture on their arrival, Luciano could tell that the door opened onto a balcony.

"Peter, I'm in a hurry," Aniete was saying. "I'm sure you must have retrieved the money when I went into hiding."

"Miranda!"

The girl on the bed turned to face Peter.

"Excuse us."

She was reluctant, but there was no way she could have missed the urgency in the command. Shutting the laptop, she left it lying on the bed and dragged her feet out of the room. On her way out, she brushed past Luciano and pretended not to notice.

"Is it safe? I mean the money," Aniete said after Miranda had left.

"Yes. It is safe."

"I need my cut."

"You should have informed me earlier."

"Things just happened fast. There was no time."

Peter shrugged and turned to the wardrobe, but then he paused in his tracks.

"News came."

"What news?"

"That you are dead. They said you were shot dead," Peter said. Aniete shrugged. "It was a good thing though, because Nku had to give up the search for you."

"You mean Silverpistol?" Luciano interrupted, showing sudden interest in the dialogue.

"What?" Peter asked, thrown off-balance by the strange name.

"The short, black dude with the trademark silver pistol," Luciano explained.

Peter regarded Luciano with disdain. He eventually ignored Luciano, turning his attention to Aniete instead. "You know it is risky coming out here."

"That is all the more reason you will have to hurry up with giving me the money. I'm going away."

"Where to?"

"I think it has to be Port-Harcourt."

Peter fell silent. "I'm just concerned about your safety, that's all."

"Hey! Cut the crap! Just give us what we came here for," Luciano said. "It isn't safe out here, you just said so yourself."

"Who is this bugger, by the way?" Peter asked Aniete.

"Listen, just forget about him," Aniete intervened. "I'm in a hurry."

"Better tell him to shut his stupid mouth."

"What is your game, man?" Luciano fired. "Why are you stalling? You don't have his money, just tell him so and don't waste anybody's time here."

"You better…" Peter trailed off, and wagging a finger at Luciano's face when a loud bang on the door interrupted. Everyone froze. They listened, unsure they had heard correctly. It came again, loud, threatening to bring down the door. Peter made for the door, but Luciano caught his arm in a firm grip.

"Where is another exit here?" Luciano whispered. His heart beat so hard against his chest that it distorted his voice.

"Why do you ask?" Peter answered, surprisingly calm.

In answer, Luciano pointed to the front door where the banging was coming from.

"It could be the landlord," Peter assured.

An alarm went off in Luciano's head. He couldn't bring himself to fall for Peter's assurances. They stank of falsehood. No landlord would threaten to break the door of his property, not in such a manner. He made for the back door. It gave way when he yanked the handle, and as he had guessed, it opened onto a small balcony. The house was built with its back facing the barbed fence such that the balcony was a few inches away from the barbed wires. The balcony overlooked a plot of land overgrown with grass and a huge mound of rubbish amassed from refuse flung out from the balconies of occupants on the first and second floors.

"Open this door!" a muffled order came through the shut front door.

Aniete hurried on to Luciano's side where he stood contemplating a jump from the balcony. The height, the barbed wires, the refuse pile - all daunted the move. They heard the lock on the front door click. It had to be Peter and he must have opened the door to let the assailants in. Aniete swung his legs over the railings. He perched on the tip of his toes on the small edge of floor space protruding from underneath the railings. Steadying himself he contemplated a leap onto the fallow plot of land. Left with no other option, Luciano cursed under his breath and followed suit. He steadied his satchel with his free hand and held onto the railings behind with his other hand. He clenched his jaw, dreading that moment when he would have to take the dangerous leap.

"*Where them?*" asked an approaching voice from inside the room.

Silverpistol! There was no mistaking the voice! Images of the silver pistol flashed through Luciano's head. He never wished to have it pointed at his chest again, and he did not want to set eyes on that menacing face any longer. There was no telling the treatment he would receive this time from the fellow, especially when found in the company of Aniete whom he had denied knowing. Heavy footsteps approached the balcony. At that instant, Luciano leaped into the air. The soles of his feet only scraped against the tip of the barbed wires, but he landed on the refuse heap, breathing in the stench that rose in protest to the impact of his landing. Aniete came sailing in the air, landing plump next to him and rolling on the refuse heap. But he was up on his feet in a flash.

Luciano glanced back at the balcony. It was Silverpistol he saw standing there, holding onto the railings in pent-up frustration. He would have stopped long enough to jeer, but he saw the fellow draw out the infamous pistol from his hip. Luciano pulled Aniete by the arm and they scampered away towards a wide exit in the fenced plot where a gate was meant to be. A shot rang out just as they rounded the exit. A bullet chipped a bit off the fence close to Aniete's head, scattering cement dust in the air. More aimless shots rang out after them as they ran into the quiet streets.

Igwemma's suitor is coming today. Ezenwanyi is happy. She is excited that her beautiful daughter is finally getting married. She was worried when Igwemma's age mates were getting married and her daughter was yet to get any suitors. She suspected Igwemma's beauty unnerved the men and that was why they settled for the less beautiful ones amongst the maidens. She was alarmed on learning that Igwemma wasn't even bothered about not getting a husband. It bothered her so deeply that she offered chickens in prayers to the gods, asking them to bring Igwemma a husband just as other girls were having.

Her prayers have been answered and Obiora is coming today. He is from a wealthy family, and he is a merchant also. Rumour has it he trades in oil and palm kernel. He is the first man to buy the white man's horse, which no one sees it eats or defecates. He sits on the horse and continuously runs his legs in circles besides it, and in this way, he travels to distant lands like Arochukwu, Emekuku, Ngwa, and the big market town of Onicha, where rumours have it that the white men come in large numbers by the Great River to buy and sell. There were just too many rumours about these white men. Some say their skins are so pale you thought they are stricken with leprosy. They say the merchants got richer in their dealings with the white man because the white man is afraid of coming off his floating house and braving the mosquitoes in the mainlands. They also say the white men wear funny clothes and hats, drink a lot of coloured hot water and speak through their nostrils. When asked how they understand the language of the white strangers, the merchants reply that the men came with interpreters who surprisingly have black skins, spoke the Igbo language like the Omambala people, but wore the same clothes like the white men and acted exactly like them. They say those interpreters addressed the white men as 'massah'.

Ezenwanyi has been cooking plenty of food all morning. She isn't the type who needs something done without other women and their daughters coming around to offer help. They respect her because, even though she is a widow, she is rich in her own right; she is the only woman in the surrounding nine villages skilled in the art of making the best wrappers. She always has people coming to pay her to make wrappers with colourful patterns for them. She makes generous gifts of clothes too. The women have come to help her to make mkpurusu, akpu, egusi and oha soups. And they will make ugba too. The girls have earlier come to sweep the whole compound and fill the clay pots with water from the Sister Rivers. Igwemma has made her hair too, the girls braided her hair into very beautiful patterns, and expensive beads wound about her hair.

It will have to be sundown when her kinsmen would begin

to mill into the compound to await Igwemma's suitor's arrival.

Ezenwanyi sighs. She is relieved to see that everything is set for her prospective in-laws' coming. The food is very much enough to feed a small crowd of famished men. Nwichi has delivered on his promise and twelve big calabashes of freshly tapped undiluted palm wine are standing, foaming in the hut she used for storing her handloom and things as needed for important occasions as this. She will just have to wait for sundown and then people will get to understand she isn't called Ezenwanyi for nothing.

Obiora is chatting excitedly with Omeudo and Obiarakara, his brothers, as they tag along at the end of the entourage going to Umuafor. Obiora is going to perform the first marriage rites on his proposed bride. He is excited that in four market weeks, the beautiful Igwemma will become his bride. He has brought along his white man's horse too; he is going to flaunt his mark of affluence in Umaufor.

"I hear she is very beautiful like a mammy-water," Omeudo says. He is the one walking next to Obiora.

"Just wait till you see her."

"You think you will win the contest?" Obiarakara teases. "We will know how beautiful your wife is and then we will try to get a wife that surpasses her in beauty."

"Be careful you don't bring in the water goddess into the family someday," Obiora says with a smile.

They were all born on the same season. They all take after

their father, Ozo Omenka, so they look like triplets. If they were, they would have been abandoned at birth to die in the evil forest whilst their mothers were purified of the abomination. The god of fertility visited Ozo Omenka one night and his three barren wives got pregnant on the same moon. The boys have grown as toddlers, rolling in the dirt together. As children, they teamed up to fight against other kids, from other families. In their teenage years they stealthily raided fruit trees in other people's fenced compounds, and when early youth came, they competed for the maidens until Obiora eventually gave up on the chase earlier than his brothers.

They tease him as they walk side-by-side. He is the one in the middle wheeling his white man's horse along. The others don't have their own white man's horses. Omeudo grows yams and Obiarakara makes tools of iron in the market square. He makes weapons too.

At the head of the entourage is a servant boy carrying a big calabash of upwine on his head. A loose wad of leaves is used as stopper on the mouth of the calabash. Behind the servant boy are other young boys of the extended household. They have on their heads long baskets containing big tubers of yams, wads of cloths, beads, chickens and many other gift items they will give to the bride and her mother. After the youths comes Obiora's mother in the company of fellow wives and other women of the extended household. Even Enyidiya, the quarrelsome woman, has been so headstrong as to come along in her pregnancy. The women are dressed gorgeously. Obiora's mother wears the ivory armlets and bracelet her son bought for her on his last trip to Onicha to trade with the white men in their big floating houses.

After the women, come the men. Some of them have their machetes and sheathed and dangling from their hips. The men throw jokes amongst themselves as they walk along. Everyone is excited about the new wife who will join the family soon. They are most excited that it would be the most beautiful woman they will have in their village. They have heard she is as beautiful as mammy-water, and the women who haven't seen her are eager to set their eyes on the famed beauty.

They have come to the top of a hill. If a good thrower tosses a pebble, it will land on one of the thatched roofs in Umuafor. They could even see smoke rising from the roofs of huts where wives cooked early suppers. Obiora feels the pressure in his bladder.

"Hold this for me," he tells Obiarakara, handing him the handlebars of the white man's horse. He stands by the road side and urinates into the bushes. Obiarakara doesn't know how to ride the white man's horse. It is nothing to be ashamed of, for only a handful of people know how to ride it in the whole of the twenty-nine villages bordered by the Sister Rivers.

Obiora doesn't trust anyone with his white man's horse, but today, he is too excited to care. As he urinate he makes sure the shrubs at the edge of the bush conceals his penis from the others' view.

Obiarakara is thrilled to hold the silver handlebars. Omeudo is concerned with an 'icheku' bush not too far into the surrounding bushes. He is contemplating risking tufts of grass *hanging onto his ceremonial clothes to get some of the black fruits he loves so much.*

Why not I try this once, Obiarakara thinks to himself. Just this once. I will just have to sit on the saddle and see what it feels like. And so he mounts the saddle. But, alas, they are at the peak of a steep hill and he is a bit shorter than his brothers. His toes cannot touch the ground. He comes rolling down on the saddle of the gleaming white man's horse as he fights to keep from falling off. The white man's horse gathers speed with every inch it moves downhill. Obiarakara screams for his father and his other kinsmen in front to scamper away from the path. He doesn't know where the bell is. He is alarmed. His eyes pop wide with fear. The wind brushes past against his ears, and he is more scared. He has never had such an experience in all his life. The old men hear him coming. They scramble for the bushes on either side of the path like frightened squirrels and Obiarakara sweeps past like the round metal bullet from a hunter's stuffed gun. He is approaching the women, but they don't see him coming. He screams to them, but the wind takes his voice backwards and away from earshot. The men behind, recovering from the shock, begin to scream for the women to flee the hilly path. They hear the men and they scuttle into the bushes too, screaming like wild fowls. The youths bearing yams and the gift items on their heads are not so lucky. The handle bar hits one in the waist and his long basket topples over to the ground. Obiarakara hits a small gully and the front tyre veers wildly to the right. The servant boy with the keg of upwine sees him coming. He scurries to safety to the side of the path, but the white man's horse comes rolling towards him. He screams in fear, but the large front tyre only brushes against his thigh as it speeds past into the dense bushes. It gets entangled in the undergrowth and falls to its side, its tyres still spinning in the air. Obiarakara has fallen onto a bed of soft undergrowth. He gets to his feet. He is lucky he is not injured, but he is very sorry. He looks penitent as he drags his brother's prized white man's horse, undamaged, out of the bushes and onto the path. Everyone has gathered around. The women are chatting excitedly. Everyone is relieved to see that Obiarakara has not broken a bone in the accident. Only two people have injuries. A boy with a scratch where the handlebar has grazed his waist, and the other, the servant boy; the tyre had given him a slight abrasion on his thigh. But the upwine. The upwine. The calabash lies in bits on the side of the path. The thirsty earth is draining off all of the spilled wine.

Obiarakara is very remorseful. He avoids the shocked look in Obiora's eyes.

"Don't worry," Ozo Omenka comforts Obiora.

"I can ride quickly back to the village and arrange for another calabash of wine," Obiora suggests, making to reach for the handlebars of his white man's horse still in Obiarakara's possession.

"Obi," Ichie Ojiakunwemba, his uncle calls him. "Are you still a child?"

Obiora is confused. He does not understand the meaning of the question. It surprises him that the men have a thoughtful look on their faces and the women now stand aloof, folding their arms, shrugging and snapping their fingers in a show of suppressed wonder. It appears as though they have been informed that somewhere in the bushes nearby, a man dangled from a tree branch.

"This is not a road we should tread," Omenka says.

Obiora fears to ask for the meaning of the proverbs. He is a son of the soil after all; if he has a proverb explained to him, it means the bride price on his mother's head is a total waste. His mother is present and he fears to dishonour her. But he still doesn't understand the words.

"My son, this is a sign. Our ancestors are kind to us. This marriage would have not yielded any good fruits and they have just told us so."

He is beginning to see the meaning.

"Do you remember that when we pray to Chukwu Okike and to ancestors, we say that 'if they chance upon us on our way to an unfruitful union, may the wine calabash be broken'? This is a prayer answered. So, my son, bear your brother Obiarakara no grudge because it is not his fault that this whole incidence has happened. Let us go home and celebrate instead. Our prayers have been answered and we are sure we are at peace with our ancestors."

The procession turns homewards. They walk not in grouped pairs as earlier, but as one mass of a light-hearted people. Obiarakara pushes the white man's horse along beside his brothers. He is not sorry anymore. He feels like a hero.

They have come to the top of another hill and Obiarakara asks everyone to step aside. He mounts the white man's horse and holds tightly onto the handlebars. He allows it to roll downhill, whooping in excitement. The others cheer loudly from the safety of the hilltop. It is only his mother, Ekemma, who holds onto her bosom in fear as she watches her rascally son takes on a most daring feat.

EIGHTEEN

They ran and ran, cutting through avenues and lanes, and never stopped until they came to the busy highway. Doubled over and panting, they looked out for any approaching taxi.

"*Shit!*" Aniete cursed.

"I told you," Luciano managed to say as he struggled with his breath. "I told you we should go to Port-Harcourt directly."

"I'm not going to Port-Harcourt."

Luciano stared hard at him. The expression on his face underwent a dramatic change. "Are you just crazy or senseless or what?"

"I am not going to Port-Harcourt. Not yet."

"When? In a coffin?"

He straightened up, only to move a distance from Luciano and then he resumed his reclined posture. "You are just suicidal, you know," Luciano said, raising his voice loud enough to be heard over the whoosh of cars speeding past. "Why do you love courting danger? That guy back there, Silverpistol, is really pissed. He looks like he wouldn't have any qualms cutting your penis and shoving it down your throat just so he can sleep properly at night. And in case you are too stupid to see, that your Peter of a guy just sold you out back there and now Silverpistol knows you are very much alive and running loose in town. He will smell you out, I know it. He will sniff every inch of ground in this town to smoke you out of any hole you run into. This place is no longer safe for you, but will you see it? No. Because the screws have fallen off your small brain and it wobbles upon one delicate hook in the large expanse of your thick skull."

A group of boys wearing their trousers pulled way down their buttocks to reveal a glimpse of their underpants walked past. They glanced back over their shoulders more than thrice to steal looks at the supposedly mad fellow raving at another indifferent one. Aniete straightened up and began to walk away. "And where the hell are you headed to?"

"I need somewhere to sleep, eat and bathe?" Aniete said over his shoulder. Luciano ran up after him, tagging along, but making no effort to halt Aniete's progress.

"And where would that be?"

"A hotel."

"How do you intend paying for it?"

"You."

"What?"

"You will pay."

"How? I don't understand you."

"You have an answer to that. You will pay for the hotel, for the food and for any other expenses."

"You are one insolent bastard."

"I didn't hear that."

"You should be thinking of keeping yourself safe. It is dangerous walking like this on the road."

A tricycle came speeding by. Aniete flagged it down. Before he called out his destination, Luciano had climbed in, hugging his satchel to his chest. In spite of his madness at Aniete, he appeared scared.

"Ama-wire," Aniete instructed the driver as he perched on the seat next to Luciano.

"Where in Ama-wire?"

"Oriental Palace Hotel."

"Two fifty."

"No problems." The driver eased the little vehicle onto the traffic.

"You didn't even bargain," Luciano said.

"Do you have any problems with paying two hundred and fifty naira?"

"And this hotel you mentioned, what about it?"

"It is a luxurious place I have always dreamt of passing a night in?"

"And why do you think we can afford it?"

"You said my father is rich."

Luciano swallowed. "Yes?"

"Then, a night at the hotel wouldn't be a problem to a rich man's contractor."

"The problem is the timing. You have all the days of your life to enjoy much luxury, but not right now. You need to be alive first."

"Who knows, we might die tomorrow. Why not we enjoy the chance we have while we still have it?"

Luciano stole a look at the driver; he had his ears plugged with an earphone. He was playing some bongo music too loudly that bits of the familiar rhythm wafted to his hearing.

"You are really as crazy as your father."

"You never told me he is crazy."

"To hell with you!" Luciano said, turning away and fuming.

Aniete chuckled. "Look at the bright side of it, The Oriental Palace is one of the best hotels in town. Their security is as world-class as their accommodation and food. We will be safe there."

"How much is the cheapest room for a night?" Luciano asked, his attention still turned away.

"I hear it is somewhere around twenty-five thousand naira."

"What?!"

"Call my *father* if that will be a problem," Aniete

said with an air of indifference. "Tell him that his son demands some good treatment for a few days. I just hope I am not creating the impression of being a prodigal son."

How on earth did I get involved with this bone in the throat? He wished he could simply drug Aniete and smuggle him speedily in an ambulance to Port-Harcourt, get his payment and then wash his hands off the troubles which the crazy fellow appeared to attract to himself like a strong magnet to bits of iron.

NINETEEN

A HOTEL ROOM IN OWERRI

Luciano parted the silky window blinds and peered into the gathering night. He wished the only window in the hotel room offered a view of the entrance instead of some greasy mechanic's workshop. It was the cheapest room they could get on the first floor, and he had nearly got into a fight at the reception with Aniete for his frivolity. He sighed inwardly, giving up the hopeless idea of scouting the perimeter of the hotel.

Aniete lay on his back on the large bed, a celebrity magazine he had picked up at the reception shielding his face. He looked like a lizard basking upside down in the stream of cold air spewing from the vents of the air conditioner. They hadn't exchanged a word since after the near-fracas at the reception.

Luciano picked his way around the room to the bathroom. The warm shower made him feel at ease. He stood still to enjoy the needle-like sprays of water that pelted his shoulders and chest like fluid bullets. A small plastic pouch on the faucet held tubes of customized liquid soap, body and hand lotions, shaving powder, and many other liquids that made one smell like they had just walked out of a perfumery. The big white towel hanging from a thin silver rail felt warm and soothing. He dried his body standing before the mirror above the faucet; he felt transformed already, but his only regret was in having to wear the same used pair of trousers again. They made him cringe; the same trousers in which he had done a long jump onto a refuse heap: it felt damp and smelt of sweat. He padded into the room and found Aniete standing by the parted curtains of the window, his face set in a distant look. A live English football match was playing on the 32-inch LED TV. Luciano's wild guess was that the boy was suffering the pain of Peter's betrayal. *Maybe he had really trusted this Peter guy so much.* He wished to let the boy wallow in his depression, but he saw an opportunity that would serve his purpose. *And he had to take it.*

"You sounded so confident of Peter," he teased as he threw himsel onto the soft bed, but Aniete ignored him. "But he betrayed you."

He reached for one of the fluffy white pillows, seizing the chance to steal a look at the boy from the corner of his eye. Aniete still stood fixed at the same spot like a statue. Luciano saw his tactic wasn't working out and tried a different one; he propped up his head with the pillow and pretended to be interested in the football match, but his mind was far away from the activity of more than twenty-two athletic men tactically vying to push an inflated piece of leather into the other's guarded goal post.

"You see, you are playing a dangerous but futile game in remaining in this town. You will have the time to carry on with all these in Port-Harcourt. There will be so much money on your hands that you will have time for nothing else."

Aniete still didn't move a muscle. Luciano was beginning to despair; the attempt at getting the boy to talk wasn't yielding any fruits. He made to reach for the remote control when Aniete eventually spoke like one in a trance:

"I never would have believed Peter to betray me."

Luciano forgot about the remote control for the time being.

"I trusted him and watched his back," Aniete continued. "I never would have done the same to him even when I could easily have done it."

"Trust is very expensive. You should have known that long before now."

Aniete ignored the sarcasm.

"We settled for a fair cut for each one of us. Why then would he desire mine too?"

"How much is this your own 'cut'?"

"Seven hundred thousand."

He turned to face Aniete. "Did I hear you say *seven hundred thousand naira* or is it supposed to be dollars or euros?"

Aniete didn't answer.

"Did you just risk my life for just that? *Seven hundred thousand naira?!*" Luciano asked. Aniete didn't say anything. "You truly must be mad."

"You won't understand."

"Understand what? Your lack of brains? You have an immeasurable store of wealth awaiting your arrival in Port-Harcourt and here you are taunting gun-wielding demons for just how much? *Seven hundred thousand naira?*"

"It is more than that."

"You are one stupid senseless Calabar boy."

"I am not Calabar. I am Efik!" Aniete fired back, turning to face him.

"You all are the same people!"

"Not exactly. You just don't know the subtle difference!"

"To hell with your lack of ambition and over-complacence!"

He got off the bed and stomped to a lone sofa at the farthest end of the room next to a wardrobe, like he was trying to stay away from Aniete.

"It is more than the money."

It was Luciano's turn to play dumb-mute. "It is all about trust and credibility."

No response came from Luciano, and it secretly stung Aniete. He didn't like that Luciano was fuming. In spite of everything he had come to develop some respect for his talkative guardian. Luciano, he had seen, was temperamental and desperate, but he had an innate sense of alertness, a valuable quality capable of getting one out of a tight corner.

"We kidnapped a man, Peter's uncle. Peter was broke and I was broke too. We involved the other guys from the Blue Hood. We needed their help with arms, safe locations, transportation and all that. We demanded a ransom and the man bargained for the much he could offer. The money came and everything worked according ..." It struck him that Luciano wasn't keen on listening to his story; he seemed too pissed to settle down to reason. "I am going down to eat," he said, changing the subject.

"Where?" Luciano asked.

Aniete nearly broke into a laugh on hearing him speak. It was elating to know that Luciano never wanted to lose sight of him, even though he was upset.

"Downstairs, of course. In the restaurant."

"We could go outside to eat at a cheaper place."

"Why?"

"Are you the one paying?"

"No. You will pay. Besides, in case you are forgetting too soon, it will be a lot safer here."

Luciano opened his mouth to curse, but he thought better of it and bit his lower lip.

Aniete saw the gesture and smiled. He made for the door and Luciano followed suit.

At the restaurant, they ate in silence, Luciano refusing to rise to Aniete's efforts to lighten up the mood. It appeared he was intent on keeping the malice. In revenge, Aniete ordered an expensive bottle of Brut and paid deaf ears to Luciano's protests.

In the dead of the night, whilst Aniete slept deeply, laden with food and wine, Luciano tapped furiously at the keys of his laptop. His resentment faded gradually as the minutes went by. Writing, to him, was therapeutic.

Ezenwanyi was worried. Her fears return; Igwemma might not get married like the other girls. Obiora and his people didn't come again and many rumours are beginning to spread through the village. They were stories she had chosen to ignore for the sake of her peace of mind. She felt guilty for Igwemma; she spent many nights feeling so. It may be my fault, she whispered to herself as she lay awake on the bamboo bed listening to noises. Igwemma's snores were part of the noises. She didn't know if she would tell her the truth. She didn't want to. But she couldn't keep it off her mind; the guilt of deceiving everybody in the village, even her husband Anayo. He died believing a lie, the lie that the beautiful Igwemma was his daughter.

She was a young girl then, beautiful too, but not as beautiful as Igwemma. She was tall and shapely; that was the enviable beauty everyone knew until Igwemma came into the world with those eyelashes, the glowing light skin, feline steps, full red lips, slender fingers and a voice with such a rare tune that only a hunter who ventures into the forests can confess to have heard birds with same rarity sing.

Ezenwanyi once went with her mother to the famous Ahiaukwu market one morning many seasons ago when she was a budding young maiden. She carried the basket of smoked fish her mother sold while her mother walked briskly ahead, humming a folk song she was so fond of.

In the market, they displayed their wares upon plantain leaves spread on the hard-beaten clay floor of their shed. People came to buy fish. But some others just came, haggled for prices and walked away. These ones, Ezenwanyi's mother would hurl verbal abuses at as they walked away. Some would return her venom and others would just ignore the indignant fish seller.

One customer came by, a man, tall and firmly built, with his hair intricately patterned. He appeared rich, like one of those men in the palm business. He asks for the prices of the fish. Ezenwanyi's mother told him. He didn't haggle but paid for the biggest three in shiny cowry shells.

"You have a beautiful daughter," he said to Ezenwanyi's mother.

"She is betrothed."

"I am not surprised," he said and bade them farewell.

"Why will a young man be buying smoked fish in the market? Doesn't he have a wife or a mother?" Ezenwanyi asks her mother.

"My daughter, I wouldn't know. Strange things do happen every time."

"Maybe he is not married and his mother might not be in the house."

"I don't know. And it is none of my business, this child!" she told her daughter. "He has gone away. Let us hope to sell as much so we can buy enough foodstuff for the week."

But Ezenwanyi could still see the man. He had not gone away, but was seated on a bench in the stall where a woman sold odudu and agidi. In a banana leaf in his hand, he had a generous measure of odudu and agidi. He was eating, but slowly and with his eyes fixed on her. She looked away, and then looked in his direction again. He was still looking at her. She was shy, but she liked it that he was looking at her. She liked his looks, his face, and the way his arms stood out, hanging at his sides. He looked like a warrior, but a gentle one, an important and rich one. He was not like Anayo. She never liked Anayo. He was not handsome. He was shy, shorter and stuttered badly whenever they met briefly on her way to fetch firewood in the bush. Many times she wished she were as lucky as Nnenna who was betrothed to the handsome Amanze or Nwanyieke or even Adanna. They had better men they boasted of and really meant it, but not her. She would boast of Anayo to her friends. She would tell stories of all the beautiful things he said to her when they were together, but in her heart she knew she was only making them up so as to feel as important as her friends.

"Nne," her mother called her. Ezenwanyi snapped off her reverie.

"We have sold some reasonable amount. Take this money, go into the market and get foodstuff. You know what and what we need." Her mother handed her a few cowry shells.

"Shouldn't we wait a little longer when we would have sold all the fish?" she asked, pretending not to appear too eager to leave. Her mother hadn't seen the strange customer eyeing her from the distance, but Ezenwanyi didn't want her to become any suspicious.

"By then other customers would have selected the choicest items at the stalls."

"Okay." She took the money from her mother.

"You will take it home. I will sell some more and then join you in the house, hopefully before the sun stands over that ukwa tree." She pointed to the large tree at the centre of the market square with its giant pods hanging tentatively from its branches. The pods had never been known to fall off in the day, but whenever they did, it was on the head of some individual who died on the spot. It is said that one would have done a wrong so grievous to die that way.

"Don't let them cheat you o, especially that tricky woman who sells ogbono."

"No, they won't. I will haggle well."

She takes one of the baskets, the one her mother had brought with her to the market.

As she walked away, she overheard her mother mutter to herself: "I wish she weren't the only one who sells ogbono at this time when it is out of season."

Ezenwanyi walked towards the stalls where women sold foodstuff. She looked back every now and again. She felt embarrassed at her disappointment in not seeing the man following after her.

He is just a stranger, she told herself. But it was just a shallow condolence. It sounded so hollow; she didn't like the sound of it. Long ago, she had known herself to be her own worst adviser. She rounded the corner where girls and women plait their hair. She would have stopped to watch the new hair patterns being worked by the expert hair plaiters, but she didn't want to get her mother angry by idling away time. She continued up the line of stalls, she wanted to buy ukpor firstly. She looked behind and felt another stab of disappointment; the strange customer wasn't following behind.

By the time she got to the stall where the slender woman sold ogbono, she had forgotten all about him. She had reserved her energy for the haggling, and such a tactical fight over a compromise it had been, with the both of them reluctant to shift grounds. In the end, the woman gave up grudgingly and Ezenwanyi had to be alert that she didn't perform a sleight of the hand with the measuring gourd.

The sun was almost high up in the sky when she bought everything she needed. She walked through the throng of people in the busy market, ducking and dodging careless limbs and unwatchful bodies, to protect the basket of foodstuff on her head from being knocked over.

She contemplated taking the shortcut through the communal farmlands, but reasoned it was at times like this, when the sun shone brightly that bushes and grasses crawled with snakes and other reptiles coming out to bask in the radiant warmth. But she dreaded the scorching sun upon her neck and arms if she took the major road devoid of shades.

She took the path through the farmlands. Her eyes darts around the bush path, she watched the ground before her very closely for anything that would rustle the underground before planting every step. The vegetation was lush. A light breeze sweeping through the farmlands made cassava leaves wave as though they were bidding goodbye to an unknown deity. Just a few distances more, she thought, and she would emerge on the village square and then take the footpath beside the giant ikoro to her house.

She heard footsteps, or was it another gust of wind? She turned and saw him! She had forgotten about him, but now she saw him walking a few meters behind, her heart leapt. She felt fear at first and quickened her steps, to create some more distance away from him. But he increased his strides too. He was fast closing the gap between them. She felt ashamed to break into a trot though he was quickly gaining grounds on her. Instead of her fear to increase, she began to feel excited. She was enjoying the chase. It made her feel precious. Wanted. Like a woman. A desirable woman.

He gripped her arm gently. Very gently. It was the arm that held the basket secured on her head. She hadn't felt such a touch. The palms were too soft for such a man. She wished it were those arms that had touched her in such places Anayo had touched her one moonlit night a few markets ago, for she would have prayed Chukwueke to halt the moon forever on its hurried journey across the starry skies.

"You never struck me as one who would run away at the approach of your customer."

Oh, the voice! Hard and very masculine. It was as soothing as shea butter on a spent body besides a log fire, and yet, like gunpowder, it blew a woman's heart to shreds and rattled her limbs.

"I was not running," she defended, trying desperately to summon up a confident demeanour. She turned around, facing him. Even though she was regarded as tall, the man was shoulders above her. She had never seen a man as tall in all her life. He truly wasn't from these parts, for such attributes wouldn't have gone unnoticed in the village or its environs. He must be one of those traders selling precious commodities.

"You are wondering who I am?" He still held her hand, but it was the wrist this time. She politely shook her hand free because his palm pressing against her skin was making her incapable of thinking straight. As suspicious of strangers as she was, she surprisingly didn't want to offend this particular one.

"My name is Obumkere," he introduced himself. "I am a traveler. I am a musician too, and a trader, a wrestler, anything that can afford to pay for meals on the way. I came to your market to buy python skin. I hear it is a very precious commodity where I am headed to."

"Are you a wanderer?" she asks innocently.

He shrugged his great shoulders. "Some people prefer to use that word."

"Do you cook on your journey?"

The man, Obumkere, laughed. His laughter reverberated through Ezenwanyi's eardrums long after he had stopped laughing. It sounded like the laughter of a romantic god.

"Is it because of the fish I bought?"

"I thought you were going home to make soup."

"No. I bought them just to get the chance to talk to you."

Ezenwanyi turned away to hide the big smile mutinously spreading across her face. She picked on a weed growing close to the path.

"I followed you all through the market. You move real quickly in a crowd. Where did you learn to haggle like that?"

A small laugh escaped her throat. It was only a small laugh; she held the rest down her chest.

"Your mother said you are betrothed."

She nodded in the affirmative, but half-heartedly. He saw the nod even though her face was turned away.

"He must truly be a lucky man."

"Are you betrothed too?" she found herself asking.

"Who will betroth a wanderer?"he joked.

"You have a home?"She turned a fraction to look him in the face, but only momentarily.

"Yes, but I'm very far away from it."

They remained silent as though they had each run out of words to feed their conversation. She thought she could hear her heartbeat against the rustle of leaves in the still, hot air. The sun was already high above the sky, but her mother was the last thing on Ezenwanyi's mind.

"You are going home, I guess," he asked finally, breaking the long silence.

"Yes."

"You mind if I walk some distance with you?"

She lowered her head to hide her face again. She was too shy to tell him so at the moment, but she would follow him across rivers and hills if only he would ask her to. He took her silence for consent. He held her hand as they walked side-by-side, but it wasn't to her house they went.

A narrower footpath veered off the main one to the right. It wound and curled like a carelessly dumped bundle of twines, cutting through a grove of bamboo trees growing in a cluster. Grey, fallen bamboo leaves formed a deep soft bed on the floor around. It was to this grove that Ezenwanyi followed the stranger. He lay atop her on the bed of leaves that rustled with their writhing bodies; he thrust into her and she reached out to receive him.

She bit her lips to stop from screaming the obscenities the wild pleasures surging through her body seemed to suggest to her head. Anayo had deflowered her, but it had been a hurried act, and she had wept for days, mourning the vain loss of her virginity. With this stranger, she knew she would feel no remorse. What she was sure to feel was an end to whatever frail feelings she had for Anayo.

Many days passed and she expected to see Obumkere again. He never came. He had disappeared just as he had appeared – mysteriously. She looked out for him every time and everywhere. When she went to the market, she would wish to see him and then she would take the footpath through the farmlands, hoping he would stalk her again. She visited the cluster of bamboo trees twice like a pilgrimage. She desperately wanted to see him again. She wanted to confess to him that she cared nothing for her betroth anymore. She wanted to tell him she was pregnant by him and that she would die if he didn't make her his wife. She would be a wife to a wanderer, a handsome wanderer. She wished to go to the ends of the earth with him, to sleep with him on the road, cheer him on as he wrestled with his opponents for their meals, and then help him haggle for python skin. She would do the same for lion's skin, alligator's, leopard's, deer's, anything. All she needed was to have him for herself at any price. Just any price; none was too steep to pay.

He never came.

She had to do something about the pregnancy before it showed.

And it showed.

To only one – her mother. And they had to do something about it.

She visited Anayo's hut one night. She hated that he trembled with fear at seeing her sneak into his hut in the cover of darkness.

"Did anybody see you come in?" he asked, his eyes popping out of their sockets.

"Of course not."

"Are you sure my father didn't see you?"

"I was careful."

"It is too risky. My father will skin me alive if he gets to know I brought a …"

"Shh!" she hushed him. "You just might wake them up with your panicking."

He calmed down a bit, ashamed that a woman was telling him to be courageous. He wanted to suggest that he sneak her back, away from his hut, but she stripped naked before him and he froze. The small lump in his neck bopped up and down as though he was perpetually swallowing a lump of akpu. There was another lump too; it rose against his loincloth.

She guided him onto his back on the bed because he was too stunned to exercise any control of his limbs. He hadn't had the privilege of a night between his erect penis and a naked maiden in the safety of a lone hut. But when she guided him into her, *he came alive. He pounded and thrust and shoved, emitting a suppressed moan until the wee hours of the morning when only palm wine tappers ventured out to check on their calabashes high up in palm trees. He was lost in exhausted slumber by the time Ezenwanyi sneaked out, looking left and right before scrambling across the compound to the main entrance. Nobody had seen her leave the compound except for a silent owl high up in a pear tree.*

Two market weeks passed.

Anayo, stricken with remorse, confessed to his parents that his woman, Ezenwanyi, was pregnant with his child. The marriage rites were hurried over. Anayo's father gave him his own share of the family farmlands, a hundred and twenty yam seedlings, two he-goats, four she-goats, and two ewes. One of the ewes nursed two young rams. Members of his age-grade built him two mud huts; his obi, and a smaller one for his new wife to sleep in. Some of them made thatch for the roofs from palm leaves, and others got mud from a quarry. They talked and joked as they worked. They built a shed for a kitchen, another for livestock and they fenced the compound roundabout with the base of freshly-cut palm fronds. It took them five days to complete the task. All those five days, Anayo's mother made them breakfast and lunch. They thanked her and ate amidst jokes. Anayo's father brought a keg of fresh wine every afternoon and the young men worked happily as their heads swooned lightly. They were happy working together for their age mate, knowing each one's turn would come for the others to return the customary favour.

Anayo never learn of the treachery against him. Only two

people laughed at his back while he boasted that he had sired the most beautiful creature on earth: Ezenwanyi and her mother. They both scorned the naïve man in their hearts even after he had long died mysteriously in his sleep.

No child came after Igwemma. No pregnancies even. It seemed that Igwemma had come through and had thrown the keys to her mother's womb into the mud-coloured waters of the Imo River.

TWENTY

Luciano slept far into the morning of the next day, having stayed up late working on *Igwemma*. The sound of running water roused him from his deep slumber, but his eyes remained closed until he heard the soft footfalls of Aniete in the room.

"What are your plans now?" he asked sleepily.

"I don't know," Aniete replied, towelling his head. He sounded sincere and his voice lacked any hint of the animosity of the night before.

"That leaves us with the option of taking the next bus to Port-Harcourt."

"Not now."

"So tell me when. Is it when they come to tell us our hotel rent is expired? Is it when you stand at the business end of a silver pistol with only a fraction of a moment to dwell on what mess you have made out of your pitiful life when you had the chance to make it end better? When? Tell me."

"I need your help," Aniete said. He settled down at the foot of the bed, the big white towel draped around his neck.

"There you go again. Are you just daft or simply acting stupid? Of course I am helping you preserve yourself. What other help are you asking for? What else do you think I can do for you? Don't you see I need help too? I need help to bundle you to Port-Harcourt. I need help to tell your rich father *fuck you* in the face and mean it this time around. I need help in having to contend with your genetic madness. If I had all the help I need right now, you and your kind wouldn't have existed in my life."

Aniete waited till Luciano had expended his frustration. "I want us to kidnap Peter."

Luciano regarded him with utter disbelief. At long last, he scoffed. "Now I know for a certainty. I thought it was just some wild insinuation, but now I know for sure that it is with insane people I have been dealing all this time. You know what? I quit. Everything. All this madness about getting you to your father. Honestly, I quit. Period."

He got up, grabbed his satchel from the sofa where he had dumped it the night before. Slinging it across his shoulder, he made for the door, shuffling his feet into his pair of shoes. But when he got to the door, his hand lingered on the door knob; he was evidently unable to bring himself to walk out of the room.

Aniete saw the reluctance. He took note of the fact that he had discovered Luciano's weakness; he would be a fool not to see that Luciano relied so much on the success of this mission he so professed to despise.

Luciano heaved a sigh and let his hand drop from the doorknob, and then he took slow penitent steps back to the centre of the room.

"Okay, what's the deal?" he asked, his shoulders drooping in defeat.

"I need …"

"Firstly," he cut Aniete short, his index finger raised in emphasis. "Listen to my terms. After kidnapping this your St. Peter, or whatever the heck his name is, there will be no more adventures. We will just take the next bus and be off to Port-Harcourt. Agreed?"

"Agreed."

He unslung his satchel, tossed it casually onto the bed and continued towards the sofa. He collapsed into it. "Now, let me hear you out."

"We will kidnap Peter …"

"May I ask why?"

"He has to give me my money."

"Is that all? I could just arrange for your father to deposit the seven hundred thousand naira into your account as a condition for seeing you in his house in the next two hours. We could sit safely in this room and await confirmation of the money transfer."

Aniete was mute for a moment. Luciano speculated he was considering the offer, and his hope rose.

"No. There is more to it than just the money," Aniete said.

Luciano was nearly successful in hiding his disappointment. "You mind telling me? Because if I am going to be your partner in something as highly criminal as kidnap, I will have to go into it with both eyes wide open."

"I have told you all."

"Don't be silly, you have told me nothing. Okay, in case you need some prodding, I think I have some for you right here. Apart from being a student, what else do you do? Who is that guy Silverpistol, and how did you come to piss him off this much? Who were those other people who shot you in the village and why did they shoot at you? How come you have become so notorious that guns blaze whenever you get to be in the open for too long? You could start from there for the moment."

Aniete tossed the towel onto the bed. It was an act of resignation; he needed Luciano's help, and if letting him in on shady details of a recent past was the price, he reasoned he could live with that. And so he began to tell Luciano about the kidnap, but with the intent of keeping back some details. Luciano listened, only interrupting occasionally to clarify some details he felt didn't quite fit in. Five minutes into the narration, it became clear to Aniete that there would be no withholding any part of the story if he was to win Luciano's trust; the fellow seemed to have a nose for lies.

He sighed and began to tell Luciano everything as it happened.

ANT-INFESTED WOODS

JUNE, 2012

TWENTY-ONE

IMO STATE UNIVERSITY, OWERRI.

On the corridors of the faculty building, two boys stood side-by-side, peering intently at the exam result sheets in the glass-cased notice board. The fact that they attended the same class in Accounting and were still total strangers wasn't out of place; the Faculty of Social Sciences housed six departments and a few thousand students, some of whom wouldn't so much as exchange a word with one another for the intended four years of their studies. It didn't help matters that the lecture halls were always crammed full, with some students perched on the shutter-less windows as they strained to hear from the lecturer hastening to escape the atmosphere made more suffocating by a heterogeneous mix of perfumes, deodorants and sweat within an airless confinement.

The boys checking the result sheets shared only one thing in common - their sullen countenance.

"*Chai!*" the one with large ears exclaimed. "Three units course for that matter!" His neighbour turned to him as though to say *I understand*.

"What's your matric number?" he asked.

"0161"

He traced with his forefinger against the glass. "Aniete Ubong?"

The one called Aniete nodded. The other boy shrugged. "You guys borrowed the course, *abi*?"

"Yes."

"What department?"

"FST."

"Nna, which one is FST?"

"Food Science and Technology"

His colleague nodded his comprehension. "You?"

"0079"

Aniete traced his forefinger against the glass too. "Peter Barry."

"Yea."

Aniete checked the grade against the name. Many other names on the list had 'F' written near their matriculation numbers; a begrudging sprinkle of A's and B's; several C's, D's and E's.

"This man wicked eh," Aniete lamented.

"All these lecturers who graduated with third class degrees are always like that. What else do you expect of them? They are sworn sadists."

Aniete hissed. "And honestly, I don't have the money to sort this man's course with."

"How much does he charge for sorting?"

"5k"

"Even if I had the money, the man has sworn to keep me for extra two years in this school."

"Why? What did you do to him?"

Peter hissed. He ran his hand along his punk-style haircut. It was a show of resignation. "There was this girl in my faculty … I didn't know he was fucking her."

"You have not gone to settle with him?"

"What's there to settle with the foolish man? He is lucky his wife is abroad. I would have taken the matter to her myself and then we would know who needs to settle issues with whom."

"Well, the thing is that if you show him some good money, he will forget everything."

"But I have no money."

"My brother, you are not alone. Me, I haven't eaten since last night."

They both laughed at each other's confession; two people drawing comfort from mutual misery. They talked some more and then shared a parting handshake.

Peter walked with an exaggerated gait. He was every bit the ladies' man and he dressed as such; colourful and pleasing to the senses.

They met again two weeks later.

The sun stood proudly overhead, lauding its fiery authority over all that lived and moved on the earth. Aniete laboured uphill in the sweltering heat on his way from the lecture halls, eager to get to his room in the hostel. He was angry at the scorching sun. The beginning of hunger pangs made him feel more miserable. But it was Professor Obidike, the Food Toxicology lecturer, who had wreaked the most havoc on his day. The man had kept them all waiting for over two hours past the scheduled time for the lecture, and when he eventually drove his rattling red Nissan onto his reserved parking space in the Faculty premises, the servile lackey of a course rep hurried to take his bag from him as was his habit, but the man waved him away. He wasn't carrying any bags, and he was not dressed for the lecture; he had on a pair of white knee-length shorts and a green polo shirt with the collars turned up. Ignoring the greetings from the waiting students, he strode into his office, picked up a badminton racket, returned to his car and drove off. Just like that. No apologies. No explanations. The students hissed their indignation but that did nothing. It wasn't the first time *Prof* acted like that.

Aniete was startled by the sound of running footsteps approaching from behind. He turned to recognize Peter.

"How far, Peter?"

"I'm cool, my man." Peter managed to pull an

exhaustive smile. Panting and out of breath, he offered his hand. Aniete resumed his uphill journey but in a stroll. Peter fell in step.

"What's up?"

"You didn't come for Dr. Ekwueme's lecture?"

"I did. I saw you in the front seat, but I didn't see you again at the end of the lecture. You just disappeared."

Peter wiped his forehead with a thumb. "Have you sorted that lecturer?"

Aniete wracked his memory, and then recalled the discussion he had had with Peter a fortnight ago. "My guy, where has one seen the money na?"

"If you get a chance to make the money, will you take it?"

Aniete chuckled. "Why not? Who wouldn't?"

Peter seemed to readjust his composure as he slowed his pace. "There is a chance. I want to discuss it with you."

The note of discretion in Peter's voice wasn't lost on Aniete. He read a faint note of hesitation in Peter's stance. The guy must have thought this moment over and over in his mind before bringing himself to play it out. "I have one rich uncle," Peter began. "He is very rich. He has hotels and houses and businesses all over this country and abroad." He paused to study Aniete's reaction. The blank expression staring back at him told him nothing. "If we kidnap him, we will get plenty money. I am talking about millions. It could be in dollars or pounds even."

Aniete's countenance remained unchanged. "It is going to be easy. I know where he lives and where he stays, everything about him. I can get you details of where exactly he could be at any given point in time."

"Why not go and ask him for the money you need. You just said he is your uncle and that he is rich."

"He is very stingy. I have not seen his one naira since I got into this university. Even when he was abroad, he never sent me anything. He is just stingy for no reason."

"Please I don't do such things," Aniete said.

Peter looked at him in disappointment. Even when Aniete offered his hand for a handshake, it had only been by the dictates of a conditioned reflex that he took it. He must have banked so much on this one move playing out. Transfixed, he stood watching Aniete walk uphill towards Bishop's Court.

There were times when Aniete hated the manner in which his mother went about issues, and this was one of those times. Two weeks had come and gone and she hadn't sent money as promised. There were textbooks to buy and he was almost starving. *If only he had a father.* If the man hadn't been too quick to die when he was but a few days old, he wouldn't have had to suffer as much as he did, especially the traumatizing childhood experience of seeing different men come to live with them in their small flat for days. There were so many of them at different times that he had lost count. He had been glad when his mother enrolled him into a boarding school. One holiday, he returned from the boarding house to see another fresh face, younger than the other faces he was used to. He hadn't attached much importance to it, but he was to come home for many more holidays to see the same face in the house and that was when he began to realize that his mother might have got herself a permanent partner. It should have come as a relief to him, but he hated that his mother had chosen to yoke with such a lazy man as Asuquo - her new boyfriend. Asuquo did nothing all day long other than eat and make his mother moan loudly from behind the closed door of their bedroom. There were many times when he walked into them making out in the sitting room, in the kitchen, and the toilet. He hadn't been able to contain his fury the day he met them on his own bed. From that day, his indifference for Asuquo turned into spite.

His mother hardly worked, but they lived modestly. He had asked her one day and she had told him that she had invested in stocks when she was much younger and worked decent jobs. He didn't press further, but he caught the hint of dodginess when he asked the question.

She had a girl child for Asuquo. Such a bundle the baby was, never ceasing to cry and depriving everyone of sleep every night. For reasons unknown to Aniete, things began to take on a different turn with the coming of the new baby. His mother began to sell crayfish and crabs by the roadside in the rural neighbourhood where they had moved into a two-room apartment. That had been in his first year in the university, and the best moments of his life because he could stay away from home as long as he desired.

Three days came and things turned worse for Aniete. It was with a stomach raw with hunger that he sought Peter in the lecture halls.

He still didn't find him on the morning of the fourth day.

On the afternoon of the fifth day, he chose to leave the campus through the Back Gate and had to pass through the wooden shacks where they sold cheap food. Somebody shouted his name. He turned in the direction of the caller and would nearly have broken down in tears on seeing Peter waving at him from the entrance of a shack. Peter beckoned for him to come over, and then retreated into the shack.

Aniete strode across the hot, sandy terrain towards the shack. Peter was seated at a plastic table across from a light-complexioned young woman.

"How far?" Aniete asked Peter, grinning as he settled into an empty seat.

"I'm okay," Peter managed to say in spite of a toothpick sticking out of his mouth

"Where have you been? You suddenly disappeared."

"Nna, I went nowhere o. I've been very much on campus."

"But I've not seen you for … how many days now."

Peter shrugged.

"Hi." Peter's companion waved at him. He had been carried away at seeing Peter that he had not paid the young woman any attention.

"Hi," he said, and turned to Peter. "Man, you guys are enjoying o."

"Do you care for some food?" Peter asked.

"You wouldn't know how hungry I am."

Peter summoned a boy waiting at tables, and in a moment, Aniete was devouring two mounds of *akpu* and a bowl of vegetable soup mixed with egusi soup. Peter engaged the young woman in a low-toned discussion.

"We need to talk," he told Peter when he was done with the food. Peter seemed to guess what the impromptu meeting would be all about.

"Let us see Miranda off," he suggested.

Together, they walked the young woman through the Back Gate and to the tricycle park where she boarded a tricycle and bade them farewell.

Aniete and Peter strolled along the street, away from the noisy tricycle park and possible eavesdroppers.

"I have given serious thoughts to what you told me the last time," Aniete said. "I hope you haven't changed your mind."

"No," Peter said after a moment of silent consideration.

"This your uncle, are you sure he has money? I mean liquid money?"

"Plenty of it, I tell you. And I am not guessing. I know what I am talking about."

"So how much ransom are we looking at?"

"Urm ... As much as twenty million."

"Wow! Are you serious?"

"Of course I am. He will pay up."

"That's a whole lot of money, my guy!"

"That man has more than that."

"So what information do you have on him?"

Peter outlined his plans. He gave detailed information of the man's whereabouts. He told him that the man had an ongoing housing project in Obigbo where he usually visited every evening from his house in Port-Harcourt to check up on its progress. He told Aniete of the routes his uncle took, the bar in uptown Port-Harcourt where he visited every evening, and the days and times he visited his hotel businesses in Owerri. Aniete did not interrupt until Peter was done with the briefing. "How come you are this exact?" he asked.

"I told you he is my uncle. I am close to him. I run errands for him and I know a lot more about him than he is willing to tell."

"So he is this rich and doesn't go about with escorts?"

"No. He likes keeping a low profile. He might even walk past without you knowing how loaded he is. He even travels to Abuja and abroad in a pair of combat shorts and without luggage. The only wealth he flaunts is his white Range Rover."

Aniete mulled the information over in his mind as they strolled along. "What are you thinking?" Peter asked.

"I'm thinking that this job is too big for the both of us to pull off alone. We will need more hands?"

"I thought so too."

"Do you have anyone in mind?"

"No. Do you?"

"I think I know some people who wouldn't turn down such an offer as this. They are known to do much more daring things for far less than one-twelfth of the money we are talking about."

"You trust these people?"

"No. But we will manage them. We will not let them do any negotiation or tell them the exact amount in ransom we are expecting. They will only be the muscle and will supply the tools. The both of us will do every other work that is to be done."

"Hold on. Have you forgotten he is my uncle? I can't show my face, you know."

"I wasn't saying you would. You will work from the inside. You will help facilitate the transaction by making sure that your uncle's immediate family pays up on time. He has a wife, right?"

"Yes."

"Fine. You will also serve to advise against their involving the police. Are you close to her? I mean your uncle's wife."

"Not too close. Just a little bit."

"That will do."

"But how come you are this tactical?"

"Didn't you believe I could do it when you came to me?"

"Yea, I know, but ..."

Aniete smiled confidently. "I was a member of a secondary school fraternity back in those days. We kidnapped our principal's imported cats only for four days. He had threatened that some of our boys wouldn't sit for the math paper during WASSCE."

"Did you demand a ransom?"

"Yes."

"How much?"

He chuckled. "Only the opportunity for all others to sit for the math paper."

Aniete and Peter strolled along the serene streets of Aladimma Housing Estate, paying no attention to the old flats that told of glory days long gone. They were light-hearted, and excited that things were about to take a new turn for them.

Things actually took a new turn, but it was a sharp one, the kind that they never anticipated.

TWENTY-TWO

Even though Aniete was not a member of The Blue Hood or any other campus fraternity, but two boys in Pentagon Hostel were loyal members of the dreaded fraternity. As long as territorial issues never came up, he was their friend, especially the friend of the exuberant guy named Hulk. They called him Hulk because of his bulging biceps which he toned religiously every morning and evening. It was either because of his biceps or the crude tattoos on his torso, but he rarely wore anything other than vests, except for those rare moments when he went into the university for lectures. He smoked so much that one would think he subsisted on marijuana, but he never touched a cigarette; he would smoke a cigar only in clubs and social gatherings just to feel important.

It was to Hulk Aniete went with the proposal.

Later that evening, Aniete and Peter stood before a smallish fellow, Nku, the top man in the Blue Hood hierarchy, narrating the details of their proposal. Aniete couldn't believe he was standing before a fellow whose existence was only spoken of in whispers. The guy was a shadow, a legend, one never to be seen but whose influence was felt. Surprisingly, the dreaded fellow didn't look as terrifying as his reputation inspired. But for the perpetual snarl on his face, he looked the kind of guy you would ignore if he sat next to you on the long benches in the ETF lecture halls. The people guarding him even appeared to be easy-going dandies incapable of soiling their palms with blood.

Nku indicated his interest in the proposal. Even when Aniete told him the ransom in view was two million naira, he did not change his mind. The money was agreed to be split fifty-fifty between the two camps and the layout of the details for the operation began in earnest. Peter's role in the operation was approved. Nku didn't object to Aniete handling the operation, but on the condition that it didn't demand his boys to be answerable to any other.

On their third meeting, they settled for a date to kidnap Peter's uncle.

TWENTY-THREE

IGBO-ETCHE: 20 KM FROM PORT-HARCOURT

The asphalt stretched ahead like a grey Anaconda basking in the sun. It cut its way through an unending expanse of lands thick with vegetation. Cars tore along the highway at top speed.

The man behind the steering wheel of the speeding Range Rover shrugged at the thought of a car breaking down on the road, in the middle of nowhere with no houses or people within sight. But whosoever drove an unreliable car along this road must be crazy, he thought to himself. A Volkswagen station wagon overtook him sharply, its driver stepping hard on the accelerator.

The thought of a cheap Volkswagen overtaking him in that manner bruised his ego. He stepped on the accelerator, and smoothly overtook the offending Volkswagen. The wild look in the driver's eyes pleased him. The poor fellow might have feared it was some highway robber's car about to double-cross him on this lonely road. He smiled to himself as he increased the speed, widening the distance between himself and the Volkswagen.

Despite the potential dangers of this road, people preferred it to the gully-ridden and flooded Aba-Port-Harcourt expressway. The last time he had plied that road, he had had to grit his teeth every time the jagged ends of the broken road scraped the bottom of his Range Rover.

The phone beside the gear stick vibrated. He took his gaze off the road only for a fraction of a second to glance at the illuminated screen; it was his wife. He allowed the phone to ring and made a mental note to call her after the meeting with his solicitor in Obigbo.

He stepped on the brakes, released it and then tapped on it again. The big SUV slowed down like a charging stallion reluctant to obey the rider's pull on its reins. It was a good thing he had seen the damaged spot on the road on time. He eased the SUV slowly along the jagged broken road, all the while wondering what could have caused the sudden damage. It hadn't been the previous day.

It happened too quickly for him to comprehend. In an instant, some balaclava-clad men materialized out of the bushes on either side with rifles trained on his windshield. He counted five of them and, in that split moment, his mind went to Johannesburg and the war with the Maputo gang; those days when he had been known as Mezkana. He had been a part of the action, the hitman for the Dogo cartel. From experience, he could tell that the men wearing the balaclavas would spray his windscreen with automatic gunfire if he proved stubborn. He brought the car to a halt and held up his hands for them to see. Panic crawled up his chest, but he fought it down. *Was this his karma? Had the Maputo guys tracked him down to Nigeria?* There was no chance it was the Maputo gang, he reasoned. This had to be a random robbery. They would only take the car, his wallet and wristwatch. *Only if he could reach for the Beretta strapped underneath his seat.*

The door on his side flew open. He hadn't seen any one of them come to his side, surely the fellow had approached from behind. The gunman motioned for him to step out of the car. He obeyed, trying to keep from staring into the white eyes bulging through the slits in the woollen balaclava.

"Your phone!"

He pointed to the car. The fellow motioned for another to get the phone. The others trained their rifles more intently on him as they marched him away from the car. A pair of handcuffs was roughly clasped to his wrists, restraining his hands behind his back, and a damp hood pulled over his head. Hands gripped his arms and marched him forward. Nobody uttered a word as they led him on.

Twigs cracked under his feet and grass brushed against his exposed arms where his shirt didn't cover. He could tell he was being led into the bush. They marched on in a straight direction. A little distance more and the earth began to sink slowly under his feet. But the vegetation had grown thicker, he could tell from the leaves brushing against the hood over his face.

He had begun to think that this could be nothing but kidnapping. But was it for ransom or was it still the Maputo guys? Could this be the price he was to pay for that night in a Johannesburg club when he pumped three bullets into Joe Da Don's chest?

They came to a stop and made him sit on the ground. The earth was soft and dense with a mat of grasses; he could feel them against his buttocks. He rested his back against what he felt to be the trunk of a large tree. They hadn't removed the hood and not one of them had so much as uttered a word in communication. He didn't say any word too, even though he suspected they were walking around him.

Night approached with the creaks of insects and chilly dampness. The mosquitoes whirred close to his ears in clueless flight. They bit and sucked as though in protest to the presence of the trespassing humans. Hunger came, and with it thirst and such taunting discomfort as he had never known all his life. It made him crave for those little pleasures he had always taken for granted; a good meal with a bottle of good wine, a bath, the feel of fresh warm clothes against his skin, a soft bed and the companionship of a woman under the cover of warm blankets. How he longed for those common pleasures. He fell asleep eventually, but in fits. The dew soaked his clothes and chilled his bones, and the night noises made his heart leap with fright every now and then. Sometime during the night, he thought his captors had deserted him, but when he attempted to struggle free, the beam of a powerful torchlight was aimed at his face. He thought it a warning against any idea of an escape. Once, he received a vicious kick to the thigh for putting up a protest against the inhumane treatment being meted out to him. In all, he resolved to remain calm.

He must have finally succumbed to the exhaustion by morning when the hood was roughly lifted off his head. He squinted in the warm sunlight. The golden brightness hurt his eyes so bad he clenched his eyelids shut for a considerable while. He hadn't known the jungle air to smell so fresh and light; he had to restrain himself from taking in too much all at once because he feared that his lungs would burst with the strain.

Gradually, he opened his eyes. They were in a small clearing in the heart of a jungle. Four youths cradling rifles like guerrilla fighters sat on a log under a makeshift tent to the left of a tree trunk against which he was rested. It felt insulting that his captors were a pack of youngsters, and amateur-looking at that.

A figure loomed in front of him; a short, dark-complexioned youth and he wasn't wearing any balaclavas like the others; their leader, perhaps. His face was set in a perpetual snarl and his eyes bespoke a mean determination. It was such a face that's the natural endowment of people who did those jobs considered dirty and which kept the machinery of the underworld functional. Such faces were never mustered up; they told of their owners' true nature.

"You have been kidnapped," the youth with the snarl said. "We will not think twice if it comes down to killing you this very moment. So, you must have to do exactly as we tell you so that you may live. I think we are clear?"

He didn't seem like he was expecting any answers for he returned the hood over Mezkana's face almost immediately. Mezkana felt the footfalls retreating. He remained still. He was beginning to wish for his kidnappers to make their demands known; he would give them anything, just anything they demanded. He didn't know which was getting to him faster; the suspenseful silence, the discomfort or the hunger and thirst that threatened to drive him insane. He simply desired to be free, to be transported to his normal life far away from the nightmare he was going through.

They gave him no food, no water and the hood remained over his face. Nobody spoke to him and he heard nobody talk to anybody.

TWENTY-FOUR

"How is he holding up?"

"Fine."

"Hope nobody spoke to him?"

"Yes. I did."

"You did?"

"I just threatened him into behaving."

Aniete fell silent as he trailed behind Nku on the footpath. The shrubs brushed against his face and tickled his ears; that was the annoying part. He slapped them away in irritation. There was no telling which was the more annoying; Nku's interrogation of the hostage or the tickling shrubs. He wanted to remind the Blue Hood boss of their agreement that he was not to exchange a word with the hostage under any circumstance. If there had to be any rules to be forgotten so soon, it shouldn't be the fact that there was only one person in charge of this operation. And that person was he, Aniete.

"How is your guy doing on his own end?"

"You mean Peter?"

"Yea, Peter."

"I spoke with him on the way. He is in position now, with the hostage's family."

"That is very impressive."

"He is waiting for us to contact the family. Do you have his phone as I advised?"

"Yea."

"We are good, then."

"Yes, we should be."

They got to a point where the path disappeared into dense bushes. Only a young, slender iroko tree with a mop of leaves on its sparse branches served as a guidepost to the clearing. They saw the landmark and knew the clearing was just around the corner to the left. In silence, they headed in the direction of their camp, brushing aside creeping plants from their faces and watching where their feet fell.

The sun rays no longer felt mild. It burned against Mezkana's exposed skin and heated up the little air trapped within the hood, but it evaporated the dewy dampness on his clothes. His arms felt heavy, like they were mortar casts attached to his shoulder girdle; the blood didn't flow within the veins any longer. It came to his thoughts that his arms might be getting gradually paralyzed. He could take it no more; the hunger, the thirst, the burning sun ... the stiffening arms.

"Who is there?" he screamed. His voice sounded muffled even to his ears. His breath entrapped in the hood stank so badly and he had to inhale it again. "I know you are there! I want to speak with your leader!"

He listened for a response, but none came. Never in all his life had he known silence to be so heavy that it seemed to be a blanket draped over his senses. He was scared of what would become of him the longer the blanket remained over him.

"Talk to me! What the hell do you want?!"

No one talked to him. He listened again. It was only the sounds of the jungle coming alive with the approach of the steadily-rising sun. Something rustled the grasses in a gliding hurry. *A snake?*

"What the bloody hell do you people want?!"

Silence still.

He began to struggle, shrugging his shoulders in a futile attempt to remove the hood. Somebody dealt him a vicious kick to the thigh, but then he struggled more, kicking up grasses and loose earth.

"Let him be!" he heard a voice command softly. The kick didn't repeat itself. He waited, breathing in his entrapped bad breath. The hood came off, a little more gently than the previous time. He blinked, adjusting his sight to the daylight. A mere youth was squatted in front of him such that their faces were level. Like the short one with the evil snarl standing a few paces behind him, he wore no balaclava. His complexion was of a much lighter hue and his face, mild-looking, with soft eyes that told of deep understanding. The prominent ears on either side of his head stood out like a ship's propellers. But the problem was that the youth's face revealed no emotion. The youth shoved an object into his face. He cringed backward to take a look at it and recognized his phone.

"Your password," the youth asked.

Mezkana's ears picked up the unmistakable lilt of either the Efik or Ibibio people; he couldn't distinguish between the two ethnic nationalities.

"Your password," the youth repeated. The short one observed intently from his position behind him.

"MEZ 4567."

The youth held his gaze for some time. It was an unspoken warning. He eventually broke eye contact long enough to punch in the code on the screen of the phone. Satisfied, the youth rose and walked away. The short fellow stepped forward and roughly replaced the hood. Mezkana kicked in protest, but nobody paid him attention. He yelled at the top of his voice. A boot kicked him hard in the stomach, knocking out his breath. He crumpled on the ground like a rag doll, wheezing. It was a miracle he didn't pass out completely. It took him a while to recover from the assault, but when he did, he gave up any idea of resistance and resolved to stay alive.

The hood was lifted off roughly again. It was the same light-complexioned youth squatting before him. He didn't say a word, but he placed the phone against his left ear.

"Speak to your wife," he ordered in a benevolent tone.

"Hello," Mezkana heard his wife's voice come through. He nearly wouldn't have recognized the voice because of the note of panic; she must have been crying.

"Nne."

"Honey, where are you?"

"Listen, just …"

He didn't complete the sentence because Aniete gave him a hard punch in the stomach with his free hand, causing him to grunt and wheeze into the phone speaker. He heard the hysterical cry of his wife on the other end as the phone was peeled off his ear. The hood was replaced as roughly again. He could hear the fellow's voice as he retreated: "If you don't do exactly as you will be instructed in the next two hours, we will help you deposit your husband in the mortuary. Stay by your phone. We will call you in two hour's time with instructions to follow." He paused. "One more thing, if I suspect you of involving the police, you won't like the outcome."

Yet again the hood was lifted off . It was the same light-complexioned fellow standing over him. He squatted down on his haunches so he could look him straight in the eyes. His face wasn't blank this time, it was searching.

"Look here, don't take this personally," he said. "I punched you then to drive home a point. It is business. You are a businessman, I am hopeful you understand that. As compensation for that, we won't be putting any hood over your head, I assure you. But then, I won't be here with you all the time. My friends over there," he gestured at the others cradling rifles a few paces behind. "They aren't as understanding as I am. It has been a long time since they shot at a man and I guarantee you they will not hesitate to put a bullet in your leg just to say *good morning*."

Mezkana nodded his acknowledgement.

"Thank you, sir, for understanding," the youth said, straightening up. He walked over to the other short fellow leaning heavily against the trunk of a palm tree. They talked in whispers for some minutes, with the short one glancing in his direction ever so often. The fair guy walked away, disappearing into the bush, but the short one stayed back.

Mezkana wished it had been the short fellow who hadn't stayed back.

TWENTY-FIVE

PORT-HARCOURT: A DUPLEX IN THE G.R.A

Three days after his arrival at Uncle's house, it happened.

He had returned from an errand: Uncle's wife had sent him to buy some bottles of cosmetics from the supermarket down the street. It had surprised him that a bottle of facial cleanser and two other bottles of what he hadn't cared to know had cost thirty seven thousand naira; the exact amount she had handed him in cash. On walking into the sitting room with his purchase in a branded nylon bag, he met Uncle's wife weeping into her open palms. And that was when he knew the ball has been set rolling.

"They have kidnapped your uncle," she said amidst sobs when she saw him standing by the door, a puzzled look on his face.

"Who? Where? When?" He appeared genuinely shocked.

"I don't know o."

He carried himself like a sleep-walker to the closest leather sofa. The leather creaked in protest to his weight.

"I told him to be mindful. I told him that we should relocate to Abuja or Calabar. There is always trouble here; it is either militancy today or an accident from bad roads tomorrow. I told him Abuja is okay, Calabar is peaceful … Enugu is fine, but would he hear?" She bemoaned in hysteria.

When she lifted her face, he was astonished; he seemed to be looking at the face of a total stranger. He had always thought her beautiful, but with the tears washing off all the facial cosmetics, and the reddened eyes bulging out of their sockets, he began to question his judgment about women and beauty. He cautioned himself to concentrate on the issue at hand.

"Have they demanded anything yet?"

"No."

He looked questioningly at her. "They said that they will call back in an hour's time."

"So what do we do now?"

"I don't know … hmmm … yes, I don't know o." She began to cry afresh, slapping the back of her palms on her thighs.

Peter said nothing. She picked up the phone on the low glass table and started punching in a number.

"Who do you want to call?"

"My brother."

Peter swallowed hard. He hadn't met Uncle's brother- in-law. He hoped the man would not prove to be a hitch in the plan. The possibility of a third party's involvement hadn't been put into account; he had expected everything to happen as easily as advising and escorting Uncle's wife to make the cash drop at the designated area. He knew he had a delicate and crucial role to play, but the tricky part would be to discharge that role effectively without compromising himself.

She put the phone to her ear and stood up from her seat. Pacing about the sitting room, she awaited the person on the other end to pick the call.

"Ehe, Kalu ... Yes... It is Ikuku, he has been kidnapped... please come now I don't know what to do ... please ... I don't know what to say ... I think I'm going mad. Please don't ask me any more questions, just come. Please ... okay."

In a little less than an hour's time, there was a knock on the gate outside. Uncle's wife hastened out of the sitting room. She returned leading a lanky, clean-shaven man into the sitting room. He had a look about him that seemed to suggest he was in dire need of food. His chequered long-sleeved shirt had damp patches under both arms and on his back. From his servile composure, it was evident Uncle's wife was his constant benefactor. While they walked into the sitting room, the man, Kalu, listened with rapt attention to Uncle's wife's briefing on the events of the past few hours. He hadn't acknowledged Peter's presence and Peter didn't bother with asserting his existence.

She wasn't crying anymore. Kalu had successfully convinced her to eat some of the plantains and eggs he had hastily fried in the kitchen. After eating only a few pieces, she had given up on the food which Kalu gratefully devoured. He still hadn't acknowledged Peter's presence.

They sat about the sitting room, expectantly waiting on the mobile phone at the glass centre table to come alive. Kalu had begun to doze from the combined effect of the full stomach and the air-conditioning set on full blast. Uncle's wife didn't bother to slap his thigh anymore to make him stay awake. At exactly twelve, the phone rang. Uncle's wife tapped Kalu's thigh. He snapped awake, wiping his eyes. She reached for the phone.

"Hello." She suddenly must have thought of the others in the room for she set the phone on loudspeaker. Everyone leaned forward to catch every word of what the kidnappers had to say. "Hello," she said again.

"Listen very carefully," the voice came through, steady and authoritative. "Because if you fail to carry out this instruction to the letter, believe me when I tell you that the outcome will be too grave for you to bear. Are you following?"

Peter nearly wouldn't have recognized Aniete's voice. It sounded so mean and devilish over the phone.

"Yes ... Yes," she stuttered, the hysteria returning.

"Good. I will be texting to your phone four separate locations. You are to drop off five million naira in one thousand naira denominations at each of these locations and at the exact time frame. I believe it will be fair to give you three hours to get the money ready and be set for the drop-offs. You should also know that in three hour's time, my patience will run out.

"Woman, don't let your husband remain in my custody after those three hours ... And one more thing, I must warn again, if I suspect any police involvement, your husband will die instantly."

The line went dead.

"Where do I get that kind of money from?" Uncle's wife asked no one in particular. She had begun to cry again, throwing her arms in the air. Kalu fell back into his seat. He had the look of a man totally clueless.

"Let us go to the police station," he suggested finally.

Peter opened his mouth to counter the suggestion, but Uncle's wife cut in immediately.

"Did you not hear what they said?" she said, and sniffed. "They will kill him if we involve the police."

"Let us give them the money *na*," Kalu said. He seemed too eager to get the unpleasant business done with.

"The only money I have in this house is forty thousand naira," she lamented. "What do I do? Who do I call?" She began to cry aloud, carrying her arms on her head. Trails of tears blackened with mascara trailed down her face.

"Don't you have money in the bank?"

"I have only seventy-five thousand naira o. That is all the money I have in my bank account o."

"Your husband *nko?*"

She slapped her hands on her thighs in despair and then heaved a heavy sigh. "My brother, I don't know anything about my husband's money or assets. He keeps them away from me. The only thing I know is the money he gives me for upkeep and the little I save from it."

"But he has plenty money *na*. He has many houses, hotels, estates everywhere?"

"I know, but I cannot point out any one of them to you."

Kalu looked at his sister in disbelief. The revelations seemed too preposterous to accept. He collapsed back into his seat and supported his chin under a clenched fist.

Peter was shocked too. They hadn't foreseen this in their plans. Somehow, he would have to let the others know of the situation without compromising himself. He remembered Aniete's warning him never to get out of sight from his uncle's family for two reasons; he needed to make sure things went smoothly; secondly, when everything must have boiled down, someone might start looking at patterns in an attempt to spot anything out of the ordinary. He couldn't disappoint Aniete; the guy had proven himself to be such a master planner.

"Yours is a sensitive role," Aniete had told him on the day he was to leave for Uncle's house. "I want you to concentrate. I will bury the money in the jungle fifty strides due east from the big mahogany tree. Only both of us know about this. Nobody will touch a dime of the money until you are back and safe."

He couldn't tell why he believed Aniete. Maybe it was blind trust he had for the guy. And he still trusted in the guy to pull this operation through with the way things looked.

"So what do we do now?" Kalu asked. His eyeballs stood reddened in their sockets and the veins stood on his forehead.

"You will have to call them and tell them so," Peter suggested. They must have forgotten all about him because they looked at him as though they were sensing his presence for the first time. "Let us tell them the situation, that you don't have that kind of money. Maybe they will understand and feel pity. Just tell them the truth."

She looked to Kalu to seek his opinion on the suggestion. He seemed to buy into it, for he nodded his assent. She reached for the phone on the centre table.

TWENTY-SIX

A JUNGLE IN IGBO-ETCHE

Aniete sat cross-legged on the bed of trampled undergrowth, across from the captive. He had removed the cuffs from the man's wrists. They both ate bananas and groundnuts in silence. Two bottles of water lay on the ground between them. The others were in the shed, feeding bananas through the mouth hole in their balaclavas. They had their rifles lying across their laps, and their eyes on alert. From the look of things, a cursory observer would have concluded that an important man was having a picnic in the jungle with his nephew, under the watchful eyes of some hired armed guards. Nku was nowhere within sight; he had gone into town.

Mezkana, famished, had gulped down the bananas, but had slowed down considerably now his belly felt almost full.

"You are a wise man," Aniete said, more like a statement of fact.

Mezkana looked at him, but it was only briefly, and then he returned his attention to his peeling of the skin of a banana. "You keep all your finances from your wife. Only strong, wise men can maintain such a rare principle."

Mezkana threw him a brief glance again and then bit into the banana. He munched away as though to spite his interrogator. He respected the youth for being too smart for his age, but then he pitied him. If only the boy knew what game he was playing and with whom he was playing. "I am demanding your ransom, but your wife seems not to be reliant enough to deliver."

He bit another mouthful of banana again. "I need the money, and I need it today." Mezkana threw some groundnuts into his mouth and chewed. Aniete made a point of note that the man was calling his bluff. "Sir, I don't like what I do, but it is something I have to do in order to survive and hopefully to become a man with some means just like you. I want you to know I have come this far to getting this money from you and I must get it at whatever cost."

Mezkana reached for the bottle of water, but Aniete snatched it away from his reach and tossed it over his shoulder. "You have to be fair with me too. I have treated you well, better than the others have done."

Mezkana studied him, as though he was deciding whether to slit his throat or stab him in the stomach.

When he finally spoke, it was with a reserved conviction, like a man counselling his godson: "I like you. You are a very sharp boy, but the game you play is too dangerous for you. You just might be playing it with the devil. My advice to you is to let me go, and then run far away where I won't see you because if I do get you, and I am certain I will, you will know who you are messing with."

Aniete got to his feet, and dusted his buttocks as he walked towards the other gang members in the shed. He talked to one of them in a whisper, and the fellow handed him something from his hip. Aniete returned to Mezkana seated on the ground and munching some bananas. On drawing close, he took aim and fired off the revolver.

Tai! Tai!

The first shot missed. The bullet dug into the soil a few inches away from Mezkana's leg, but it was the second bullet that got him just above the ankle of his right leg. Mezkana cried out in agony, holding onto the injured leg. His cries came out muffled by the pulp of bananas filling his mouth so it sounded like a goat being strangled. Aniete stood over him, pointing the revolver to his chest. Mezkana raised his hand as though to fend off any oncoming bullets. Aniete fired another shot point-blank at a finger, sending a spray of blood and bits of shattered bones into the air. A hoarse cry escaped Mezkana's throat as he spat out the messy pulp of bananas from his mouth.

"Please don't kill me," he begged, tears streaming down his face. "I will give you anything you want. Anything. Please."

"Now we are talking," Aniete said, lowering the gun. "I need the money I asked your wife for."

"How much?"

"It is not in your place to know. Just tell her where and how to lay hands on plenty cash."

"I don't have any cash in the bank."

Aniete raised the revolver again. "What will I stash money in the bank for?" Mezkana cried. "I am a businessman, for Christ's sake."

Aniete pressed the muzzle of the gun into the man's temple. "Wait! I can arrange for somebody to give you all the money you need."

"Where does this person stay?"

"Here … In Port-Harcourt."

"Perfect," Aniete said, lowering the pistol. "Call him immediately." He fetched the phone from his pocket and tossed it onto Mezkana's lap and then watched on as the man grabbed frantically for the phone with his good hand. The other one looked too messy, a good fraction of his index finger completely gone. Mezkana tapped clumsily at the phone screen and then put it to his ear.

"Onwa." He winced into the phone. "Don't worry... I am just in a very difficult situation right now…"

Aniete snatched the phone from Mezkana's ear.

"Listen very carefully," he said into the phone. "This bastard, whosoever he is to you has been kidnapped. As I speak with you, he has only four hours after which you should start preparing for his funeral. Now, call his wife immediately and follow her demands. Make sure not to try anything stupid, and be fast about it. Your friend here has only one bullet in him now, in four hours time, he would have twenty-four in places where an instant death would be an act of kindness."

He ended the call, pocketed the phone and looked at Mezkana clinging onto his bloodied hand in shock. "Give me one minute to bind your wound as a show of appreciation for your cooperation." With that, he strode towards the makeshift shed. He congratulated himself for being thoughtful enough as to have brought along a first aid kit. It was snake bites and maybe light bruises he had had in mind; he had never planned for any interrogation to go this far, but then he had done what had to be done and things looked better for it.

Uncle's wife paced about the sitting room, her eyes glued to the phone on the centre table. She bumped her knee against a sofa but paid no attention to the bruised knee. She wrung her hands in panic hoping she hadn't made a wrong move in telling the kidnappers that she didn't have access to any of her husband's money. Kalu tried to calm her but gave up on the futile effort and relaxed into the chair instead. He too had his eyes on the phone.

Peter was shaking. Things had taken a different turn than he had anticipated. *Uncle's wife not having access to Uncle's money?* It sounded too absurd, moreso because it had foiled his plans. He feared trouble might come out of this thing, and he wanted none of it; he would surely be twice doomed than the others if this were to backfire. He caught himself closing his eyes and mumbling a little prayer that the others in the jungle be resourceful enough as to conclude this business quickly. All he desired was an end to everything without his involvement getting known. It never mattered if Uncle died in the end; the man and all his worldly goods had never been of any significance to him. His death wouldn't change much either.

The phone rang. Uncle's wife dove for it on the first ring. "Hello … yes … Please …okay … twenty million … but… are you sure they will … please I don't want them to kill my husband …okay … But … Okay, I will try to be calm … okay … Thank you sir. God bless you, sir. " She removed the phone from her ear and slowly leveled herself into the closest settee. The others stared, visibly surprised that he was calm and not trembly.

"It is Onwa," she explained to their silent enquiry.

"Sorry, who is Onwa?" Kalu asked, straining forward in his seat as though he feared the consequences of missing any word.

"He is Ikuku's friend. The kidnappers contacted him."

"What did he say?" Kalu pursued.

"He said he will be handling everything. He said I shouldn't worry."

"That is good news." Kalu breathed his relief.

"But he said he will be negotiating the ransom with the kidnappers, and that there is no way he can lay hands on the twenty million within the time frame."

"How much is he saying they can come up with?" Peter asked without thinking.

"Three million."

He felt the fury heat up in his chest, but he cautioned himself to hold it down.

The phone rang.

Aniete recognized the caller to be the same Onwa whom the hostage had called earlier. He hadn't been expecting the call so soon. Wondering what could possibly have gone out of line, he punched the answer button and put the phone to his ear.

"Hello," the voice from the other end broke through a slight static.

"You were supposed to do as I said and not call me."

"Please I rallied around for cash and all I can lay my hand on is three million naira."

"Do you think I am negotiating?"

"No, … but please, this is the much we could lay our hands on. We will need more time to get twenty million."

"How much time are you asking for?"

"Two weeks tops … the banks … they will need some clearance to move such amount of money."

Aniete's head was working overtime. He never wished this whole deal to linger for more than a day. He feared that the longer it tarried, the more careless they might become and the more things stood a chance of getting out of control. *But Peter had said the man had plenty of money?* He kept quiet, thinking hard. Only the caller's breathing told him the connection was still live.

Three million? Ridiculous!

It was clear to him that his leverage lay in the hysteria of the paying party and he feared that with time its effect would wear out and they might become calculative. If things should turn out so, he knew the chances of getting double-crossed would increase. He wasn't ready for that. The odds would be against him if he let that happen.

"Get the cash ready in one-thousand naira denominations. In exactly twenty minutes, I will be calling to tell you where to bring the cash to. Don't try to be smart. If I get suspicious, then rest assured you have landed yourself a job of comforting your friend's widow."

He severed the line and cursed inwardly. Every hope for a huge pay-off had just died like a hibiscus flower in the heat of the tropical noon sun.

Aniete glanced at the watch strapped to his wrist. He breathed deeply and drummed his fingers nervously on his knee. The interior of the red Toyota Camry felt hot and stifling. He glanced at the driver, one of Nku's boys. The fellow nervously ran his sweaty hands along the steering wheel and looked every now and then at the rear-view mirror. They were parked in the deserted premises of an oil wellhead, waiting for the man who was to bring the ransom.

"Any signs?" Aniete asked the driver.

"None."

The boy blew out a stream of air from his mouth and fingered the balaclava he wore like a beanie. Aniete disliked the fellow. His tension was beginning to wear off on him too. He glanced at his watch again and found that five minutes were left. He willed himself to stay calm. Nothing in the deserted environment held his attention, only a heavy-looking iron pipes in the middle of a fenced-in rectangular perimeter with grass growing tall in places where the concrete flooring was broken. The place, a deserted oil wellhead, gave them a sense of privacy and concealment from cars that sped past.

When he looked far enough, he could make out the flame of natural gas being flared in a Shell flow station in the distance. He thought of Nku at that moment. The man was with the hostage in his Range Rover, parked at a distance close to the wire fence of the flow station, awaiting his signal.

A black Nissan Armada slowly moved into the perimeter. It parked back-to-back with the Toyota Camry as the driver had been instructed. Aniete waited and saw the boot pop open. Everything was going according to instructions. He gave the driver the go-ahead sign. The boy rolled down his balaclava and then left the car. He walked briskly to the Nissan, lifted the boot open, took out a black duffle bag and hurried back into the Toyota Camry. Aniete did a random check on the cash; there weren't any counterfeit notes found in between the crisp bundles of one-thousand naira notes. He had heard that people placed tracking devices amongst ransom. There seemed to be no hint of such devices between the wads of money. He felt the bag. Clean.

"Let's go."

The driver shot the car forward, did a wild U-turn around the oil wellhead and headed for the perimeter exit. Aniete shot a glance into the parked Nissan Armada. There was an elderly man holding the wheels in a quivering grip.

Soon after they had joined the road, the driver

peeled off his balaclava. Aniete reached for the phone in his pocket and dialed a number.

"I have the cash ... It is confirmed. I will tell the man where to pick up the hostage." He severed the connection and dialed another number. "Drive towards the gate of the flow station. I believe you will recognize your friend's car. He is inside. Good doing business with you."

He severed the connection, removed the SIM card from the phone, broke it and tossed the pieces out of the speeding car. A few metres further, he hurled the phone far into the bush and then sat back with his gaze fixed on the bush on his side of the window.

"Pull over," he said to the driver. The driver flashed him a questioning look. "Now!"

The driver tapped on the brake and guided the car to a stop by the roadside. Aniete grabbed hold of the bag, and got out. "Don't wait for me. I will meet you at the hideout." He waited for the surprised driver to drive away into the distance, and then he disappeared into the thick bush, keeping a huge mahogany tree in sight.

Shortly after the clock on the sitting room wall chimed one, the phone rang again; Uncle had been released. The caller, Onwa, took his time to complain how the heartless criminals had the patience to confirm that the money wasn't counterfeit notes. Aunty collapsed back into the chair and wept afresh. Neither Peter nor Kalu bothered to comfort her; they could tell relief from grief.

"When do we get paid?" Nku asked Aniete.

They stood side-by-side in the clearing in the jungle, two commanders watching the foot soldiers pack up their gears for evacuation after the ransom had been collected and the hostage deposited for pick-up. Nobody wore any balaclavas, but cheerful looks adorned their faces in anticipation of a payday.

"The mission is not yet over. My man is still in place. We have to be patient until he gets back so he doesn't blow his cover in haste."

Nku regarded Aniete closely, the whites of his eyes moist and reddened from smoking marijuana. There was something about the look in his eyes; it was a warning to Aniete never to attempt a double-cross. "I know your concerns. The money is safe. Nobody touches it for the moment."

Aniete wasn't foolish; he never would conceive the idea of double-crossing anybody on this deal, especially not someone as important as the top man of the Blue Hood fraternity.

TWENTY-SEVEN

A DUPLEX IN THE G.R.A

Mezkana lay on his back, propped against a white pillow on the king-sized bed in his bedroom. His injured leg and finger were swaddled in thick white bandages. He had spent only three days in the hospital and had insisted on convalescing at home. Luckily, the gunshot wounds weren't as serious as he had feared; the bullet hadn't shattered any bones in the leg. The trouble was with the finger; the doctors said he would have to live with the stump

He had hardly uttered a word since his release, not even in reply to anyone's greeting, and he instructed that his new phone be turned off all the time. The only time he talked a little was when Onwa visited, but then he had begged the older man to keep the news of his kidnap secret. The visiting doctor had said it was post-traumatic stress and not the mental problem his wife had feared.

Uncle's wife was in the kitchen this afternoon. She could see, through the open window, that the sun had dried up the dew on the grass and parked cars. The hired nurse had left an hour ago to be back in the evening when she would redress the wound and set up another bag of IV fluid. Peter sat on a chair beside Uncle's bed, watching the IV fluid drip through the transparent tubing on its way into Uncle's arm. The silence was unnerving. He would have turned on the TV just to listen to anything other than Uncle's conscious rhythmic breathing, but he was afraid to provoke him.

"Has somebody held a gun at you before?"

The unexpected question startled Peter and left him dumbfounded. He could only shake his head. Uncle turned his head to flash him a look and then returned to staring at the ceiling. "Do you know what pains me the most?"

"No." His voice seemed to have worked of its own accord. It sounded strange to his ears.

"Those were little boys. Amateurs. They don't know what they have gotten into."

Peter nodded as though in assent. He could see that Uncle's wound was uch more psychological than physical.

"Peter."

"Uncle?"

"Do you know that those boys were about your age?"

He shook his head. Uncle must have anticipated his answer, for he never turned to look at him. "But they were good enough for their age. I have been thinking of how to trace these guys."

"Will you go to the police?" Peter asked, trying to sound genuinely naïve.

"If I go to the police, the news will become public. Some other criminal groups will see me as a means of making easy money. No, I will not go to the police. I will get them on my own terms. "

Despite the air conditioning, the room felt suffocating. Peter sat still, scarcely breathing.

"Peter," Uncle called, breaking the momentary silence.

"Uncle?"

"Do you know how I made my money abroad?" Peter gulped down an imaginary lump, but he couldn't bring himself to say anything. "I was a hit-man for a drug cartel. I shot people when they least expected. I killed for other cartels too. The people I killed were very mean people, the ones who wouldn't think twice before they took a fellow man's life." He chuckled. "I will get those boys. All of them, I swear. They will know who they just messed with."

A shiver shot down Peter's spine. He had always known Uncle to be a tough guy; he knew Uncle kept a shotgun in the house. Before now, he had harboured the suspicion that Uncle did drugs or some other tough stuff in his time abroad. But killing for money? They really were in deep trouble. Every one of them.

The remainder of the day was unsettling. Images of himself and the others in police custody flashed through his mind. As he lay awake on his bed that night, he brainstormed on ways of saving himself should everything come crumbling down on the kidnap deal.

One week later Uncle gave him money for his fare back to Owerri.

Peter breathed a sigh of relief when the bus eased out of the motorpark; he was tired of constantly having to put up appearances in Uncle's house. His mind went to the ransom. It hurt that he was to get less than he had anticipated. He flirted with the idea of having all of the three million naira to himself; after all, Aniete and the others didn't know that he was coming back yet.

By the time the bus moved into Owerri, Peter had conceived a plan; it sounded fool-proof enough. Uncle needed his captors so much he would be willing to pay some good money to know their identities. He would have to be the one to make that revelation and get paid for it. But first, he needed to get hold of the ransom all to himself before he set the others on the run for their lives. It all needed careful execution so he wouldn't in any way give himself away. He considered involving Miranda, but he had reservations for her capabilities. He never trusted her that much either. Still, no better option seemed to present itself.

The ITC bus spluttered into the rowdy motor park late in the evening. He alighted with his sparse luggage – a black knapsack – and headed towards a girl seated under a big yellow umbrella set over a round plastic table of the same colour. On the table before the girl were arranged stacks of SIM packs according to their different network providers. Next to the stack of SIM cards was a black HP mini laptop equipped with an external webcam.

"Do you have MTN SIM card?" Peter asked the girl.

"Yes."

"How much?"

"Two hundred, plus one hundred naira for registration."

"Give me MTN."

Peter hastily dug into his pocket for the money. He was proud of himself for his smart action. After here, he would be heading straight to the site where the ransom was buried. As always, it was first things first.

TWENTY-EIGHT

Gud day. It isn't necessary to no me. I've valuable info 4 u in exchange 4 300k. I no wia u can get d kidnappers, including the 1 who shot u. They're all students in Owerri. They are my colleagues. Don't boda calling me. Text me if interested in paying 4 more info. Tanx.

Peter hit the 'send' button and then began composing another text:

U just executed a deal. U've been betrayed. Ur life is in danger. I offer my help for just 50k. Don't boda calling. Text me if interested 2 no more.

He hit the 'send' button and then collapsed back on the mattress, staring at the familiar ceiling in his room. His eyes wandered to the polished door of the built-in wardrobe. Behind the doors, a small bag was safely stashed. It held the ransom. *The naïve Aniete!* The guy had buried the cash in the exact place in the jungle as he had said he would. Peter chuckled to himself. It felt good to be at the top of the game and calling the shots. He had rolled the dice and he would have to keep his eyes wide open.

The phone beeped. He shot up from the mattress, frantically feeling the sheets for the phone:

I'll give u 400k. Give me their identities and locations, all of them.

A second message arrived almost immediately: *Interested. Let's meet immediately.*

His heart thumped violently against his chest. His armpits felt damp with sweat. It was all happening too fast, faster than he had anticipated. He admonished himself to think fast and very carefully.

With shaky hands, he managed to tap the keys on his phone.

5674352629, Miranda Ilo, Access Bank. Pay in half the amt n I'll tell you wia 2 find each 1 of them.

Send.

To the second message, he composed a reply: *There's an Anglican Church @ Orodo. Every1 knows there. Bring the money along at 7pm 2moro.*

Send.

He stretched on the bed, listening to the thump of his heart. It wasn't fear he felt. Far from it. He felt excitement such as he hadn't known before. It made him feel very alive, and in control, like a man. He knew he had played into a dangerous game, but the music had begun and he would dance merrily to it.

The room grew dark with approaching nightfall, but he didn't bother with the light bulb; it would give away his presence. Not one of his friends, not even Miranda knew of his return. He desired for it to remain that way for the time being. If the experience of the past few days hadn't taught him anything, it had at least taught him discretion. He made a point to call Miranda later to notify her of a deposit that would be made in her name. But in the meantime, he slept off in the growing darkness of the room.

TWENTY-NINE

The watch on Aniete's wrist told him he had been sitting in the church pews for a whole hour. As the informant had said, the church hadn't been difficult to locate. It was too big an edifice to miss. Already, it was thirty minutes past the agreed time of meeting and the fellow was yet to show up. He didn't have the fifty thousand naira on him, but he believed he could convince the guy to be a little bit patient.

Time was running out and he was beginning to get worried. He reached for his phone in his trouser pocket and composed a text: *Wia are u? been w8n @ d church.*

Send.

He exhaled and settled as he waited for a reply. If no replies came in twenty minutes, he resolved, he would leave the church.

His phone beeped.

It isn't safe 4 me to cum 2day. sorry. We meet 2moro, same time & place.

He hissed in disappointment. He strongly suspected Nku was the person betraying him, and obviously one of his boys was about to snitch on him. *But then, what if he was wrong?* Nku knew where to get him if he wanted him. The Blue Hood boss knew where he stayed and where he attended lectures. If he really wanted him picked up, he would have done so in a twinkle of an eye. True. But then the mean fellow might be waiting for his own cut from the kidnap deal before swooning in on him. Nku could still be the one, or he could not. He was confused. These conflicting thoughts barraged his mind as he exited the church through the southern doorway.

He hadn't noticed the priest walked in just then through the eastern doorway.

The phone rang. It was Miranda.

"Hello, baby."

"Hello." Her voice sounded drowsy, even though it was evening.

"Are you okay?"

She giggled. "I was sleeping. The money you told me to be expecting has been paid into my account. I just received an alert."

"How much?"

"Two hundred thousand."

"Okay. Keep it. I'm coming back from my brother's place in Abuja tomorrow."

"Okay. But I want to take seven thousand from the money to make my hair."

"No, no, no. I want the money for something. It isn't exactly mine."

"Pleeeaaassseee."

He hated it when she sounded like that. It turned his will into jelly. "Don't you want me to look fine for you again? Will you want to see me wearing my old hair? You wouldn't like it, believe me. It is too rough now."

He could feel his will melting already. "Okay, don't take more than seven thousand."

He could tell the glee in her voice. "That is why I love you," she cajoled. "Buy me *kilishi* from Abuja when coming."

"I will. Take care of yourself for me."

"And you too."

He cut the connection. He smiled as he composed the text message. It took him a little less than fifteen minutes to type in the names and nicknames of six boys, and their hostel addresses. He hit the 'send' button and stretched on the bed.

His groins stirred with passion. Obviously, the thought of victory was responsible. At that moment, he wished he hadn't lied to Miranda that he was in faraway Abuja.

THIRTY

A mosquito buzzed around Aniete's left ear. Instinctively, his palm flew in the air, to swat the life out of the insolent thing. *Twack!* It landed on his ear. A hum went off in the assaulted ear as though a lawn mower had been turned on in that part of his head. He turned onto his side to ease the aching in his back, but the hardness of the long wooden desk threatened to crack his ribs.

Ever since he received the text message from the unknown fellow, Aniete had kept away from his lodge and the lecture halls. He had distorted everything about his established routine. At night, he slept on the long desks in the school auditorium when the other students came to read. And in the day, he would wander around the campus with his eyes open for Nku or any one of the Blue Hood boys he knew.

That night, a handful of students were scattered about the auditorium reading by the lights of hurricane lanterns, some burning candles and the white fluorescence of rechargeable lanterns. Just like on most nights, the campus power generator had been put out. The auditorium was silent and still. Only an occasional murmur escaped an anonymous person's lips. It would normally be like this until sometime past 2 a.m when the nocturnal readers would begin to discuss in whispers, crack hushed jokes, or snore in exhausted slumber. At that same time a boy would attempt passes at some girl, and the more acquainted pairs would slip out to seek some secluded corner for hurried sex.

Aniete grunted as he turned on the hard bench. The back of his head had begun to ache where it had come in contact with the wood. Even the blissful act of sleep had become a torture. He removed his shoes and used them for a pillow. The ease he felt was nearly absolute. He must have begun to drift off to sleep when a mosquito bit his exposed foot. Cursing, he reached for the assaulted foot in a flash. The malicious thing had already taken off in contentment. He could swear the mosquito had fangs because of its excruciating bite. He hissed, got off the bench and put on his shoes. There was not going to be any sleep for him tonight, he thought, as he walked about the auditorium.

Near the podium at the head of the auditorium, two girls chatted in low tones while their burning lanterns idled beside open books that littered the desk in front of them. Curious, Aniete slowed his steps to get a hint of their discussion.

"Hmm. Are you serious?" the one said, a comment on something the other had said.

"My dear, they just came into our lodge and shot Flames and Danny."

"These cult clashes, they have started it again. What could possibly be the problem with these boys this time? Don't they get tired of killing themselves? Or is there something else they gain from cultism that nobody is aware of? "

"My dear, I don't know o. I didn't stop to ask. I just carried myself and started coming for night class, *jeje*. I no want wahala, abeg."

"My sister abeg o, nobody want wahala. They should just let me graduate and leave this place in one piece. There is a bigger world out of this campus."

"Your own is good na. At least you will be graduating in eight month's time. Me, I have one more year and eight months to go."

"That is if nobody decides to go on strike, you mean? You know how it is with Nigerian lecturers and the government. Nobody knows that exactly any of them wants."

"Please. I don't pray for any strikes. They should just allow me to graduate on …"

Aniete walked away. He had heard enough, enough to get him thinking. He knew those two, Flames and Danny. They were members of the Blue Hood and they had been part of the kidnap team. If anybody was betraying them, it sure wouldn't be Nku betraying his own boys. But then, there was never a time when criminals had honour amongst themselves. *Who could be the Judas behind this betrayal?* He needed answers to this whole deadly puzzle, and quickly. Peter flashed through his mind, and he wished the guy would be alright. Everything would have to be on hold until Peter was back and safe. But in the meantime he would have to seek out the one setting the whole gang up.

The illuminated hands of his wrist-watch read 1:43 a.m. Dawn seemed too far away.

Evening descended.

Aniete was in the church waiting for the informant. The informant never showed up. Disappointed, he left the church but was shot on the steps and left for dead.

On that same evening, Mezkana raised a glass of his favourite whiskey in the air and drank to his heart's content. At dinner time, he surprised his wife when he ate everything on his plate. She noticed his light mood but gave up on the idea of pursuing an enquiry into the sudden change over her husband. There was no point in making any attempts in that regard, knowing how well he kept her in the dark when it came to his dealings. In her silent appraisal, she underestimated her husband's mood. In bed that night, she moaned and squealed like she had never known in a very long time.

By the morning of the next day, his mood suffered a relapse. The assassins hadn't brought the prime target's head as proof. Infuriated, he sent them back to collect it, but they hadn't found the body. He was beginning to lose his sanity. *If only his leg would heal quickly.* He couldn't wait to teach these dumb amateurs what it meant to be a contract killer.

THE LIZARDS
COME TO VISIT

THIRTY-ONE

Igwemma is happy to be amongst the beautiful people again. She missed them; the palace, the woman with the crown, the people in their beautiful dresses, her sisters and all their shiny jewels. Igwemma is sitting at table with her sisters. It is made of gold. The woman with the crown is not seated with them; she's high up on her glassy throne.

"I want some of that red wine," Igwemma says to her sisters.

They giggle amongst themselves. The woman with the crown smiles. They are happy she loves the wine.

"Of course, you will have it, my dear," the woman with the crown says to her. She waves her hand and a door opens. Maids, very beautiful in their fine clothing that do not look like calico, glide into the court in a single file. The one in front bears a big glittery jug and a goblet in a platter. The others each have a goblet on glittery platters. There are twelve of them, each to serve a princess. Igwemma spots Myeine, who gives her a warm smile. Igwemma smiles back. They are both happy to meet.

Myeine presents her a silver goblet, with a bow. She recognizes it to be the one she used on her first visit. Her sisters are each handed their own goblets. The wine is poured. Igwemma sips the wine, and thinks it's excellent. She drains her goblet and asks for more. Everybody is pleased. Myeine fills her goblet and she drinks.

The woman with the crown claps her hand and the servants leave the court. Myeine smiles at Igwemma as she leaves. Igwemma smiles back again. They love her here, she thinks, and more than she is loved in the other world. The door closes.

"Daughters of the Sister Rivers, Princesses of a great kingdom," *the woman with the crown addresses everyone.* "I have to summoned you all today to bring you great news." *Everyone is quiet. No one is sipping from their goblets; they are all listening intently to her.*

"The full moon approaches, and soon mortal men will come to seek favours from this kingdom. With blood they will come; blood of sheep, rams and of birds of the air. There will be women amongst them too, daughters of men with gifts, to appeal for many favours. I have to warn you all to be very careful this period. I know how proud you all are, and I know that there are a few mischievous ones amongst you. I have to say it now: do not stir the waters! Never make known your appearance by day or night! Haunt no man's head upon his pillow. Let no mortal behold your glory by day or night! You all shall go about your tasks amongst the sons and daughters of men until the period of the full moon is over. Daughters, stir not the wrath of your *mother with disobedience. It would never be my pleasure to exile you to wander amongst mortals for twelve seasons. Daughters of the Sister Rivers, I welcome you once again."*

The sun had just peeked out of the misty skies when Aniete and Luciano laid in wait for Peter. Like two ordinary fellows waiting for another, they idled next to an abandoned sun-beaten kiosk. Luciano had halfheartedly come along with Aniete on the plan to lay ambush for Peter; he still believed Peter would have gone into hiding with Aniete running loose. But Aniete wouldn't hear of that theory.

They saw Peter approach with some girl whom Luciano, from the distance, recognized to be Miranda. Quickly, they ducked by the kiosk, and waited, and when Peter drew abreast, Aniete fell in step beside him, subtly sticking the tip of a pen-knife to his ribs. Peter froze in shock.

"Act normal!" Aniete warned. He turned to Miranda who stood paralyzed with fright. "Run for your life and don't ever tell anybody what you have seen or I will personally come for you."

Too grateful to be exonerated from an unpleasant situation, Miranda fled back the way she had come without looking back.

"Follow me!" Aniete ordered Peter, driving the tip

of the knife a bit further into his skin. They marched into an incomplete four-storey building at a narrow side street a few paces away. The building looked like one whose owner had given up on at the time the carpenter was supposed to have come in. It stood like a ragged old giant, without the shed of a roof. It was to the topmost floor that they marched their prisoner, with only the sky above them.

Aniete roughly shoved a frightened Peter against the mossy unplastered wall hard-beaten by the elements. "Sit down!"

Peter obeyed, sliding against the wall until he came to settle upon a scattering of rodent droppings and bits of rotting planks.

Luciano stood by the open gap of what was meant to be a window, scouting the grounds below for anything out of the ordinary.

"So it was you who betrayed those boys?" Aniete asked. "They died because of your treachery. Why?"

"No, it isn't what you think … I … I …"

"You should have seen how your uncle begged for his life, but I won't give you that benefit of negotiating for your life."

"Ah! My brother. Please. It hasn't come to that … We can settle this thing between us."

"This fellow is one bloody fool," Luciano cut in, stealing his attention from the grounds below. "How did you ever partner with him? I was thinking he would change his routine knowing how fucked up he is at the moment."

"Please," Peter begged, looking from Luciano to Aniete. "Let us settle this matter like brothers. Please, I beg you."

"Where is the money?" Aniete asked.

"I don't have it … please …"

"Who has it?"

"Me … But I have spent it."

"What did you use it for? New clothes? Women?" Luciano cut in again. Aniete shot him a warning look; it was the warning a commander would give a sentinel for neglecting his watch. Luciano took the cue and returned his attention to the ground below, his face set in a sickened frown.

Aniete returned his attention to Peter. "Who has the money?"

"I placed an order for a new ride."

"My God!" Luciano exclaimed, peeling his eyes from the grounds below yet again. But it was only momentarily, for he returned his attention to his duty. His face looked like he was suffering from nausea.

"Where is the ride?"

"It is on transit from Cotonou."

"You spent all the money? All of the three million?"

"It is a Toyota Avalon. I got it cheap for two point five."

"This guy is an idiot!" Luciano cursed, leaving his post by the window to serve Peter a vicious kick in the stomach. The blow knocked the air out of Peter; he writhed in pain amongst clutching his stomach and gasping for breath.

"Now listen," Aniete said to the agonized Peter. He didn't appear pleased at having Luciano interrupt his interrogation again. "That isn't the reason for which we are having this discussion. I brought you to the top of this floor because I want to toss you out a window when I am done with you. I just don't want the dirty blood of a snitch soiling my hands."

"Please ... please..." he began to plead, forgetting the pain in his stomach. "Don't do this to me, I beg you in the name of God."

"But we can still negotiate if you tell me what I need to know."

Peter nodded his acknowledgement. "Please, anything. Anything at all. I will do ... I will tell you."

"Who are those other people after me?"

"What people?"

"Remember, if you leave me unsatisfied, I will toss you out headfirst through that window." He pointed to the window where Luciano stood watch, muttering inaudible curses under his breath.

"I don't know who is looking for you, but I think it is my uncle who sent them."

Aniete inhaled deeply. His eyes were narrowed as though he was mulling something over in his head. "How did your uncle get details of me?"

Peter hesitated.

"I think I know the answer to that one," Luciano cut in yet again. "It was you!"

Peter's gaze fell to the ground at Aniete's feet.

"Were those people the same ones who killed those Blue Hood guys?" Aniete asked.

"I think so."

"And you framed me before Nku too?" Aniete asked. Peter's face didn't leave the spot on the floor next to his interrogator's feet, so Aniete raised his voice: "Did you?!"

Peter nodded.

"Okay, I have gotten all I need from you. You are of no use to me anymore."

Peter looked up at him with eyes wild with fear. Aniete held out a hand and Luciano passed him a coil of three-cord rope from his satchel.

"Please," Peter pleaded. "We don't have to do this … I beg you … Have pity, please, my brother …"

"Shut the fuck up!" Luciano cursed. "It is either this or the flight through this window. Left for me, I will opt for the latter."

That seemed to quieten Peter. The thought of falling several metres onto the ground below strewn with steel rods, heaps of gravel and stacks of cement blocks must have advised his sudden calmness. They bound him hand and foot and gagged him with his own pair of socks, and abandoned him high up in the building under the mercy of the elements. They didn't hear his muffled screams any longer as they descended the second landing of the steep stairs.

"We have a deal, remember?"

"What deal?"

"Don't tell me you have forgotten so soon. We agreed that after this, we are going straight to Port-Harcourt."

"Of course." Aniete spoke like one suddenly recalling something but ashamed to admit it. They were standing by the roadside, their backs to the dwarf ornamental trees dotting the small strip of grasslands. Ever since they interrogated Peter, Aniete had been silent in a disturbing way.

"So, we are going to the motor park right away?"

"Sure."

Luciano nodded his approval and concentrated on keeping an eye open for any oncoming tricycles.

"Peter's uncle must think that I am dead," Aniete thought aloud.

"No. He thinks you are alive, that is why they were breaking into houses in search of you."

He seemed to ponder on the theory. "You are right."

"For once, thanks for the compliment."

"But I need another favour."

"No."

"Why? Shouldn't you have heard me out first?"

"I say *no*. And I mean it. I don't need to hear you out first."

Luciano flagged an oncoming tricycle, but it whirred past, the driver ignoring him.

"Just this once," Aniete pressed. "I swear on my life, there will be no more after it."

"What is this favour you talk about? Let me hear it."

"I want to see my mother, and then we can continue on to Port-Harcourt tomorrow."

"Where does your mother live?"

"Ikot Abasi."

"I don't know where that is, but I know that we will be going out of our way."

"It is in Akwa-Ibom, and yes, we will be going a little bit out of our way."

The frustration seething within Luciano was noticeable from his momentary silence. "Why should I grant you this favour?"

"Because we are partners. We watch each other's back."

Luciano paused for another considerable. "You are attempting to flatter me. But I am not falling for it. To be clear, I am not your partner. I am just a hand hired to get you to your father."

"Thank you."

"What for?'

"For being honest and for granting me this favour."

"Keep it." He flagged down an oncoming tricycle. It slowed down gradually until the driver braked to a stop few inches from their feet.

"Fire Service," Aniete called out to the driver

"*Unu abuo*? The two of you?"

"Yes."

"Two hundred."

"One fifty." Luciano cut in

"One eighty."

"One fifty."

The driver waved them in. They clambered onto the scratched black leather seats. Nobody said a word to the other as the tricycle whirred along the road, giving speeding cars a wide berth.

THIRTY-TWO

IKOT-ABASI

So much had changed about the city of Uyo from the last time Aniete visited. Everything looked new and different; the miles of new roads, the streetlights and overhead bridges. Luciano himself was spell-bound at the scenery that greeted him. He had never seen any town so clean, orderly and beautiful. It was so as to enjoy the scenery that he fought to take a window seat when they boarded another bus to Ikot-Abasi.

It was late afternoon when they walked along a street in Ikot-Abasi. The neighbourhood bustled with rural life. Clusters of plantain trees separated one shabby bungalow from the other. There were no fences about any of the houses and the place had the feel of a community where everyone knew everyone. Luciano could see them seated on the verandas of their houses. A woman in a dirt-coloured bra fed a nipple into a naked infant's mouth.

Little children clad in soiled pants darted up and down the street, calling out to playmates, screaming their glee and protests, and crying. A mere girl, heavily pregnant, sat on a low stool chopping the ends off periwinkle shells. A group of men sat on benches, sipping shots of local gin mixed with plant extracts. They appraised the approaching strangers.

Luciano tagged along as they approached a young man idling on the veranda of a small bungalow. The black vest he wore revealed sinewy arms speckled with heat rashes.

"I am looking for my mother," Aniete said to the man. There was no mistaking the air of indifference with which he regarded the man.

The man appeared lost. "Your mother?"

Luciano had begun to panic. He looked to Aniete but couldn't read the meaning behind the loathsome expression on his face. Just then, a woman parted a new-looking silk curtain as she emerged from a doorway. She stood for a moment like one transfixed, gazing at Aniete, and then she let out a joyous scream as she charged towards him and swept him up in a hug, lifting him a few inches off the ground. It began to make sense to Luciano; apparently the woman was Aniete's mother, even though she looked very much younger than he had thought her to be.

Her screams had attracted the neighbours so that in a short while, the compound bristled with a small crowd of women, men and children all appraising Aniete. None of them paid Luciano any attention. They commented on Aniete's sudden growth and handsomeness, and then they apologized for failing to recognize him at first when he walked past. Nobody chided him for not greeting them when he walked by them earlier.

After the excitement had died down and the neighbours returned to their business of living, Aniete's mother ushered them into the house. Luciano tagged along and sat down when Aniete did.

The sitting room was small and the cushioned armchairs, bright-coloured and cheap-looking, took up most of the floor space. The man they had earlier met on the veranda entered and settled into an armchair across from Aniete. He had an air of importance about him, like he was trying to assert his position in the scheme of things.

"You don't know him any longer, *eh*?" Aniete's mother asked the man.

"He has grown so much," was his excuse.

Luciano appraised Aniete's mother. So this is Uduak, he thought to himself. The woman who was once Chief Ofodile's cook and lover back in the days.

"Who is your friend?" she asked, taking notice of Luciano.

"He is not my friend. He said a man paid him to convince me that I am his son. Is he saying the truth?"

Uduak sized Luciano up. She adjusted in her seat, assuming the pose of a mother hen when the shadow of a hawk sweeps across.

"Mr. Man," she addressed Luciano. "Who is this man who says he is my son's father?"

Luciano smelt danger. There would be time enough to spank himself for being too stupid by walking into Aniete's snare. But for the moment, he thought it best to speak up and hope it didn't turn out as bad as he feared.

"His name is Chief Ofodile," he answered with confidence. "He lives in Port-Harcourt. He told me a story about how you became his lover when you were his cook. He said that he had had to send you away when his family was to come back home from a long holiday abroad. It was he who told me your name is Uduak." He rummaged nervously in his satchel and held out the photograph of Aniete. "He gave me this."

She stared at him, and he found himself swallowing and wiping his brow. In a flash, she snatched the photograph from his hand when he was beginning to think she wouldn't bother about it.

"How is he now? Has that his nonsense oyinbo wife left him finally?" she asked, staring at the photograph. Her voice had mellowed as her countenance; it told of a distant emotion like a dying ember in the path of a light breeze.

"Yes, and his children too. They have all left him."

She nodded. "And he is lonely. That is why he wants his second-hand son."

Luciano said nothing.

"Is he telling the truth?" Aniete cut in. "Does it mean I have a father?" He had been silently following up the conversation all the while, just like his stepfather seated like an idol cut in stone.

"Yes. The man made me pregnant and then he sent me away when it wasn't any longer convenient for him to have me around. All he did was to send me money and that was it. He was just too embarrassed to want anybody know of your existence."

"So why should I mean anything to him now?"

The defensiveness in her voice was gone when she spoke again: "Aniete, you are my son. I am not the best mother in the world and I know that I have not been a good one to you either. I know my shortcomings, but honestly, there is nothing I can do about it. And if I haven't given you any good advice before, I am giving one to you now. You should go to him and accept him. He is your father."

"Why? Why should I accept a man who has rejected me from birth?"

"You are a proud person Aniete, just like him too. Listen carefully in case you haven't noticed, the world is a very difficult place for a fatherless boy. It is even worse when you don't have money. That man, I mean your father, he is a very important man, a chief. He has money, lots of it and he needs somebody to take charge over it now he is getting old. You have to be amongst those to inherit his money and at least for once, I will not only be a rich man's mistress but a rich man's mother."

Aniete fixed her a shocked stare. "So this is all about you?"

"Don't be stupid. It is mostly about you too. You will become rich and will only have to take care of your mother. Or is that too much to ask?"

Aniete kept silent.

"So my dear," she said, facing Luciano. "When are you taking him to meet his father?"

"We were supposed to have done that a few days ago, but we will leave as soon as he is ready."

"He will be ready first thing tomorrow, you hear?"

Luciano nodded, and his face stopped short of breaking into a smile. A deep love had sprung in his heart for this spontaneous woman. "Let us get you people something to eat. Asuquo," she called the silent man. "Where is that money I gave to you to keep for me?"

"What do you want it for?" Asuquo asked.

"To cook soup for my son and his friend. I don't want them to eat the old one."

"Don't cook any soup. We are making 404 for them."

"Which of the dogs do you want to kill?"

"The useless one." He got off his seat and disappeared

into an inner room only to re-emerge seconds later, an axe in hand.

"Come and see how we kill dogs," he said to Luciano. Aniete and Luciano followed Asuquo outside.

Luciano saw the apparent reason the dog had earlier been referred to as 'useless'. It lay snoozing under the shade of a dwarfish plantain tree, its hind nestled in a hollow which it had made in the earth. Flies crowded on a sore drooping ear, but it never bothered to flap the ear to ward off the flies. But for the measured rise and fall of its belly, one would have thought it lifeless.

"It remains like this every day and night," Asuquo whispered for Luciano's benefit as they approached. "It only gets up to look for food to eat and then it goes back to sleep. It won't fuck, it won't get pregnant, it won't bear children and it won't pursue any thief."

Signaling for them to halt, Asuquo stealthily came up behind the lying dog. He raised the axe and brought it down in one savage blow on the dog's head. A spray of blood and the brain spurted into the air. The dog let out a short whimper, convulsed, and then lay still. Asuquo grinned and wiped off a spray of blood on his biceps. Luciano fought the nausea that rose to his chest. Aniete's countenance gave away no emotions; he felt his mouth water at the prospect of tasting *404* after such a long time.

For dinner, they ate pepper soup cooked with dog meat and boiled rice in the sitting room. The yellow glow of the incandescent bulb overhead lit up the room.

"You didn't ask about Eka?" Uduak asked Aniete.

"Who?"

"Have you forgotten your baby sister so soon?"

"Oh," Aniete exclaimed with indifference. He remembered the baby who deprived the whole neighbourhood of sleep and with whom he shared the same mother. "Where is she?"

"She went to stay with Asuquo's sister for some days."

"Okay."

It was a relief he wouldn't be setting eyes on her.

"You don't like *404*?" Asuquo asked Luciano. Luciano had been eating the rice but couldn't bring himself to eat the dog meat. He thought the very act barbaric, as much as doing the actual killing.

"We cook it well with *kai-kai* and plenty pepper," he explained to Luciano.

The condiments seemed to repel Luciano further. He couldn't imagine that meat could be seriously cooked with gin. "It is good for the body," Asuquo went on. "It fights against malaria and typhoid and it makes you strong like a man should be with his woman."

Luciano felt embarrassed. His embarrassment mounted as he realised that he was the only one who felt the weight of the unexpected words.

"It is your first time, but try it," Aniete urged him. "You will like it."

Emboldened by the amiable invitation, Luciano lifted a chunk of the meat in his spoon and bit into it. He had expected something gross or bland, but the spicy hotness appealed to his taste buds. He bit off a piece and chewed. The others smiled in silent commendation. Dinner continued over free-flowing conversation.

When night came Luciano lay on a mat spread out on the sitting room floor, but he couldn't sleep. Aniete's light snore and the rhythmic squeaking of the bed in the adjoining room became parts of the night. He reached for his satchel, got out his laptop, and powered it on.

It is very early in the morning, at that time when little children are still scared to venture out of their mother's huts for fear of seeing ghostly shapes. Igwemma creeps out of the house with her calabash. She plans to stay by the Sister Rivers until it is daylight when she will come home with some water so Ezenwanyi will think she went to the river much later.

She has not been able to sleep; she wants to see the woman with the crown and the princesses and all their maids and all the beautiful things. She wants to taste the wine again. The woman has told them that there will be no gathering until the full moon is over. She has to go to the Sister Rivers and sit on the bank and watch the waters in quietness.

She walks down the path that leads to the stream. She is not scared. She meets some people on the road from the stream, but she does not recognize any one of them. She sees them – women, children and men. They walk as if they're floating in the air, and they speak in a strange tongue that sounds like people whispering into hollow calabashes. They seem to talk about her as they walk past. Maybe they know her, but she doesn't know them. Some of the women are coming from the direction of the market; they bear long baskets laden with things on their heads. Some are chatting excitedly and others wear gloomy faces. Maybe they are not happy with their transaction, she thinks.

A cock crows in the distance. They all begin to hurry. The women call out to their children and the small children run excitedly behind their mothers, tugging at their wrappers and giggling excitedly in their strange fashion.

Igwemma continues her walk. She takes the straight path down the hill. She hears the murmur of the Sister Rivers; of Ahama quarrelling with Ukpokiri. She loves the sounds of the quarrelling rivers; it is beautiful music that seems to beckon to her. Her heart feels light and she breaks into a trot towards the Sister Rivers. She sees them. Their waters glitter like crystals in the fading moonlight. The noises of their quarrel are loud, very loud and she hears them clearly. She sits on the shores, her legs in the water. She hugs her legs and smiles to herself. She loves the waters, but she loves the people of the water more. She wishes she wouldn't ever have to leave this place.

She calls for Myeine the way the beautiful maid taught her to. Just call me in your heart and I will come, she told her. She calls out to her a second time, a giant ripple spreads over the calm waters. Myeine emerges from the water. Her wet hair clings to her bare shoulders and covers her naked breasts. She smiles.

"My mistress, I am at your service."

Igwemma smiles; she is happy to see Myne, her servant-friend. "I just wanted to see you and talk with you."

Myeine bows lightly.

"I was feeling lonely. I don't like to have to leave all of you people."

"It is a burden the daughters of the household have to live with every now and then."

"What about my sisters? Do they have to leave too? Do they live amongst men?"

"All of them, at one point, have lived amongst mortals, my mistress."

"Did they like their stay amongst men?"

"Their loyalty to the household comes first. I can't say for sure, only their servants can tell."

"Do you know how long I am to stay on earth?"

"I don't know, my mistress?"

"The woman with the crown, the queen, does she know?"

"I don't think so either."

"I thought she would know?"

"All we know is that you will stay for as long as it takes Ezenwanyi, your earthly mother to live. That is the covenant."

"Does she know who I am? Who I really am? I mean my mother."

"Yes. She only got to know when your sojourn amongst mortals would have ended ten seasons ago. She appeased the household with great offerings."

"What if I kill her so I return immediately?"

"You will only anger the queen."

She keeps quiet, deep in thought. *"I saw some people on my way down here. Who are they?"*

"Many things walk in the shadows, my mistress. Many things strange to the eyes of mortals, fellow custodians of the earth."

"They spoke in a strange tongue and they hurried on when the first cock crowed."

"Oh! They are the lost souls. They dwell in trees and hidden caves, both great and small. They are never sacrificed to and they only strike fear in the hearts of men and children."

"Are you saying they are not powerful?"

"They are as much powerful as they can wield the weapon of fear."

"Can't they strike men dead?"

"Men are very powerful beings, my mistress. The Creator made them so and gave them very great powers. Their ignorance is also our fortune."

"Why did The Creator make them so? Why did He give them great powers?"

"He is partial to them. I think He loves them."

"Who is The Creator?"

"The never-ending source of everything. He made all and created boundaries. Everything is sustained by Him."

"Have you seen Him?"

"My mistress, it isn't safe here anymore. I will have to leave, if you won't count it against me. It is my pleasure being of service to you."

Myeine dives into the water. A great tail fin beats the waters, dividing it in two. All is quiet again. The moon has disappeared and the sky is beginning to look ashen with the approaching dawn.

Igwemma reaches for her calabash, to fetch some water. She does not notice the fear-stricken hunter concealed behind a raffia palm, watching everything.

Luciano shut down the laptop and let out a suppressed yawn. His shoulders ached from lying propped up on his elbow, and his eyes felt like they had grains of sand in them. The night would be far gone, he thought. The squeaking from the adjoining room had long died out. In its place was a fierce snoring competition, as though two contestants were intent on outdoing each other. He stashed the laptop into the satchel, snuck the precious parcel under the cushioned chair closest to his head and snuggled into the neat but threadbare sheets given them for the night, using one of the chair cushions for a pillow. It all seemed quiet and peaceful. He let out a sigh and shut his eyes, beckoning on sleep to come.

"I'm sorry."

His eyes flew open. He thought Aniete was talking in his sleep, but the voice didn't sound dreamy. Could it be that the boy had been awake while he was working on *Igwemma*? Had he been too carried away to not have noticed the boy had ceased snoring?

"What for?" he asked in a hushed tone, turning his mouth away so his foul breath didn't hit Aniete in the face.

"I am sorry if you feel played."

"I understand your paranoia and lack of trust. It is an occupational hazard with you."

"What do you mean?"

"There wasn't water in my mouth when I spoke."

They both fell silent. The background snoring complemented the sound of their breathing.

"I am not a criminal, you know," Aniete said.

"Yes. I know."

"I did what I had to do because I needed money."

"I never judged you."

"Thank you."

Luciano didn't answer. He was spent, the way he always felt after a spell of intense work on a story. He shut his eyes again, willing sleep to come, but it was becoming apparent that he was in for a long wait.

Aniete took a deep breath. "The book you are writing, it seems … unusual. Very different."

"Do you really have a taste for literary works?" he asked.

"I read sometimes."

"What sort of books do you read?"

"I can't say for sure. Anything new and interesting."

Luciano fell silent again. "The story, what is it all about?"

Luciano opened his eyes, staring into the dark void of the room. "It is a work of fiction, magical realism to be precise. I know of only one Nigerian writer, Ben Okri, who has done something of the sort with his book, *The Famished Road*. Soyinka did the same with his poem *Abiku*." Luciano found himself talking in subdued excitement. "My book is about a girl. She is mammywater, but doesn't know it. When she finds out who she really is, she comes to despise the world of men and begins to harbour a strong desire to return to the water world."

"Did she return?"

"I don't know."

"But you are the writer. You should know."

"To be honest with you, I thought I knew the end before, but I am re-writing most parts of the story, especially towards the ending. I go after a story idea without a view of the end. I just follow whatever path a story leads onto."

"This sounds weird, but I guess it is your thing and you understand it better."

"Every writer has a technique that best works for them. I enjoy groping in the dark."

"I am scared of the dark myself."

Luciano chuckled. "Figuratively?"

"For real. You should even see how scared I am now with this mammywater story you just told. I am scared that I may have a nightmare."

"Are you being serious?"

"Yes. When I was a child, *Willy Willy* made me hide behind the couch when it played on Thursday evenings. You know, you couldn't escape it then. Even though you didn't turn on your TV, every of your neighbours did, so you just couldn't shut out the scary soundtrack from your ears. If you chose to go out in the streets, you would hardly find anyone outside, because everyone would be watching *Willy Willy* in their homes."

Luciano laughed into the sheets. He had forgotten about the weakness in his eyes and body. "It is surprising to know a tough guy like you would be scared of childish things."

It was Aniete's turn to laugh. He did so softly, careful not to be loud.

"Well, I think it was Shakespeare who said it is the eye of childhood that fears a painted devil," Luciano said.

"But those things, are they real?"

"What things?"

"Ghosts, mammywater, ogbanje."

"Well, I don't know. We have heard too many testimonies about their existence, until they have come to stick onto our minds."

"Are you saying they are not real?"

"I didn't say so. I just don't know."

"I believe ghosts to be real"

"What are your reasons?"

"When I was a child, there was this neighbour who lived with his wife in the flat next to ours. She died one day; we didn't know what killed her. Her corpse was taken to her hometown and buried. Many months later, news came to her husband that his dead wife ran a prosperous restaurant in Mbiama. Her husband doubted it, but his kinsman who had brought him the news took him there to see for himself. And just as they had said, it was his wife that the man saw. She saw him too and fled. That was the end. They never heard of her again."

Luciano fell silent for a moment. "You believe the story?"

"The husband was our neighbour."

"Hmm. This is interesting."

"You don't believe it?"

"There are many unanswered questions on this earth," Luciano said. "Seeking for answers is a journey few men are willing to undertake."

Aniete didn't answer. "Aniete."

"Yes."

"Oh, I thought you have slept off."

"No. I was thinking?"

"About what?"

"You."

"Me?"

"Yes."

"What about me?"

"Why did you take on this job to come look for me?"

"Why wouldn't I?"

"You don't strike me as a policeman or anything of the sort, not even one with criminal tendencies. You are only a little sharp. Moreover, you are just inexperienced."

"Thank God your father hadn't taken it to heart when I pointed out my shortcomings to him."

"But then, you went ahead with it even when you found out what risks you were faced with."

"I needed money. I still do. I need to publish my manuscripts, and your father is willing to pay."

"How much is it?"

"It doesn't matter. What matters is that your father is paying me."

"Why did you choose to become a writer? I have never known a rich writer. They all look introverted, poor and melancholy, and many of them look like they have yet to make up their minds whether to commit suicide or to hang on a little while longer."

"Those traits are not unique to writers, my dear. Given that there are many poets who are melancholy, there are melancholy doctors and poor lawyers and suicidal businessmen too."

"But why did you choose writing?"

"I never chose it. It stood pure and true beside me when every other option had failed me."

"Don't you want to be rich?"

"Sure, I do. But I seek a wide audience for my works too. True riches, to me, go beyond having to bother about building an electric fence around a huge pile of money."

"Well, I don't seem to understand you."

"Just let it be."

"Yea. I will take your advice. I will let it be."

A cock crowed in the distance. Another one answered farther away.

"It is nearly morning," Luciano observed. "Good night."

"But you just said it is morning, yet you say *good night*."

"Just shut up and sleep."

"Arrogant, suicidal writer," Aniete muttered under his breath as he turned away from Luciano. Luciano chuckled, and they slept off.

THIRTY-THREE

Igwemma is dreaming. In her dream she is standing by the river. She sees the woman with the crown; she is standing with her feet in the water. She looks fierce and cross. Igwemma doesn't see her sisters, she doesn't see Myeine. It is only the woman with the crown.

"I commanded you not to show yourselves! I gave an order and you flouted it. How dare you?" Her voice sounds like the rumble of distant thunder. The wind howls around her as she speaks. Her eyes look like the red-hot metals in the village blacksmith's furnace.

"Queen Mother, I am sorry. I only needed company. I was bored."

"You have no excuses. You must prove your worth on your earthly sojourn else you are unworthy to take your crown amongst royalty."

"Queen Mother, I won't do it again."

"I will make sure you don't! You are not to see the kingdom for seven seasons!"

"Please, great queen," Igwemma pleads, falling to her knees.
"Please have mercy on me."

"You are still entitled to the company of your servant
Myeine, but that will be the extent of your privileges until the
seven seasons are over."

"Please have mercy."

She doesn't see the queen anymore. She has gone with the
wind. Igwemma is crying. She falls to the ground and rolls in the
sands. She cries and cries.

And then she wakes up with tears streaming down her face.

Uduak roused them. "Wake up! Wake up!" They sat up
on the mat, rubbing their eyes, stretching and yawning.
"It is morning. I've made breakfast. Are you bathing cold
or hot water?"

"Good morning," Luciano said. His eyes looked
wild with the struggle to stay awake.

"Good morning," Aniete said, rubbing his eyes.

She didn't acknowledge their greetings. "It is
morning. Go and take a bath, you have a journey ahead
of you."

Luciano bathed first.

Uduak had led him to the bathroom; a confinement
made of tarpaulin wrapped around four stakes driven

into the ground to form a square frame. It had a big rotting plank for a door. A similar structure stood by the bathroom. It was a pit latrine. The sight of the whiffs of smoke wafting from the gaping pit had stayed Luciano's desire to defecate.

He bathed hurriedly with the perfumed soap Uduak had given him; he didn't want to create the impression that he took so long in the bathroom. Aniete bathed next while Luciano waited in the sitting room nursing a bowl of steaming *jollof* rice with two metal spoons sticking out of it. He guessed the pieces of meat with which the food was garnish were remnants of yesterday's dog.

Aniete returned from the bathroom, dressed and settled down for breakfast on the cushioned chair, besides Luciano. Uduak sat across from them.

"What happened to your ear?" she asked, noticing his chipped right ear for the first time.

Aniete's hand reached instinctively for his ear. "Nothing. Just a small accident. Where is Asuquo?" he asked in pidgin.

"He left early to see somebody who owes him money. When will you come again?"

"I don't know?" Aniete said.

"You won't come to see your mother again? You don't know you have become a big man now?"

"I will come."

"Are you sure?"

330

"Yes," he answered before spooning some rice into his mouth.

"You will buy a big house for me?" she asked, and when he shook his head, she frowned. "Why not?"

He swallowed. "Why did you lie to me that my father is dead?"

"What did you expect me to do under the circumstance? I was protecting you from rejection. He didn't want you at the time."

"Why did you get pregnant for a man who wouldn't want the child?"

"My son, that one is one long story I don't want to talk about at the moment."

"But I want to hear it."

She heaved a sigh, re-arranged the folds of her wrapper around her plump thighs and then sat back into the chair as she began to narrate how as a teenager she had worked as a live-in maid in a household. How she ran away when the man of the house tried to rape her. How she lived off the benevolence of lovers who were married men until fed up, she had gone searching for a job. How she ended up in Chief Ofodile's employ as a cook, and soon afterwards becoming his comforter in his vulnerable moments until she began to share his bed.

THIRTY-FOUR

The bus bound for Port-Harcourt travelled at a fair speed along the interstate highway.

Luciano wished the driver would go faster. He had notified Chief Ofodile on their current progress but left out the trip to Ikot-Abasi. He fought the sleepiness that was spreading over him; it had already claimed Aniete who was seated beside him. His folded arms against the backrest of the seat in front was his makeshift pillow.

The driver suddenly stepped hard on the brakes, causing the passengers to lurch forward in their seats. He swerved widely to his right to keep the screeching bus from ramming into the black BMW SUV in front whose driver had braked suddenly on sighting a large pothole. The passengers screamed, "Jesus! Blood of Jesus! Holy Ghost fire!" as the driver struggled to gain control. When the bus finally came to a halt and the fear gone, everyone began to analyze the near-accident; the SUV's brake lights hadn't been functional and so the bus driver had noticed a bit late that the vehicle wasn't in motion. The driver of the offending BMW had continued, speeding away into the distance and oblivious of the near-crash he had caused. The bus driver stepped on the accelerator in hot pursuit, paying deaf ears to his passengers' pleadings, curses and threats for him to slow down. He caught up with the BMW.

"Thunder fire your generation!" he screamed into the driver's startled face when he had drawn abreast him, flashing him his open palm. The BMW driver returned the gesture and then concentrated on the road ahead. "Na God go punish you, bastard!" the driver cursed again, and then daringly overtook the man in such a way that made him swerve sharply to avoid a brush with the scratchy bus. He sped up, leaving the BMW driver far behind. As though the incidence had loosened some restraints in him, he sped along, swerving to the left and right as he dodged the many potholes that riddled the highway. The passengers gave up the idea of pleading with him to slow down, for it had become clear he was bent on ignoring their pleas. A few relaxed, elated they would likely get to their destination earlier, but most of the women were unsettled. A woman mumbled prayers and fingered her rosary.

Igwemma sulks all day. She refuses to do anything in the house but would go and sit alone by herself beside the river.

It is evening. She is seated by the river. The other girls are washing up the river. They are looking surreptitiously at her and she knows it; she doesn't care. They have all been avoiding her. Her clay pot lies beside her on the sand; she has come to fetch water, but Mama would have to wait. She doesn't want to go home, not while it isn't yet dark. A wind blows from the Sister Rivers, bringing to her ears their quarrelsome murmur. She longs to see Myeine, she longs to visit the household again, to see all the beauty and splendour. If only the woman with the crown can pardon her. The past two moons have been like many seasons.

The troublemaker comes along, humming a tune a bit too loudly and swinging her hips with every step. Everybody knows her. They either seek to be in good terms with her or avoid her; she fears none, respects none and picks fights and quarrels wherever she meets with those whom she feels are in need for some humiliation. She has no friends, for mothers dared not see any of their daughters in the company of the disrespectful Nwodoro. That bad daughter of Nnedi will never amount to any good, the women sometimes say to her back. They too are afraid of her because she beats women old enough to be her mother, too. The men are also cautious not to get into a word-battle with Nwodoro; no man wants to be humiliated by a disrespectful girl. The judgment itself will be a public disgrace in itself, an indelible stigma which will make tongues wag for many seasons to come.

She walks up the sands. She pads noisily into the water,

close enough to the melancholy Igwemma. She kicks up the water so that it splashes on Igwemma. Igwemma looks up at her. She doesn't meet Igwemma's gaze but sings the tune she was humming. Igwemma recognizes the popular lyrics:

The one who gets heartache at my deeds

May she die of heartache

Begrudging he-goat

May she die of heartache...

Nwodoro wags her stiff hips as she fills her claypot. She hefts the full pot to her head and wades out of the river, still humming. It is not in any way by accident, but Nwodoro tilts her full pot slightly so that some of the water splashes onto Igwemma's braided hair. Nwodoro pretends not to notice but continues walking away. She doesn't know that Igwemma has sprung to her feet and is charging at her from behind like an angered ram. She pushes Nwodoro hard, sending her stumbling forward. Her clay pot falls on the sand. The water gushes from its small mouth in spurts. Nwodoro recovers from the fall and charges towards Igwemma in retaliation. They clash and fall to the ground, grunting, slapping, and clawing at each other's hair. The other girls down the river have abandoned their washing. They gathered around the fighting girls, enjoying the fight. They will absorb every detail of the fight so as not to miss out any part in later gossips. The fighters roll in the sand. They fight determinedly as though their lives depends on the outcome of the fight; this fighter would be on top the other this moment and the next moment, by sheer will, the other will get the upper hand. It seems like the fight will go on forever, with nobody winning or willing to give up until Igwemma sinks her teeth into Nwodoro's forearm. Nwodoro's cry reverberates through the forest of raffia palms that border the rivers, but Igwemma doesn't let go. She sinks her teeth deeper and deeper and Nwodoro's cry rings louder and louder as she begs for help from the bystanders. Igwemma's teeth get tinted with the red of the troublemaker's blood. The other girls see the blood and they intervene, but they don't know how to break the fight now, with one person's teeth sunk into another's flesh.

They say, "Igwemma, biko let her go."

They say, "You will kill her o".

The empathy is evident in their voices. For the first time, they get to feel something other than dread for the troublemaker. Some have begun to shed tears at the sight of the blood trailing down the arm of the screaming girl.

They plead and plead until Igwemma lets go. Nwodoro gets off the ground and flees homewards, clutching her bloody arm. The other girls keep their distance from Igwemma. They break away from her. She looks like nothing they have seen before; the sand in her dishevelled hair, the bloodied scratches on her face, the blood stains on her lips, the ferocity in her eyes. She doesn't care; she walks away from them, towards the path winding uphill amongst the dense raffia trees. She is going home without her clay pot. She licks her lips. She likes the taste of Nwodoro's blood. It tastes nearly like the wine she drank with her sisters, the wine she loves. She wants some more to quell her rising appetite. She walks home, but she cannot stop thinking about the troublemaker's sweet blood. Just a little honey to it and her seasons of exile will be made much easier, she reasons.

We're on our way 2 PH. Expected to arrive in about an hour.

He hit the 'Send' button. But moments later, when his phone beeped, he startled. The incoming message read:

Good news. I'll be waiting at Eleme Junction.

Luciano pocketed the phone and exhaled, elated that the adventures of the past few days had come to an end.

Aniete still snoozed beside him. Luciano turned his attention to the plans for the money. Once more, he went through them in detail and realized that he hadn't planned farther than having *Igwemma* in print. He gave up the mental exercise, adjusted in his seat and then settled for the scenery fleeting past. He thought how much of his recent frustrations had fleeted past just like the scenery of lush vegetation. And then he thought of Oge. Ah, Oge!

He hadn't had much success with women; there hadn't been any more than three of them in his life. Of them all, Oge had been with him the longest. She had actually stolen his heart, and then shattered it; at least that was the safest way to put her disavowing of him. He wouldn't blame her; she was a woman after all, and one who had loved with high hopes and great expectations.

He only wished it had not turned out the way it did; that she had not been pressured by the demands of society to live with no ambitions other than getting married and bearing children. He had loved her. She had been his Rachel, his Abigail, Cleopatra, but only when she still had faith in him.

THIRTY-FIVE

The village is thrown into mourning. Everybody is afraid; maybe some evil has been let loose on the land. Maybe someone had committed some great ill, some taboo of some kind, to anger the gods. What offence could it be? Nobody can tell. Nobody can tell if the offence had been incest, or something more grievous. Maybe it was a theft of some sort or some great injustice to a stranger, an orphan or widow. Was it committed by man, woman, or child? Nobody knows. The elders have embarked on a journey very early that morning to see the Afa priest. He will tell them the answers and solutions to stop the mysterious deaths.

First, it was Nwodoro. She had been found lying lifeless in the bushes where she had gone to fetch firewood. Nnedi, her mother, has refused to be comforted. She wails and cries, rolling in the sand in grief for the death of her troublesome daughter. She has forgotten all about the troubles her daughter brings home with her every day; how mothers would come banging on her bamboo door almost every evening with complaints of what damage Nwodoro had done to their daughters' faces. Everyone is quick to believe that it is the Amaoza people at it again, but while the Amaoza people were yet taking an oath of innocence in the market square, a small girl was found dead in the bushes.

Everyone is stricken with panic. A curse has been let loose, they say. Everybody dreads the bushes and the farmlands. Nobody, small or big, ventures away from their compounds without the company of another grown man armed with a sharp machete.

Igwemma is scared too. She lies in her bamboo bed, even though it is morning. Ezenwanyi has forbidden her to go out to fetch water because of the unknown evil that kills young girls.

She hasn't been able to stop herself from doing it. The taste of blood is too overpowering, and she has succumbed. She attacked Nwodoro with a piece of rock when the girl was bent over, tying her bundle of firewood. Nwodoro fell lifeless to the ground with one blow of the rock to the back of her head. She slit the girl's wrist with the small knife she had earlier stuck in the fold of her wrapper. Her blood tasted warm and sweet. Only if she brought some honey. She lured the second girl to come and pick udara with her in the bush. She killed the little girl and drank her blood too. She doesn't like the pains she caused the mothers. She doesn't like it that the village is in panic, but the taste of the blood comforts her. She is scared too, scared of the beginning of the longing for a taste of blood yet again.

"Are you having 'iba'?"Ezenwanyi asks. Igwemma is startled; she didn't see Ezenwanyi come into the hut.

"No."

"Are you sure?"

"I don't have 'iba'?"

"I have warmed the pottage. You can take yours in the pot when you are ready to eat. I am going to Oyiriugo's house. If anybody comes looking for me, tell them to meet me there."

"Ngwanu."

Ezenwanyi leaves the hut. Igwemma bites her nails and spits out the bits. An idea hits her. She gets off the bed. She will visit the river now Mama is leaving to gossip in her friend's house. She knew Mama, an ardent gossip, who will not return until late in the evening, especially now there is some juicy news in the village to nibble at.

Igwemma leaves the house for the Sister Rivers. She will stay at the banks until that time when the sun hangs high up in the sky, and then she will walk home before Mama returned from Oyiriugo's house.

Chief Ofodile stole a glance in the rearview mirror at the passenger in the backseat. So this was him, he thought to himself. The young man, Aniete, was looking out the window, a distant look on his face. Chief Ofodile had earlier been confronted with a riot of feelings at the prospect of getting to meet with his grown son for the first time. But as the hour drew nearer, everything narrowed down to a bout of panic so strong his hands shook as he waited in his car for their bus to arrive. It felt like a day not long ago when he had delivered ransom money for the release of a friend; his hands had shaken just like that while he prayed silently for his heart not to give in.

They both had identical ear, except that Aniete had his right one chipped. He also recognized in the young man the strides of Udoka his cousin who had returned from a German prison ten years ago, insane, and then died shortly afterwards from some inexplicable health complication.

Aniete hadn't said anything. Not even a word had escaped his lips as they rode in Chief Ofodile's car. So this is the man who had sired him, he kept thinking. The man whom he had presumed dead a long time ago. He felt nothing, no emotions at all on seeing the man they said was his father. He was surprised to see that the man drove himself and, Luciano and his mother were keen on making him believe the man was royalty; the type who would have fleet of cars, and not a single Nissan, waiting to give his new-found son a colourful reception complete with traditional dance troupes and lavish feasting.

Luciano had observed the cold re-union of father and son. It was a story which, if written by him, would sound so ridiculous and implausible that he wouldn't dare seek an audience for it. He had watched the boy clamber into the car without a word in greeting to Chief Ofodile, his biological father. Chief Ofodile hadn't reacted. Instead, the old man had waited for them to climb into the car and then he turned the key in the ignition and drove off, like some hired chauffeur. As the big car moved leisurely along, Luciano looked out of the window to his side, in a bid to escape the tension in the car. They were driving along the flyover at Eleme junction. He peered down the maze of roads below and at the people walking past. They appeared tiny, like soldier ants furtively walking along, striving towards things which mortal men lack the patience to understand.

Eleme junction appeared to be a simple network of roads, but it was one part of Port-Harcourt he still hadn't brought himself to master. He was enjoying the view and the light breeze blowing in his face through the window when the screeching of tyres caused his heart to skip a beat.

A round of automatic gunfire rent the air just as a Chevrolet SUV double-crossed them in a nerve-wracking screech of tyres against asphalt. Panic struck as cars screeched to a halt, bumping against each other. Drivers fled their cars and some others yet at safe distances changed gears in quick reverse. Another round of gunshots rent the air and two men jumped out of the Chevrolet, brandishing AK-47 rifles; one was short with bowlegs and the other, tall and slender. They hurried towards the Nissan with their guns at the ready. The short one sporting a pair of big, white canvas shoes pulled open the door on Aniete's side.

"Come on, come out!" he ordered Aniete who had his hands in the air as much as the car roof could allow. He made to come out but the impatient gunman roughened him out and shoved him onto the hot asphalt.

"Shebi you be Rambo? You no dey die abi?" he said, training the rifle at Aniete while his tall mate stood aloof, his alert eyes scanning about the perimeter for the slightest hint of interference. There was none. Nigerians love their lives so much to interfere with gunmen's business; the flyover looked deserted and people below were scampering to safety. Chief Ofodile cowered behind the steering wheel, stunned. Luciano, scared out of his wits, managed to feel grateful that the gunmen had a particular target which fortunately wasn't him.

The back door of the Chevrolet opened and Mezkana eased out of the car. His ankle and the index finger of his left hand were swaddled thick with bandages. A denim satchel hung across from his left shoulder. Limping on a black cane, he approached Aniete, wide-eyed with fear.

"Put his head on the ground!" he ordered. The short gunman slung his rifle across his back and hurriedly set out to do Mezkana's bidding. Mezkana transferred his walking stick to his armpit, and reached inside the satchel. When he withdrew his hand, he had a small axe in it. The sharpened edge gleamed in the sunlight. Aniete put up some resistance at the thought of his head being chopped off, but the short fellow had him pinned down. "If he gives you any troubles, put two bullets in his ankle and two in his hand," Mezkana ordered.

The short man eagerly set out to unsling his rifle.

"Ikuku!"

Mezkana turned sharply in the direction of the Nissan. "Ikuku!"

"Onwa? What are you doing here?"

"Ikuku, please. He is my boy," Chief Ofodile pleaded. His confidence had returned, even though he shook visibly. He stepped out of the car.

"Are you ..."

"Chairman," the tall thug called. "There is movement around. We have to move out now."

True enough, the ground below was beginning to bustle with renewed activity; the police, maybe.

"We will sort this out at your place," Mezkana said, and then began hobbling towards the waiting Chevrolet. The gunmen covered him. Chief Ofodile stood transfixed as though he was trying to come to terms with the beheading that he would have witnessed.

Just before his thugs helped him into the waiting Chevrolet, Mezkana turned to face Chief Ofodile. "Can I still trust you?"

A rattled Chief Ofodile nodded. The Chevrolet screeched away down the flyover, with the gunmen releasing sporadic gunfire into the air. Chief Ofodile ran over to Aniete, helped him onto his feet and into the car. It was their first bodily contact, ever.

Luciano's heart still thumped hard against his ribs. He thought he could hear the surging blood in his ears. This was another close brush with danger and he sincerely hoped for it to be the last. He would distance himself from this crazy man and his son; they seemed to attract danger wherever they went, like flies to faeces. They were cut out for the kind of troubled existence which he wasn't.

THIRTY-SIX

The thunder still rumbles in the dark, cloudy skies above. It appears the skies aren't yet satisfied with drenching the world with torrential rains. It drizzles lightly. It rained all noon and now that the earth has taken its fill of water, little streams flow along the footpaths in tiny gullies. A streak of lightning flashes across the skies, briefly illuminating the world in a dangerous flash of white light. Igwemma smacks her lips and ducks. The deafening sound of thunder strikes in the distance. Amadioha, the god of thunder might have executed some justice with his infamous bolt of lightning, she thinks. It is a good thing that she isn't on the temperamental god's list. Obviously, it hasn't come to her turn yet; maybe it will never come to her turn while she still has the queen to intercede on her behalf. Another streak of lightning flashes and she smacks her lips again, the way she has come to know as a child; people said it stops the lightning from striking one.

Igwemma is walking down the slippery wet path. She has been walking all morning. When the rain started she didn't seek any shelter. Little beads of rainwater stand out with the goose pimples on her skin. She shivers now and then and hugs herself as her teeth clatter. She is cold but keeps on walking, away from the village. She isn't sure, she hasn't ventured this far away, but she has heard that this path leads to the shrine of Idemili far away in Ubiino. She once heard that it is across three rivers, on the other side of the dreaded valley which gets flooded with fast-moving currents of water that sweeps along logs of wood and broken branches whenever it rains even for a short while. She is going there with a plea; she hopes Idemili will help her win the queen's forgiveness, even though she doesn't know how. She wants to leave the world of mortal men forever, and never to return again, because she is afraid. She is afraid of what the villagers will do to her when the elders return from the Afa priest's. She doesn't want to think of the things they will do to her when they learn she is the cause of those two deaths.

The thunder rumbles overhead again. She looks at the sky; the clouds are moving to the right across the sky as though they are summoned by Amadioha or whichever of the gods claims the territory of the vast skies. They are moving hastily, but the sky is not getting clear. Another flash of lightning strikes against her path. She smacks her lips and ducks away from the path, hugging the bushes on the edges of the path.

Taa! Taa! the thunder strikes. It is the sound of a strong man splitting the wood of an oilbean tree with a great sharpened axe. The slender over-hanging branch of a whistling pine by the path ahead falls off the tree and onto the path. Igwemma's heart *lurches. She is scared. This might be an omen. She turns into the bushes. She will have to cut through the bushes, away from the path where Amadioha's careless messenger might be travelling along on some errand.*

She doesn't like the wet leaves brushing against her bare body and her face. They irritate her senses and make her skin itch. The undergrowth is slippery with the wetness too, and she has to travel slowly to avoid slipping and falling. She will endure it all to keep safe and alive on her long journey. She is beginning to feel hungry. She didn't prepared for this journey; she fled when the panic overtake her. She has no food and water; she hopes to come by some wild fruits along the way.

It has begun to rain again. She sticks out her tongue, tilts her head back to catch the drops of water falling like blunt pins. The bushes have become denser; she parts the leaves as she proceeds. She blames herself. If there is anything she shouldn't have forgotten to bring along, it is a machete or a knife.

She continues.

She doesn't know it, but she has become a wanderer.

The rain continues, the daylight begins to fade, gradually and with disregard for the safety of a cold, hungry and lonely beautiful girl wandering alone in the thick of the bushes and for a destination very far away; a place whose existence she has only heard of in stories.

"It beats my imagination that someone like you would have such a cold-hearted son."

"One cannot always dictate what he gets to be blessed or cursed with," Chief Ofodile replied.

Luciano looked on, observing the men talk in tones that told of seasoned familiarity. They were in the sitting room of Chief Ofodile's house. Mezkana had come without the company of his misfit thugs. They had all listened to Chief Ofodile narrate his romantic relationship with his cook and house help with the outcome of the son whose existence had been much of an inconvenience to him until a short while ago when all he held dear had crumbled into hopelessness. Aniete, from his seat high on a bar stool, listened to his own history as he sipped straight from a bottle of Moet.

"This boy, your son," Mezkana said without looking in Aniete's direction, "is the brains behind my kidnap."

Chief Ofodile looked at Aniete with disbelief. "That kidnap?" he asked, and turned to Mezkana.

"Yes, you can ask him. He is the one who shot me in the leg and wasted my finger." He held up his bandaged finger. Chief Ofodile stole a momentary glance at the boy taking a swig from the half-empty bottle.

"I will return the money," Chief Ofodile promised Mezkana.

Mezkana mulled over the offer in his mind. "I'd have accepted, but considering our friendship and your sacrifice at the time, let's just say that one good act from the same blood canceled out the evil act. After all, had you not helped out immediately, your son would have executed me without any reservations."

"I can't thank you enough."

"You don't need to. We are even now, at least I no longer owe you from that day in Toronto."

Chief Ofodile laughed nervously. It had been a long time ago, but he vividly remembered that morning in North Vancouver when Mezkhana went on his first visit to Canada to establish contacts with a local drug cartel, but had run into a trap instead. It was Ofodile, a delivery truck driver at the time, who sensed a total stranger in trouble and smuggled him out of the spot in his van. A friendship began right away - one that endured even as Mezkhana returned to South Africa the next day and, many months later, Ofodile flew back to Nigeria. "I hope you find some fulfillment in this boy?"

"I will try," Chief Ofodile replied.

"I have some valuable information for you, sir, as restitution for my offenses," Aniete told Mezkana. It was the first time he had spoken that evening.

"And what would that be?" Mezkana enquired, a hint of apprehension evident in his countenance. It appeared the thirst for vendetta hadn't cleared away from his mind, at least not totally.

"I could give you the others involved in the kidnap."

"And why do you think I will be interested?"

"I don't know. For me it is restitution."

"Why are you snitching on your colleagues? What's in it for you? Tell me."

"One of them wants me dead."

"Why would they want you dead? You double-crossed them or something?"

"No. A third party betrayed us, and then set us against each other."

Mezkana nodded knowingly. "I'm aware."

"I am not surprised," Aniete said. "Because I am sure that that is the only way you could have gotten to me."

"Never mind. I know your worry, I will sort it out."

"I could give you information on this fellow's schedules. He is their leader."

"I have it already."

"No, you don't sir. If you had, you would have nailed him already."

Mezkana regarded Aniete silently for a while like a man weighing his options before making an important decision. He was clearly a man who never liked being challenged especially when it came to the profession of tracking and hacking down people.

Finally he said, "Let me see what intel you've got."

"Only on Wednesdays and Fridays does he come for his lectures in the Architecture Studio, from ten in the morning to one o'clock. But on Sunday afternoons, you can find him practising in the old studio, the last in the studio halls. He will always be alone then, except for a handful of his boys hanging about in the open premises. You will normally mistake them for ordinary students idling away a lonely Sunday afternoon. That is his most vulnerable moment. Another option would be to storm his hideout, an abandoned fenced-in house in Orji, but then you will have to go in with an infantry because not only are there always sentinels about the place, but there are more options for him to escape, unlike the studios with only one door and burglary-proofed windows. Any option other than the studio will be a big gamble because this guy we are talking about is the wind."

All eyes in the room refused to leave Aniete even after he finished speaking.

"If I should consider living up the old days, I will surely have you close," Mezkana said at last. He stood to his feet.

"I won't need to live that dangerously. Luciano here tells me that my old man is rich."

Mezkana stood to his full height, leaning on his cane. He turned to Chief Ofodile and said, "Onwa, my good friend, you have a son whose criminal tendencies will avail much for good as long as he is fed and satisfied. I envy you."

Chief Ofodile laughed like someone flattered. He rose to his feet and clasped his friend's good hand in a firm handshake. They made for the door.

Aniete continued with his drink.

Luciano patted his satchel. The feel of his laptop was comforting. He ran his palm along the satchel as though soothing it. *Don't worry*, he seemed to say to the laptop in the satchel. *Everything is almost alright.* He would wait for Chief Ofodile to return from escorting his friend and then they would discuss his payment. Getting *Igwemma* published was all that had mattered to him. It still did. He had come a long way and the future now looked certain.

THIRTY-SEVEN

Ezenwanyi's pounding can be heard from the distance. She is making dinner, even though it is not yet dusk. She makes dinner very early ever since Igwemma's disappearance.

Igwemma, she sighs. A teardrop rolls down her cheek and into the ukazi leaves she is mashing in the wooden mortar. She loosens the edge of her wrapper and dabs at the wet trail on her cheek. She has always caught herself shedding tears since two moons ago when she came home to meet her daughter's absence; the girl was acting strangely a few days before her disappearance. On coming home that evening she thought Igwemma had gone out to the river to while away her time; she had earlier got the news that Igwemma used to stare into the waters of the Sister Rivers for hours. Some speculated that Igwemma was a mammywater. Ezenwanyi didn't pay any attention to such gossips. She had given many more offerings to the water goddess not to take back her blessing, Igwemma, while she still lived. When Igwemma disappeared, she laid gifts of eggs, clay, and hens by the riverside as offering to the water goddess, but nothing happened.

Many gossips are beginning to trail her as she walks to the stream and to the market. She is beginning to feel childless. She goes to the river to fetch water, to the bushes to get firewood, sweeps the compound, washes her clothes, feeds the hens and goes to her neighbours' homes to collect live coals for making fire; all the tasks which Igwemma used to do. She overheard a man in the market square talking about the famous travelling maiden who had once stopped by his village many miles away. He regaled his listeners with tales of the travelling maiden's charming beauty and her fearlessness, and his listeners listened on, enchanted by the tale. Ezenwanyi waited patiently until the man stood up to leave. She approached him when he walked away, out of sight of his listeners.

"Please tell me about this maiden you talk about," she told him.

"She still remains the most beautiful thing that walked the earth in my village."

"Does she have a name? Did she give any?"

"No. Nobody ever has the patience to ask her name. Wherever she goes, the people are so enchanted by her beauty that they name her as they are inspired. We called her 'mkpuru mmiri' when she travelled by my village."

And Ezenwanyi left.

She knows it is Igwemma. She feels happy and comforted that at least Igwema is alive. Still, she can't keep from shedding tears whenever thoughts of her beautiful daughter cross her mind. She once thought her daughter was ravaged by the mysterious *death that swept through the village at the time when she disappeared. The elders came back with no news from the Afa priest's. They only suggested an elaborate offering to all the gods and their ancestors; perchance they would appease the aggrieved one amongst them. The sacrifices were made, and a costly one it was. It seemed the elders were wise, for gradually, life returned to normalcy after many market weeks passed without the deaths recurring.*

So Igwemma is now a wanderer. Ezenwanyi can't stop from wondering most times; she must have taken over from her father. She still remembers that handsome young traveler who left her body still yearning for him all these many long years. She still wishes to see him again. In her heart, she will always wait for him, to set eyes on him again, to see how much change age has done to his handsome features as it has done hers. She is getting old, but she is learning to be patient in waiting for both lover and daughter to come walking into the compound someday.

The old architecture studio bespoke total neglect. Thick films of dust covered every surface: the burglary-proofed windows, the chipped linoleum and all the broken drafting tables stacked haphazardly like some massive wreckage at one end of the studio hall. The studio blocks had been abandoned some eight months back when the Vice Chancellor commissioned the new three-storey Faculty of Environmental Studies building that housed six modern architectural studios. The old studios had then been converted to storerooms for broken furniture and fixtures.

At one end of the studio, Nku sat on a high stool, hunched over a drafting paper spread on a drafting table. The window louvers were open to let in fresh air. It was a Sunday afternoon when every one of the halls on campus served as a venue for Christian gatherings. He liked studying in the dusty studios on Sundays; the distant clapping and singing of the worshipers was music to his ears. Secondly, the place was always deserted at this time except when you ventured into the new studio halls. And it was the seclusion that appealed to him the most. It made the job easier for the four boys watching outside.

There were times he wished for the life of the ordinary student, for then he would have been bothered with nothing other than tests and exams, nightclubs and hostel parties, and the hottest girls on campus. Campus fraternities had held a strong appeal for him when he was but a boy in the village. Back home, the younger boys revered the university guys who had risen through the ranks of The Black Axe, Vikings and Buccaneers confraternities. They would covet the air of invincibility with which the frat boys carried themselves. Those times, he had his eyes on the Vikings because of their reputation for ruggedness. And they said you had better chances of landing jobs as a Norseman when you graduated and became a Lord.

In his freshman year, he lived up his wishes, and it was with the Blue Hood he pitched his tent. On the night of initiation, he recalled, the full moon stood out in the sky. Blindfolded, his sponsor led him along a path in a thick bush, and when the blindfold was removed, he saw himself standing with others like him around a small bonfire in a jungle clearing. The older members stood in a ring around them. All the candidates, ten in total, and just like himself, were instructed to strip to their undershorts and then beaten with the flat of machetes while forbidden to cry out. When the beating session ended, one boy was unable to stand up when the command was given; he lay lifeless and never budged even when one of the frat boys roused kicked him with a command that he stopped being a sissy. They lifted the limp boy away and the initiation ceremony continued. Each candidate was made to take an oath of allegiance before a carved idol. Nobody heard anything about the limp boy who had been taken away from the initiation ground anymore, but by the evening of the next day, the news made the rounds on campus about a third-year History student who had been abandoned lifeless before the gates of a hospital somewhere in town. His obituary poster, which appeared all over campus the following week, said he had succumbed to internal injuries from an attack by unknown hoodlums.

Nku recovered from his initiation wounds, even though on most nights, he feared he would die from the pains that tore at the insides of his body. The experience made him more ferocious, especially with the *brothers* promising him protection and total absolution from every consequence of his actions for the fraternity's cause. He no longer feared any man; he robbed students of their mobile phones, extorted them and made himself available to whip any erring *brother* back on track. Once he had gunned down a top-ranking rival cult member on Convocation Day, coerced a lecturer at gunpoint into giving good grades to his *brothers,* and fended off a contingent of policemen who would have arrested his *brothers* one initiation night. These sterling qualities didn't go unnoticed within the ranks of the fraternity. Two years afterwards, he plotted a mutiny that overthrew the sitting headman. He had thought that to be the height of his achievement and that it would give him unlimited access to fame and respect, but he hadn't known better. The new position stole what semblance of peace he had left. Fear became the only emotion he knew. He feared mutiny from his *brothers*; he feared attacks from the rival cult groups as his head was his weakness in the structure of his fraternity. Twice he had escaped attacks targeting him, and so he never slept at a place more than once. He was always on the move. Tests and exams coincided with inter-fraternity wars, and the call of duty had already cost him two extra years in school, and counting.

"Everybody dies," his sponsor, Jaga, told him. "But you have to choose how to die."

"And what if I choose to die peacefully?"

Jaga laughed. "Peace doesn't exist for a soldier. Everybody must go down, one way or another. But as a strong man, you will have to go down with as many people as you can so that the gods will give you a place of honour."

Two weeks later, Jaga was found by the roadside, the blade of an axe buried in his head. It was said that the incident happened the night before when he was returning from a nocturnal visit to one of his girlfriends.

Nku grew to hate the life he led, the futility of cultism and all its vain promises at the cost of life, peace and happiness. The memories of intelligent, promising lads who had been struck down with malicious bullets or hacked with axes made him cringe with remorse. Those boys had all suffered dishonourable deaths so some ambitious rascal would gain some recognition from his own camp. He believed that if there was a Hell in the afterlife, there surely would be a large reservation for those who died for such vain things. But he dared not let his rioting emotions show. Many of his comrades had gone down for this vague cause already and many more would, but the ones still standing would never endure a leader who had suddenly grown soft in the core. They would be too glad to hack him down and take his place, content in the justification that they had done the fraternity a service in pruning off a weakling in the chain of command.

"Good afternoon, I am looking for somebody."

Nku's heart froze. He looked up to the speaker who appeared to have materialized from nowhere. The speaker was a man dressed in a purple blazer and leaning heavily against the termite-eaten doorpost. He tapped a black cane rhythmically on the floor like one biding his time.

Nku uttered no word. He couldn't even bring himself to breathe. Like one transfixed, he stared at the strange dandy looking so out of place in the environment. Recognition began to set in.

"Actually, you know you are the one I am looking for," the man said with an air of leisure. "Of course, I recognize you, even if you were dead and back from the abyss, blackened all over with hell's soot." He walked labouriously into the studio, one arm hidden behind his back. A few paces from Nku's drawing table, he halted. His eyes were wolfish with scorn, and they regarded Nku with measured hate.

A gun! Nku's heart thumped too loudly that he could swear the man could hear it from where he stood. Sweat broke out of his every pore and his dampened shirt clung to his skin. He cursed himself for having not kept his pistol within easy reach. He had been too confident in the boys keeping watch outside that he had left the pistol in the bag propped against the rusty metal legs of his draft table. He looked out the window at the dwarf cashew trees outside; none of his men was in sight. It dawned on him that he might have been sold away.

"Never bother about them," the man said to him, evidently reading his mind. "I took care of them just as I will take care of you. It used to be my profession, *taking care of people.*"

The man brought his arm around. He had a silenced pistol which he brought up level with Nku's face. He took aim with a hand so steady it seemed like a lifeless appendage.

That bastard! Nku cursed under his breath. He was thinking of Aniete. It pained him that the bloody civilian would outplay him just like this and at his own game. In all his life, he hadn't thought this moment would come when he would have to stare down the barrel of a gun, waiting for when the bullet would come flying in to put an end to his life. So this was what his victims had felt in that moment before he executed them?

"I thought you would be saying some prayers?" Mezkana teased, never letting down his aim.

Nku said nothing. He couldn't bring his patched throat to labour for any speech; he was only bracing his body for the final moment. If this was to be his end, he would not meet it begging and whimpering as some others whom he had encountered and who had elicited nothing but spite from him.

"You still think I will shoot you?" Mezkana asked.

Nku's sweaty head could only move a fraction to the left as though he were indecisive. Mezkana let down his aim, inhaled deeply and flashed a wide smile like one enjoying a winning game. Nku realized that he hadn't been breathing all the while. His lungs ached with the renewed effort.

"I am not a clown, neither do I earn my bread by being talkative. If I had wanted you dead, you would have been getting stiff by now. I would have put a bullet here," he tapped the barrel of his gun against his temple. "Through that window," he said, and pointed to an open window to the right of Nku.

"Thank you," Nku breathed. He was surprised he had said those words. It felt as though someone else had taken possession of his willpower.

"You are welcome, but you can thank me later after hearing me out." Mezkana shifted his weight, throwing a foot forward. Nku caught a glimpse of a bandaged ankle. He looked on, wide-eyed and attentive.

"Here is the deal. That boy, what is his name again?" He tapped the barrel of the pistol against his head. "Aniete. Yes, your partner. I learned you are after his head."

"He betrayed me," Nku managed to say. His composure was gradually returning on realizing that death for him had been postponed for another day.

"I doubt it."

"How …"

"Shhh," Mezkana hushed him, halfheartedly waving the pistol at Nku's face. Nku gulped down his remaining words. "If he had betrayed you, death wouldn't have waited for you until today. He is one hell of an efficient chap in case you haven't yet noticed. But that is not why I am here. You will live for today on one condition, that you stay away from him. It is a very simple and single commandment. Hence, I don't expect you to forget it. I am not as patient or as forgiving as God. If you so much as violate my commandment, I guarantee you, you will forever watch over your back. If you don't have any questions, I have an appointment elsewhere to keep."

He turned around and limped towards the door.

"What about my men?" Nku asked.

Mezkana paused in his tracks. "What men?"

"The ones outside."

"Oh! Them? They are outside, in friendly company. You can see them if you stretch your gaze further … towards that water tank." He chuckled, swaying his head in mirth as he stepped out of the studio.

Nku couldn't hear the man's footfalls as he walked down the hallway. He could have been a ghost. Nku got off his stool and peered through the open louvers in the direction of two rubber water tanks farther away from the cashew trees. He saw them seated on a pile of concrete blocks. Two strange men stood before them, talking elaborately while his men appeared to be listening. To a cursory observer, six fellows were having an animated discussion, but he knew better. The two men must have bullied them into striking the pose. He could even make out a small bulging outline at the hip of the short one with the bow legs and oversize white shoes.

He sighed. He hadn't prayed in a very long while, but he pressed his forehead against the metal burglary proof, shut his eyes and muttered, "Thank you, God."

ACKNOWLEDGEMENT

I was passing through an uncertain moment finding, without success, a publisher to take a look at the first novel-length manuscript I had written. The year was 2014 and months had passed since, as one of the selected emerging writers, I had participated in the Caine Prize Short Story Surgery in my city, Port-Harcourt. The euphoria of meeting the other twelve selected writers and the workshop's facilitators - Ellah Wakatama Allfrey, Adam Abubakar Ibrahim and Stanley Kenani - had died down and I was left with the silence that attended the self-doubt building up with each passing week. One morning, I listened to Tuface Idibia's 'Dance In The Rain', and the song held a new meaning for me in that moment. In its lyrics, I found myself being told that I must pick myself up and soldier on; that I must write my next book rather than keep on whipping myself for my inability to win the attention of a publisher for my novel. And that was how I began to write this novel.

Johnson Maduabuchi Iroegbu made sure that in the time I wrote this book, I lacked for nothing.

Karina Olajide, my darling sister, was the first to read this manuscript and gave her approval of it.

Akor Oche believes so much in this manuscript and insists that this is the best thing I had so far written. Mrs Ngozi Ebubedike insisted on doing the first round of edits on the manuscript. I must thank her for her generousity and unwavering support.

Every writer wishes to have that one person who believes in the potential of their writing long before the world gets to discover it. I found such a person in Chukwunyere Emenogu. He had read the manuscript of this novel and was totally taken by it. I remain eternally grateful for the three years he granted me sanctuary in the serenity of his spacious flat, rent-free, so I could write in peace and comfort.

To my editor, Ebelenna Tobenna Esomnofu, I am grateful.

This novel is about the struggles of a writer to have his book published. Therefore I owe a debt of gratitude to Dr. Onyeka Nwelue of Abibiman Publishing UK, who also is my publisher, for betting on this manuscript.

www.ingramcontent.com/pod-product-compliance
Lightning Source LLC
Chambersburg PA
CBHW051317190726
48290CB00001B/198